THE THEORY OF EARLS

KATHLEEN AYERS

Copyright © 2020 by Kathleen Ayers

All rights reserved.

No part of this book may be reproduced in any form or by any electronic or mechanical means, including information storage and retrieval systems, without written permission from the author, except for the use of brief quotations in a book review.

Editing by Midnight Owl Editing

Cover by Covers and Cupcakes

1

LONDON, 1839

"Stand up straight, Margaret. Good Lord, if you slouch in such a manner, you'll make everyone think you have a physical deformity. It has been difficult enough to find you a suitable gentleman this season. Impossible in fact, but Lord Winthrop has expressed an interest in you, and we don't wish to scare him away."

Margaret Lainscott gave her aunt, Lady Dobson, a strained smile. "Of course, Aunt." Winthrop *wouldn't* do. If she could terrify him into fleeing England, Margaret would do so.

A trickle of perspiration ran between the small hollow of her breasts. Margaret could feel it sliding down her skin in a most unpleasant manner. The ballroom was dreadfully hot even though the doors had been thrown open to the gardens outside. The crush of the *ton* was stifling. The only thing worse than being paraded around her aunt's little ball like a half-lame mare no one wanted was enduring her aunt's company.

If only her father hadn't decided to inspect the new vein of tin on his own that spring morning three years ago, Walter Lainscott would still be alive. Margaret would be at home in Yorkshire playing the piano and drinking tea instead of having Aunt Agnes dangle her before every eligible but uninterested bachelor in London. It was no secret Lady Dobson could barely tolerate the reminder of her younger sister's shameful and unfortunate marriage to a tin miner. Not only was Margaret the byproduct of a union with a common tradesman, but she was too long in the tooth at the age of twenty-six to attract more than passing attention. In addition to her age, Margaret was only passably pretty in comparison to this season's crop of debutantes. Most of the *ton* considered her to be shockingly plain. Margaret's only redeemable qualities, according to her aunt, were that she could play the piano and possessed an obscenely large dowry.

"Oh, look, there's Lord Winthrop now." Aunt Agnes flipped her fan and widened her eyes in delight.

Bollocks.

Margaret ran her gloved hands down the folds of her gown, leaving indentations in the lush fabric. Best to get this over with as soon as possible.

"Miss Lainscott."

The smell of pomade and talc instantly reached her nostrils. Winthrop smelled like a sweaty infant. The impoverished heir to an earldom had rapidly become her aunt's favorite potential suitor for Margaret's hand, though why she favored him was a mystery.

If given the choice, Margaret would prefer not to marry at all, but Aunt Agnes had made her expectations clear in that regard. She had no inclination to allow Margaret to continue living on her charity which meant Margaret had to marry. Margaret had reconciled herself to such a fate. It was the only way to escape her aunt and possibly give herself some control over her life. But not just any gentleman would do.

She dropped gracefully into a curtsy and lowered her eyes, lest he see the distaste hovering in them. "Lord Winthrop."

"How are you finding the weather, Miss Lainscott?"

Margaret gave him a timid nod, careful not to meet his eyes, pretending extreme shyness in his presence. "Very fair, my lord."

Limited intelligence was Margaret's first requirement in a potential husband, for such a husband would be easier for her to control. He must be pleasant, polite, and somewhat attractive. She preferred he have a passion or hobby he adored. Hunting, breeding horses, fishing. Perhaps carpentry or playing chess. Something which would compel him to spend the bulk of his time away from Margaret. Of course, it would also be lovely if her future husband possessed a country estate where Margaret could take up residence and escape the confines of London. But that last requirement was the least important.

Margaret regarded Winthrop with a keen eye, taking in his massive, sweating form. He more than surpassed her first requirement. The piece of toast she'd had for breakfast that morning possessed more brains than he did. Winthrop was polite and appeared pleasant, but Margaret thought his good humor to be false. She sensed cruelty and malice in his eyes, as if his true nature was hidden behind a pompous demeanor. And he possessed no interests outside of playing cards or betting on horses that she could see.

Winthrop would be *intolerable* as a husband.

There was also the question of children. Winthrop was an only child. He'd want an heir. Margaret wasn't opposed to performing her wifely duties, she was only against sharing a bed with Winthrop.

Thankfully, after expending a small bit of his limited

attention on Margaret, Winthrop proceeded to ignore her and struck up a conversation with Aunt Agnes. Margaret allowed herself the small victory. She had perfected the ability to become invisible by adopting an excessively reserved demeanor. Such a thing came in handy when dealing with the Winthrops of the world.

Another whiff of talc met her nose.

She found *nothing* even remotely appealing in Winthrop's appearance, even overlooking the sweating and the smell of powder. Narrow shoulders sat atop a thickened waist and rounded bottom, reminding Margaret of a pear. Ham-fisted, Winthrop's hands were often clammy. The damp feel of his fingers was noticeable even beneath the costly gloves he wore. He also favored what Margaret considered to be rather dainty shoes instead of boots, which looked ridiculous for he had rather large, duck-like feet.

No. Winthrop would not do at all.

"Miss Lainscott?" Winthrop interrupted her reflections of his person, suddenly reminded of her presence. "Would you care to take a turn about the terrace with me?"

And endure the smell of your pomade? It's nearly worse than your conversation skills.

"I don't—"

"Of course she would," her aunt said, interceding before Margaret could decline. "Margaret could benefit from some fresh air." Aunt Agnes fluttered her fan toward the doors. "I must see to my guests, but I leave my niece in your capable hands."

Could her aunt be any more obvious? Margaret had to keep herself from voicing a strident objection to being forced into Winthrop's company. But if she dared make the slightest protest, her aunt would punish her.

"Enjoy yourself." Aunt Agnes smiled indulgently, giving Margaret a pinch to the arm before fluttering off in a whirl of dark purple skirts, the large turban atop her head tilting at a dangerous angle.

Margaret stared at the turban, silently commanding the headdress to topple off her aunt's head and roll across the marble floor, shocking the crowd of guests and exposing the bald head Margaret was sure lay beneath. No one wore turbans and hadn't for at least twenty years. Not unless they had to.

Lord Winthrop's giant paw took Margaret's hand and placed her fingers on his forearm. "Shall we?" He nodded down at her, sweat glistening on his forehead.

There was no escape.

Steering Margaret expertly through the crush, Lord Winthrop guided her to a set of tall French doors and out into the blissfully cool terrace. A breeze gently buffeted her face as she looked out into the gardens. The strains of the orchestra filtered through the open doors and Margaret swayed in time with the music, mentally wincing as she heard one of the violins hit a wrong note. No one would likely notice but her.

Music was the only thing which kept her sane during events such as these. Whenever she heard music, the sound of each instrument filled her mind with a swirl of colors which in turn formed themselves into notes. The notes would intertwine and split to become a melody, while her fingers itched for a pen to write everything down. She had a special book for such things, large and shaped like a ledger one might use for household accounts. It had been a gift from her father several years ago when Margaret had studied music with Mr. Strauss, her neighbor in Yorkshire. The elderly Austrian gentleman had once been a composer of some renown on the Continent before coming to England to live with his daughter.

Winthrop propelled her in the direction of a stone bench

at the edge of the terrace, annoying her with his presence and his sweating. Margaret found herself praying for a plague of locusts or some other more welcome rescue.

"We can dance later if you like." He'd apparently seen her moving in time to the music and had mistaken it for an invitation.

Margaret's eyes slid down Lord Winthrop's oddly shaped form. The very thought of being clasped to him while dancing a waltz was abhorrent. And he was still sweating profusely; surely that couldn't be normal. She kept her eyes down, pretending to be too timid to reply.

An exasperated sigh left him, just as she'd expected. Perhaps if she bored him, he would simply go away.

"Your aunt has given me leave to call on you." Lord Winthrop nodded for her to sit. "I shall come tomorrow."

Good Lord. Winthrop *was* going to court her.

If she didn't want to be stuck with the repugnant earl, Margaret had best choose a gentleman herself. And quickly. The combination of *title* and *stupid* should be easy to find within the *ton*. She just hadn't tried hard enough. Margaret had hoped to make it through another season before her aunt would force the issue of marriage. But clearly, time had run out.

Her mind ran through a host of acquaintances she'd made since coming to London who had professed interest in her. There weren't a great many, the only disadvantage to her strategy of intentionally falling beneath notice. Several possessed the same entitled, cruel nature as Winthrop. One or two exhibited a sign of intelligence, which wouldn't do. Most were in need of a fat dowry. Margaret was an heiress; her money had attracted nearly every gentleman who bet on the horses too often or carelessly gambled. She'd have to be discerning.

Winthrop had begun to bore her with the details of a

party he'd recently attended. She ignored him and continued searching her memories, discarding one gentleman after another. This was more difficult than she'd anticipated. Suddenly, a pleasant face swam before her. Kind. Vacant eyes. *Enamored* of the outdoors. Spoke extensively of a hunting lodge. She'd made his acquaintance at Gray Covington last year during a house party she'd attended. He would suit her perfectly if he were still unmarried. His name was Carter... Carson? *Bollocks*. She should have made more of an effort.

Unfortunately, Margaret drew a blank at his name. Not an unusual occurrence. She was terrible at names.

Cool air blew against her face, helping to banish the smell of Lord Winthrop's overuse of talc. As he stood before her, droning on about his own self-importance, wrongly assuming she was interested, Margaret decided to tackle the problem at hand. She needed a suitable excuse to make Winthrop go away, lest he try to steal a kiss and attempt to compromise her. Aunt Agnes would be thrilled.

Margaret went with a headache. Overused by ladies in her situation, to be sure, but she wasn't feeling especially creative tonight.

"Oh, my." Her fingers fell against her temple. She looked up at Winthrop from beneath her lashes. "My lord," she said in a voice barely above a whisper, "you have my gratitude for seeing me out into this blessedly cool air, but my headache has not abated."

Margaret hoped Winthrop had paid so little attention to her earlier that he wouldn't remember she'd not mentioned a headache. She cast her eyes down as if mortified to be in such a state.

"You should have asked me sooner to escort you out." The reprimand, coming as it did from the pompous, overstuffed pear, was a bit unwelcome.

Margaret bit her lip to keep herself from giving him a

sharp retort. Sometimes it was very difficult to pretend to be such a milquetoast. Touching him tentatively on the forearm, she murmured, "Would you grant me one more favor, Lord Winthrop?"

He stepped forward, his heavy, velvet-clad form far too close for comfort.

"I'm so *terribly* thirsty. Would you mind fetching me a glass of lemonade? I am certain such refreshment and the cool air will revive me. I would be incredibly grateful."

Disappointment mixed with annoyance on his florid features. But Winthrop, thankfully, was too much of a gentleman to decline. "Of course, Miss Lainscott. Sit here and I shall return promptly." He dutifully waddled back inside to find the refreshment table.

Once he was gone, Margaret breathed a sigh of relief, leaning back against the stone wall. There was a path leading to the servants' entrance just down the steps before her and through an opening in her aunt's wisteria. She would be upstairs in her room within a matter of minutes. Eliza, her lady's maid, could send word to her aunt and Lord Winthrop that she'd regretfully had to retire for the evening with a headache. Aunt Agnes would be furious tomorrow, but Margaret couldn't tolerate Winthrop's presence any longer.

Standing up, she brushed her skirts and hurried down the steps leading into the gardens. Her aunt hadn't instructed the servants to light torches in the garden, not wishing to incite any young gentlemen inclined to ruination, but there was moonlight and Margaret knew the way by heart. This wasn't the first time she'd escaped into the wisteria. As she slunk along the wall, careful not to tear her gown, she caught the scent of a cheroot mixing with the aroma of the garden.

A dark shape moved along the vines and blooms, startling her.

"Nicely done, Miss Lainscott."

Margaret froze at the greeting, allowing the deep baritone to melt into her skin. She forgot names with regularity. Titles. Sometimes faces. But *never* the *sound* of a person. And especially not the resonance of this man's voice, though they'd only been in each other's company one other time. An odd fluttering started low in her belly.

A large, impeccably dressed form moved out of the wisteria and into a patch of moonlight. The cheroot clutched between his teeth dangled from a wide, sensual mouth as he smiled at her.

"Lord Welles." Margaret's blood pulsed louder in her ears. He was as beautiful as she remembered, even more so with moonlight creating shadows across the sculpted lines of his handsome face. She hadn't seen Welles since Lady Cambourne's house party at Gray Covington when Margaret had made such a spectacle of herself.

"You seem unsurprised to find me lurking about your aunt's garden." A dark lock of hair fell over his brow as he tilted his chin to take her in. He pulled the cheroot from his mouth with an elegant wave of his hand and tossed the stub to the ground.

"This particular bit of wisteria speaks to me often." Margaret's blood hummed louder, lighting her nerves on fire. Her attraction to him, which she equated to a feeling of intoxication, hadn't abated in the least since she'd last seen him. During the house party, Margaret had convinced herself the racing of her heart at his nearness was only a schoolgirl crush. The feeling would disappear in time, certainly by their next meeting. Which was now.

I was terribly mistaken.

"I assume Winthrop will find only an empty bench upon his return." Welles shook his head and made a tsking sound with his tongue. "Not very nice of you, Miss Lainscott. But then," his voice deepened until the vibration caressed

Margaret down to her core, "I'm certain you aren't as agreeable as you pretend to be."

His comment surprised her. Margaret's timid mouse disguise had served her well during her time among the *ton*. No one, except perhaps her friend, Lady Kilmaire, suspected she was anything else. It was far easier to deal with her aunt as well if she was beneath notice. Even worse, Margaret knew that at the slightest sign of rebellion, Aunt Agnes would take her piano away.

"Why would you say such a thing, Lord Welles?" She deliberately kept her voice meek and timid.

"Because it's true?" Soft laughter bubbled from the depths of his chest. "I'm not fooled, Miss Lainscott. I *see* you."

A flutter started low in her stomach at his amusement, the sound filling her senses with a harmony of swirling purples, blues, and greens. "I don't think we are acquainted enough, my lord, for you to infer such a thing."

A quiet snort of disbelief followed her declaration. "True, Miss Lainscott. But during our brief time together at Gray Covington, you made an indelible impression upon me and it was not that of a timid, reserved young lady."

She had made a *cake* of herself during the house party with her performance on the piano; still, Margaret couldn't, for the life of her, remember making any sort of impression on Lord Welles. The thought caused another round of fluttering inside.

The pale light of the moon shifted across his eyes and she caught a glimpse of sapphire.

Margaret purposefully looked down to study the toe of her slipper, not willing to meet his gaze. His eyes were famous among the women of London. She'd heard young ladies swooned at only a glance from Lord Welles. Margaret was glad she couldn't see the startling rings of blue, each one successively darker as they neared his pupils, the deep color flecked with bits of gold. One pea-wit debutante had even written a poem about Welles and his eyes, much to the *ton*'s amusement.

"Your performance at the piano, the *passion* you exhibited..." He halted for a moment as if weighing how to express himself. "I found it all quite captivating."

Welles had the most *glorious* tonal quality to his voice, as if Margaret were being addressed by a large cello. She could have stood there and listened to him speak all night.

"It was the highlight of my stay at Gray Covington," he finished.

And meeting Welles had been the highlight of Margaret's stay at the Cambourne estate. The invitation to the house party at Gray Covington had been unexpected but welcome. At the time, Aunt Agnes had wanted to dangle Margaret before the Earl of Kilmaire who was seeking a wife and would be in attendance. Her aunt's idea had been to have Margaret give the guests an impromptu performance on the piano to gain Lord Kilmaire's attention, a futile effort because the earl was already in love with Lady Miranda Reynolds, whom he'd married not long after the party.

The performance had been a disaster.

"I fear I may have played a bit too...*forcefully*," Margaret said, understating the truth. The impromptu recital had resulted in embarrassment to both herself and Aunt Agnes. Margaret *did* play with passion, so much so that she sometimes forgot everything but the music. She and the piano would fuse together as her fingers flew over the keys, the notes pulsating through her.

I may have writhed against the piano bench.

"My aunt was not pleased with my performance." Heat washed up her cheeks.

"I don't imagine she was."

Margaret had been banned from the piano for the

remainder of their stay at Gray Covington. She'd been made to embroider instead. It had been pure torture.

"You are masterful on the piano." Welles had moved a step closer to her, trapping her amid the wisteria.

"I didn't realize you cared so much for music. Do you play?" Certainly her...*emotional* display while playing had been mortifying, but she couldn't fathom why Lord Welles had found it so memorable. Even before coming to London, Margaret wasn't the sort of young lady who attracted attention from a man like Welles. Aunt Agnes claimed Margaret to be so drab, she faded into the wood panels of the dining room during a dinner party.

"I learned as a child. My mother adored music." A frown tightened his wide mouth. "But I've never played as you do. That is a level I could never hope to achieve."

Welles *had* been enamored with the music. Even as absorbed as she was, she'd noticed him watching her, his eyes half-closed in pleasure while his friend continued to speak to him.

His friend. The dim-witted gentleman she'd met at Gray Covington. He'd been in the company of Lord Welles.

"Carstairs," she abruptly blurted out.

"I beg your pardon?" His mouth curved upward, brow wrinkling slightly in confusion.

Finding Welles hiding in the wisteria was far better than the plague of locusts she'd been wishing for earlier. He was an associate of Lord Carstairs. "The gentleman who accompanied you to Gray Covington. Lord Carstairs."

"*I* know who Carstairs is, but what has he got to do with anything?"

Footsteps sounded on the terrace. *Winthrop.*

"I beg your discretion, my lord." Margaret placed a hand on his forearm as she peeked through the wisteria at Winthrop.

"Why, Miss Lainscott, are you being hunted?" Welles shot a pointed look at her fingers, a lazy smile tugging at his lips. "And I stand corrected. You are incredibly timid."

Margaret snatched her hand back and lowered her voice. "I have a strong desire to renew my acquaintance with Lord Carstairs."

Welles hovered over her, so close she could feel the heat coming off his larger form.

"For what purpose?"

"Marriage. To me."

"I see." Welles sounded more amused than outraged by her admission. His smile stayed in place as he nodded. "Do go on. I confess I'm speechless."

"I know this isn't exactly the type of thing to discuss at the present time," she waved her hands about, "while hiding from Lord Winthrop in the wisteria."

"*You* are hiding. I was merely enjoying a cheroot."

"I would ask your assistance in reintroducing me to Lord Carstairs—"

"For the purpose of marrying him, due to husbandly qualities which I can only assume at this point?"

"Miss Lainscott?" Winthrop called from the terrace. "Are you in the garden?"

"Damn and blast," Margaret swore under her breath as she glanced at Winthrop and then back to Welles. "Yes, my lord. Please pay attention. I haven't much time to make my point." She stamped one slipper-clad foot.

Welles chuckled softly. "There she is."

"There who is?" She had only precious moments to spare before Winthrop's velvet-clad form pounced upon her with lemonade clutched in one moist hand.

"A most interesting young lady."

"I'm not at all interesting, my lord."

"I beg to differ."

"My aunt has decided I must marry, and I fear her choice for me is Winthrop."

"I can see why you would be less than enthusiastic about such a match. And your aunt's desire to marry you off is common knowledge." His voice lowered, humming deliciously in the small hollow of the wisteria. "I'm not sure what your requirements are, but I'll assume Winthrop doesn't meet any of them?"

Margaret was rapidly becoming horrified at the turn in conversation and slid further into the blooms and vines. This was the last thing she'd ever thought to discuss with Lord Welles. "He only meets one of my criteria."

"Lack of intelligence? Poor choices in footwear?"

A sound of surprise escaped Margaret at his correct assessment of the situation. Lord Welles was not only handsome but astute as well. "And Winthrop is...*oddly* shaped," she added, casting him a look to see if he took offense from her description.

"Don't forget his overuse of talc; certainly that detracts from his suitability." Welles brought a tapered finger to his lips as if deep in thought. "I wish to make absolutely certain I understand. You find Lord Carstairs attractive, and not the least bit shaped like a pear; you are relieved he prefers boots and most importantly," he leaned down, close enough Margaret could smell the light scent of his shaving soap, "he's not nearly as intelligent as you are."

With his face in shadow, Margaret could only see the outline of Welles's patrician nose and the curve of his chin. If he neglected to move for a few moments, he could easily be mistaken for one of her aunt's Grecian statues. Possibly Zeus or Apollo.

Hades would be a better comparison.

"Am I correct, Miss Lainscott?"

His breath tickled the fine hairs dangling above the curve

of her ear as the low timbre of his voice slid down the length of her neck. The fluttering inside her stomach increased.

Definitely Hades.

It was becoming increasingly difficult to think with Welles so close to her. Everything about him was seductive, from his scent to the decadent richness of his voice. Margaret prided herself on not being just another pea-wit young lady, but even she had her limitations.

"Yes, my lord. Your assessment of my situation is correct."

Winthrop was coming closer. She could hear his ridiculous shoes striking the pavement.

"I realize I am being presumptuous. We don't know each other well enough for me to ask for your assistance." She hurried her words, ignoring the way her skin was tingling from Welles's nearness. "But I would beg your indulgence. I've not seen Lord Carstairs at any functions I've attended."

"Miss Lainscott?" A peevish voice bellowed into the darkness. "Is that you in the wisteria? I have your lemonade."

"Damn," she uttered without thinking.

Welles laughed softly, more beautiful than any human being had a right to be. "Don't worry, Miss Lainscott. I'll make sure you get away." Snaking an arm about her waist, he pushed Margaret deeper into the wisteria. His hand, warm and strong, flattened against the small of her back then slid down across the tops of her buttocks and squeezed gently.

Margaret gasped at his boldness.

"Don't make a sound, Miss Lainscott," Welles admonished. "You wouldn't wish Lord Winthrop to spot you." The large hand slid up to the small of her back. He gave her a gentle shove in the opposite direction.

"You'll help me?"

He didn't answer. Instead, he stepped out of the wisteria. "Winthrop? Are you spying on me?" Welles managed to sound imperious and outraged.

Margaret slid beneath the vines, listening to Winthrop sputter like a teapot at the implication that he'd interrupted an assignation. At least she wouldn't have to endure him again this evening.

"Thank you," she whispered before slipping through the gate, wondering at the wisdom of confiding her plans to Lord Welles.

2

"Oh, miss. If your aunt finds you gone..."

Margaret gave an exasperated sigh and placed a hand on her slender hips. "She won't find me gone unless you *tell* her, Eliza."

"What if *something* happens?"

"Nothing is going to happen." Margaret was not about to be deterred. Today was very important. Much more important than whatever punishment Aunt Agnes would mete out if she found her gone. "She won't even know I'm not here. All you need to do is lock the door behind me." She tied the bonnet snugly beneath her chin.

"Miss, what if Lord Winthrop calls?"

Margaret hesitated. "He won't." Winthrop had called the day after her aunt's ball to take her for a ride in the park. The entire experience had been awkward. Uncomfortable. *Intolerable.* He'd returned just yesterday to repeat the horror by taking tea with her and Aunt Agnes. If anything, the two instances had solidified Margaret's determination *not* to allow herself to be married to Winthrop.

"Eliza, I am leaving. Lord Winthrop has already paid two

calls on me this week. He won't do so again. If *anyone* knocks, which they won't," she assured her maid, "remind them I've a terrible headache today. You already made such known when you brought up my breakfast tray, didn't you?"

The maid nodded.

"Then no one will disturb me. I'll be back for tea. Possibly. I'm not certain." Margaret shrugged and walked to the door. "Lock this behind me," she instructed the maid again.

The maid nodded. "Yes, miss."

Margaret slipped out into the hall and made her way downstairs and through the kitchen, avoiding anyone who might remark on her appearance, especially her aunt's lady's maid, Oakes. Carefully, she made her way up the stairs of the servants' entrance and into the early afternoon.

Aunt Agnes wouldn't ask after her, no matter Eliza's fears. Margaret's request for breakfast in her room signaled to the staff that she was suffering from one of her headaches, an affliction she'd convinced her aunt she suffered from over the last two years. Then she'd instructed Eliza to mention her headache to Cook while bringing Margaret tea *and* inform Oakes that Margaret was ailing. Aunt Agnes would be gone most of the day paying calls and was likely relieved she wouldn't have to drag Margaret with her. No one would miss her.

Margaret smiled as she made her way around the corner to the mews. She meant to take the alley down to the next street and hail a hack. She quickened her steps in anticipation of the day's events. It wouldn't do for her to be late.

3

"It's much too early for you to be here."

Anthony Marcus Barrington, Earl of Welles ignored the grouchy tone in his brother's voice.

"It's after twelve; I was leaving another meeting and thought I'd stop by." His 'meeting' had been leaving the bed of his latest mistress, a Parisian ballet dancer who had wept rivers of tears as he'd tried to disengage himself from her naked form to leave the bed. Claudette had become needier in the last few months and finding out about her affair with one of her fellow ballet dancers had given Tony the perfect excuse to end their association.

A snort of disbelief came from the man who approached him with a crystal decanter and two glasses. Leo looked well-rested despite his objection to the hour. His brother rarely slept more than five or six hours and never sought his own bed until just before dawn. "Your mistress, I suppose? The French girl. Did you finally end it?"

"Yes." Tony pulled off his gloves and laid them on the table. "Bring that over here." He waved at the decanter. "No more pretending to enjoy pretentious French wine for me."

"You don't mind if I call on Claudette then, do you?" Leo smiled, showing a row of even, white teeth.

"No, she probably wouldn't know the difference."

Tony's resemblance to his brother was rather uncanny, considering the two weren't twins. Leo was an inch shorter and slightly broader through the chest than Tony, but the eyes were the same, as was the rich brown of their hair. He and his bastard half-brother looked so much alike most people mistook one for the other, especially at a distance.

Tony took the proffered glass, inhaling the contents with a smile. "Well-aged scotch."

"I don't *really* mean to call on Claudette," Leo stated. "She's delicious, but I believe we share enough."

That was certainly true. "It's just as well; she's been tupping one of her fellow dancers."

"Another ballerina?" Leo sounded hopeful.

"Sadly, no. The leading man."

"Well, then she definitely has no appeal for me." Leo settled into the chair next to him and they clinked glasses.

Leo Murphy, not only his brother but also Tony's closest friend, took a sip of the scotch, shivering as the liquid slid down his throat. "*Christ,* I wasn't ready for that."

He and Leo had spent their childhood together, running through the woods and staging mock battles on the Duke of Averell's country estate. The duke's heir and the son of an Irish housemaid had never known they were blood until the death of Tony's mother. Having had a relationship with Leo's mother prior to his marriage, the duke decided to keep both his wife and mistress under one roof rather than break things off. Molly eventually became lady's maid to Tony's mother.

It was a convenient arrangement for Marcus, the Duke of Averell, until it wasn't.

"Averell sent me word again. Another letter full of platitudes. Wants to grant me one of his unentailed estates." Leo's gaze fell to the fire in the grate. "I wish he'd stop. Give up. I've no desire for a relationship with him after everything that happened."

"The old prick is tenacious, I'll give him that." Tony sipped at his drink.

"Fat lot of good it will do him. I didn't even take the money he offered me so I could start Elysium."

Instead, Tony had given Leo the funds for a share of the business. He'd already made his investment back many times over and never regretted it. Besides, the heir to a duchy becoming a partner in a notorious pleasure palace had infuriated the duke.

Molly had been devastated by the death of Tony's mother, Katherine. Despite her lengthy relationship with the duke and the affair, Molly had cared deeply for her mistress. After Katherine's death, Molly had become incredibly religious and moved herself and Leo to the outskirts of London. She had then met and married a hack driver who had provided her and Leo with a comfortable home, but little else. Leo didn't have fond memories of his stepfather, a brutish man who had been free with his fists. Thankfully, the marriage hadn't lasted. Molly's husband had fallen down the stairs one night, drunk, breaking his neck.

Tony had serious doubts the death had been accidental. Leo blamed the duke for all of it.

Glancing at Leo, Tony took in his brother's garishly patterned waistcoat with a small frown of distaste. Leo had always favored such clothing; often it was the only way patrons of Elysium could tell them apart. Today's waistcoat was particularly loud, consisting of a swirling mass of mustard and pale blue silk stitched with gold thread.

"If *you* would just capitulate," Leo continued, "he'd leave *me* alone. I told him to bugger off. I've more than enough money to buy my own bloody estate if I wish to do so. And I don't. What would I do in the country? Traipse about the gardens? I also don't need him spouting off to everyone that he's my father. Other lords don't acknowledge every extra branch on their tree. Why must Averell do so?"

"I've no intention of ever giving him what he wants." His father wanted Tony to marry and provide an heir for the prestigious Averell dukedom. But Tony was filled with loathing for his father for all the wrongs done to his mother. "I enjoy informing the duke, on the rare occasions we speak," Tony rolled the glass between his palms, "that I'll *never* produce his bloody heir. It delights me to tell him the legitimate line of the Duke of Averell will die an untimely death, just as my mother did. It is my father's misfortune the title can't go to some obscure cousin living across the ocean in New York."

"Is there really some unknown distant relation of your family moldering about in America?"

"It's *your* family as well." Tony waved his hand. "*Our* father's elder half-sister caused quite a scandal when she married into a prominent New York family. Jilted a marquess to do so. She has sons. An entire army of them. Pity one of my cousins isn't free to inherit."

Leo snorted and poured them both another finger of the scotch. They sat in companionable silence for a few minutes, both lost in their own thoughts, before Leo said, "The girls and Amanda are in London."

Tony already knew of his stepmother's arrival for the season, as well as that of his younger sisters. No matter his hatred of his father, Tony loved the girls and adored his flighty stepmother, even though Amanda certainly had poor taste in men as evidenced by her affection for his father.

"She sent a note asking me to stop by and visit," Tony said. "I told her I would come only if she promises not to discuss the duke. I've no desire to hear how our father's declining health would improve if only he could reconcile with his sons."

Leo snorted. "How long does a duke linger on his deathbed until he finally succumbs?"

"Apparently such a thing can go on for years." Tony knew it was a ploy on his father's part. The man was capable of all sorts of deceit. "I'll pay the duchess a call today. I'm certain she'll extend an invitation for me to dine at some point this week. Your presence will be requested as well."

Her Grace, the Duchess of Averell had brought the girls to London without her husband, who was deemed far too ill to travel with his family. The oldest of the girls, Andromeda, or Romy as she was called, had been eager to make her debut so she could enjoy the season. Not because Romy wished to marry, but rather for the fashion opportunity presented by the round of balls, recitals, fetes, evenings at the opera, and visits to the theater. Romy adored gowns, hats, gloves, and the assortment of fripperies which constituted London's season. But it wasn't just wearing them; Romy's true passion lay in the design of the gowns and accessories, an admirable talent and something she was quite good at. She often created lavish costumes and gowns for her mother and sisters.

Unfortunately, the daughter of the Duke of Averell would have little opportunity to practice such a trade.

"Do you want to review last night's receipts while you're here?"

Tony nodded.

Leo stood and brought over a stack of markers, placing the sheaf of papers on the table between them. Taking a ledger, he took notes on each patron's marker as Tony shuffled through the stack. Leo wrote down whose membership should be terminated, which gentlemen Elysium would continue to extend credit to or what assets the establishment would accept as payment. Horses, houses, carriages. Cufflinks were popular. Hatpins. Brooches. Once Leo had accepted the services of a mistress as payment.

"Winthrop." His brother snorted.

"Winthrop?" Tony recalled the waddling lord who had hunted the delicious Miss Lainscott with such determination at Lady Dobson's ball. It had been a fluke that Tony had even attended and reacquainted himself with Miss Lainscott, though he'd never forgotten meeting her at Gray Covington. The delicate pianist had made an indelible impression on him. He shifted in his seat as a sharp throb of arousal shot between his thighs at the mere thought of Miss Margaret Lainscott.

"He wants an extension on his account."

Tony shook his head. "Has he any way to secure such credit?"

"Winthrop claims he'll be marrying soon, and his future bride is an heiress."

Miss Lainscott was an heiress. Tin. "Did he mention the girl's name?"

"Refused to give it to me. Claims I won't know her, but he said she's rich as Croesus. Bragged about bagging her and then shipping her off to one of his estates so he wouldn't have to deal with her." Leo shook his head. "Poor girl."

Tony's fingers tightened around his glass of scotch. It appeared Miss Lainscott's instincts had been spot on. "But he failed to give you a name? Sounds as if the marriage is not assured."

"No. I suppose after disparaging her in such a way he became fearful I'd inform the unlucky heiress of his intentions." Leo gave a soft chuckle. "He's a buffoon and a poor gambler. I'm sure he'll run through any fortune she has in a fortnight."

Tony took another sip of scotch. He liked Miss Lainscott, probably more than she would wish him to, and had been toying with a way to see her again, though Tony knew he shouldn't. But he felt oddly protective of her, in addition to wanting to bed her. Besides, he disliked Winthrop; the man was an overindulged windbag determined to fritter away what was left in the family coffers on gambling and mistresses.

"Maybe you should give him a small extension," Tony replied to his brother. Miss Lainscott *had* asked him for help in securing another, less repulsive suitor. Truthfully, he'd been a little put out she hadn't considered Tony to be suitable, only Carstairs. Not that it mattered. Tony's intentions toward the delectable Miss Lainscott were anything but honorable and most definitely wouldn't result in marriage.

He'd wanted her from the moment he'd seen her, ridiculously pretending to be a timid little mouse and fading into the tapestries at Gray Covington. When she'd practically made love to the damn piano while performing for the guests, Welles had nearly snuck into her room at the house party and ravished her.

The dull ache between his thighs had become a persistent throbbing.

"The color of your waistcoat is a bit much so early in the day," Tony said to Leo, determined to distract himself from thoughts of Miss Lainscott. The cut of his trousers wasn't very forgiving.

"Bugger off, Tony." Leo's lip curled. "I like a bit of color; it's better than dressing as if I'm about to attend a funeral." He nodded to Tony's perfectly tailored suit of indigo. "You look like an undertaker."

"There's always a widow who needs consoling at a funeral. Though I suppose you sniff out widows whether at a funeral or not," Tony said pointedly. His brother was easily baited.

"Don't," Leo warned. "I'm fulfilling a promise to her late husband. Nothing more."

Tony tipped the scotch back to his lips and drained the

glass. "Of course you are. You're a paragon of virtue. Honorable to the core. It's one of the first things one realizes about you."

Leo scowled. His fingers drummed against the crystal in his hand as if he was considering throwing the glass at Tony's head. "I've work to do. You can see yourself out."

Tony chuckled. Leo had always possessed a temper. Standing, he bid his brother goodbye, carefully adjusting his coat.

Tony meant to help Miss Lainscott, but in return, he would also make a request of *her*.

4

Margaret handed the hackney driver a handful of coins and looked up at the dark stone mansion sitting by itself at the end of the street, wondering if she'd gotten the address incorrect. A home this large couldn't possibly belong to a fellow musician, which she assumed Mrs. Anderson's friend was. She looked back down at the note clutched in her hand. This *was* the correct address. The mansion before her would dwarf her aunt's home. She turned to ask the hackney to wait, but he was already trotting off in search of another fare.

Taking a deep breath, she climbed up the steps to face the double doors. Lifting the heavy silver knocker, she rapped sharply, prepared to beg the occupant's forgiveness for being given the incorrect address.

Margaret hadn't been sure what to expect when she received a note from Mrs. Anderson after having casually met the well-known pianist at a charitable tea. She couldn't remember what charity, nor anyone else's names, only that watercress sandwiches had been served with lemonade.

Meeting Mrs. Anderson had made everything else fade into the background.

Lucy Anderson was respected by men and women alike for her talent as both a performer and teacher. Not only had she played with the Royal Philharmonic, but she taught lessons to the sons and daughters of London's elite. When Aunt Agnes had slipped away to fawn over a towering woman draped in silk, Margaret had taken the opportunity to engage Mrs. Anderson in conversation.

After chatting for some time, Margaret had been asked to join Mrs. Anderson and a group of like-minded ladies for an afternoon of tea and music.

Margaret placed a hand over her heart. *Fellow musicians.* She hadn't had the opportunity to play with another artist since she'd left Yorkshire. Aunt Agnes frowned on such a thing. She preferred all of Margaret's thoughts to be in the direction of finding a suitable husband. It was one thing for Margaret to play the piano well, that was acceptable, but anything beyond that might interfere with a future husband's desires. Her aunt had even prohibited any *further* study of music, something Margaret had discreetly shared with Mrs. Anderson.

The door swung open. A dour-looking butler, thin mustache sitting atop a twitching upper lip, viewed her with superiority. "May I help you, miss?"

"Good afternoon, I—"

"She's joining our gathering, Pith." A beautiful woman came forward, her voluptuous form showcased to perfection in a swathe of buttercup silk. There were daisies embroidered along the hem of the dress and actual flowers placed strategically in the coils of her reddish-gold hair. She looked as if she should be skipping through a field, picking berries, and singing with the birds. Smiling broadly, she reached out her beringed hands to Margaret in welcome.

"Of course, Your Grace." The butler bowed and ushered Margaret inside.

A duchess? Mrs. Anderson had failed to mention such a thing.

"You must be Miss Lainscott." Her Grace clasped Margaret's hands. "I'm delighted you could join us. Lucy was concerned you might not be able to slip away."

Margaret dropped to a curtsy. "Your Grace." As she stood, she took in her surroundings, appreciating the wide foyer painted the color of pale yellow. Decorated with strategically placed *objets d'art* and tall vases of roses, the entire hall and foyer smelled like a summer garden. The floor beneath her feet was pale pink marble shot through with gold which Margaret assumed was Italian in origin. Everything around her spoke of powerful wealth and understated elegance.

"I'm the Duchess of Averell." A copper curl fell over her forehead. "Patroness of the arts and dear friend of Lucy. Though not a musician." She gave a graceful shrug.

Margaret wasn't familiar with the Duchess of Averell. If she'd heard the name before, she'd forgotten it. A common occurrence. But Margaret was sure Aunt Agnes knew the duchess. Her aunt knew everyone in the *ton*.

"I'm fortunate to have a conservatory." The duchess winked in a very un-duchess like way. "The moment I arrived in London I offered its use to Lucy and her friends. I do wish I played an instrument myself, but alas, I show not an iota of musical talent." She took Margaret's arm and led her up a wide flight of stairs sporting an ornate, carved banister smelling of beeswax. As they reached the landing, the lilting melody of a flute followed by the plucking of violin strings floated into the hallway.

"Oh, there you are, Miss Lainscott." Mrs. Anderson left a plush sofa covered with pale blue damask to greet her.

Several pairs of eyes looked up as Margaret entered the conservatory.

A slender, dark-haired young girl stood off to one side, a flute clutched in her hand. She looked at Margaret with interest for a moment, nodded shyly, and picked up the flute again. The grandest piano Margaret had ever seen sat directly behind the girl, dominating the far corner of the room. She moved toward the piano as a moth to a flame but hesitated, stopping herself from doing something so improper.

It's magnificent.

Aunt Agnes did have a piano, stuck unceremoniously in the back of an unused parlor as an afterthought. Margaret wasn't even certain the piano had ever been tuned. She was only permitted to play when no callers were expected. Her aunt's piano was certainly nothing like this gorgeous instrument, shining like a beacon to Margaret.

"Mama, who is this?" A pretty girl of about fourteen with wide blue eyes interrupted Margaret's lustful stare. A violin dangled from one slender hand.

"Phaedra, darling, this is Miss Lainscott. A pianist. Miss Lainscott, my daughter, Lady Phaedra. And our flutist is my ward, Miss Olivia Nelson."

Miss Nelson nodded her head. "Greetings, Miss Lainscott."

"A pianist? Oh, thank *goodness*." Phaedra gave a great, dramatic sigh. "We won't have Romy pounding at the keys and torturing us. No matter how many lessons she takes from Mrs. Anderson, she rarely gets better."

"Phaedra," the duchess admonished her daughter. "Behave."

"I heard that. At least I'm not screeching away like an annoyed cat." A stunning young woman popped up from the other side of the piano, where she'd apparently been searching for something on the floor. "Found it," she said, holding up a pin. Her eyes were also light blue, but with a circle of darker blue around the iris. There was something familiar about her, but Margaret didn't think they'd ever met.

"Andromeda, this is Miss Lainscott," the duchess said. "My eldest daughter, Lady Andromeda."

"Greetings, Miss Lainscott. In case you were wondering, our other sister is named Theodosia. My mother's adoration of Greek culture extended to the naming her children. Papa indulged her, much to our mutual dismay."

"Don't forget the barn cats," Phaedra interjected. "Do you remember Hermes and Aphrodite?"

"Oh, yes. I still miss Hermes." Andromeda turned back to her mother. "Theo sends word she *may* appear for tea. She's busy with her miniatures."

"Then I daresay we won't see her until dinner this evening, sporting paint under her nails." The duchess gave a frustrated sigh. "You, Andromeda, are excused from your duties at the piano today," she announced with a wrinkle of her brow. "Most thankfully."

"Welcome, Miss Lainscott. It is lovely meeting you," Andromeda said to Margaret over her shoulder as she skipped out of the conservatory, her elation at not having to play the piano evident. "I'll return for tea. Cook made those tiny cakes with pink icing I adore."

The duchess placed a hand on her temple. "I pray daily for patience."

"Come, Miss Lainscott." Mrs. Anderson took her hand and pointed to two women, nearly hidden in the corner by a large potted fern, arguing over a page of sheet music.

"Ladies." Mrs. Anderson clapped her hands with a wry smile. "I'm sure you're both correct. May I present our pianist for today, Miss Lainscott. Miss Lainscott, I'm pleased to introduce you to Mrs. Mounsey and Mrs. Adams."

Both women greeted her politely then immediately went back to their discussion.

"It's not really an argument, you understand," Mrs. Anderson said. "It is more a difference of opinion. Mrs. Mounsey usually wins."

Margaret was beside herself with joy. Not only was she in the same room as Lucy Anderson, renowned pianist, but Anne Mounsey was also here. Mrs. Mounsey was a female composer and Mrs. Adams, a soprano.

She had never, *ever*, been so happy in her entire life and nearly giggled with the joy of being here. When asked to sit at the piano, Margaret sucked in her breath at the gold lettering above the keys that labeled the instrument as a Broadwood and very expensive. Margaret nearly expired on the spot.

The next two hours passed swiftly as the women combined their efforts on several well-known pieces before attempting one of Mrs. Mounsey's recent compositions. Mrs. Anderson played the Broadwood as Margaret watched in adoration, eagerly awaiting her turn.

Miss Nelson turned out to be a gifted flutist, though Lady Phaedra was far from mastering the violin. While she played with enthusiasm, Margaret had to admit she needed much more practice. When Mrs. Anderson gestured for Margaret to come and sit next to her on the piano bench, she eagerly complied. As Margaret joined Miss Nelson and Phaedra on a simple piece, Mrs. Anderson gently corrected her on her form and technique, making several suggestions. Margaret's fingers didn't leave the keys again until the tea cart arrived.

Mrs. Anderson gave her a quick hug and said, "You have a gift, Margaret. Your passion for music is evident in every keystroke. Do not let *anyone* deter you from continuing to do what you love."

Margaret nodded solemnly, her eyes welling with tears. It

had been so long since anyone had praised or complimented her for anything.

Except Lord Welles. He had admired my playing.

She ran her hands over the piano, caressing the fine wood with her fingertips. "I daresay anyone would sound like an angel on an instrument such as this."

Mrs. Anderson frowned. "Surely your aunt possesses a piano?"

"She does," Margaret assured her. "But nothing so fine. The poor thing is ancient and out of tune. But I do my best."

Mrs. Anderson stared at her thoughtfully for a moment before saying, "I'm sure you do."

The butler, Pith, presented the tea cart with a flourish. The tray was piled high with a vast assortment of sandwiches, pastries, honey, and clotted cream in addition to the tea.

The duchess clapped her hands. "Ladies, a *symphony* of delights awaits you."

Mrs. Anderson laughed at her friend's little joke and made her way to the sofa. Chairs had been arranged around a low table in the center of the room. Dropping the violin, Phaedra raced to the tea cart but slowed down as the duchess tilted her head. The other ladies approached in a much calmer manner.

Margaret had been so focused on the Broadwood and the music filling the room she'd given little thought to anything else. Reluctantly, she left the piano and took a place on the sofa where her stomach proceeded to grumble in hunger at the repast laid before them.

Accepting a cup of tea, Margaret bit into a flaky currant scone, so light it melted in her mouth. Her aunt's cook was not nearly so skilled at baking. As she savored her treat, Margaret listened in rapt attention to the conversation around her.

The Duchess of Averell, she soon found out, had always

been a patron of the arts. Her support of female artists was well known. She and Mrs. Anderson met when the latter had come to teach both the duchess and Andromeda, whom everyone referred to as Romy, the piano.

Mrs. Anderson rolled her eyes at the recollection. "Your Grace was kind enough to end her lessons after a time."

The duchess burst into laughter. "And it *was* a kindness," she said, eyes twinkling. "I was quite terrible. I believe my husband begged me to stop, promising he would gift me with a large diamond if only I would cease my attempts at playing. His late wife was musically inclined, and I had wished to impress him. My lack of talent, however, does not preclude me from encouraging others." She nodded in the direction of Phaedra, who was licking frosting off her lip, and Miss Nelson. "Artistic pursuits should be nurtured, no matter what form they take, whether you are male or female. When I learned that *all* women, no matter their skill, were denied membership in the Royal Society of Musicians, I was outraged. An artist is an artist and should receive the support of their peers, despite their gender. When my dear Lucy informed me the Royal Society of Musicians would deny assistance to a violinist or pianist purely because that person was female, I was outraged."

"Outraged is a much more polite term for my emotion at the time," Mrs. Anderson chimed in. "Mrs. Mounsey and myself, along with another friend, decided to form our own society to assist female musicians in need. Her Grace has thrown her support behind us." She took her friend's hand. "And we are *most* grateful."

The duchess blushed at the attention and squeezed Mrs. Anderson's hand. "You shall always have my support."

After tea, Mrs. Mounsey and Mrs. Adams saw themselves out with hugs and a thank you to the duchess.

Mrs. Anderson smiled and stood, patting her stomach.

"My compliments to your cook on the scones, Your Grace. And I am so happy you could join us today, Miss Lainscott. I fear I won't see you again for some time. I'm to start rehearsals for my next appearance with the Royal Philharmonic Orchestra."

"Thank you for inviting me. I will look forward to spending another afternoon such as this." Today had been amazing and Margaret would never forget the kindness of Mrs. Anderson and her friends. Nor of the duchess for having her. She was loath to leave the sunny conservatory and return to the exhausting task of avoiding Winthrop.

The thought brought Lord Welles and their conversation to mind. She hadn't given up on becoming reacquainted with Carstairs.

The duchess walked Mrs. Anderson to the door, hugging her tightly. Margaret saw her nod as Mrs. Anderson said something in a low tone, then her gaze landed on Margaret.

"I fear I must take my leave as well, Your Grace." Margaret stood, knowing she'd stayed far longer than was prudent. It wouldn't be wise for Aunt Agnes or any of the servants to see Margaret sneak back to her room.

"A moment, Miss Lainscott." The duchess motioned for her to sit back down.

Surprised, Margaret did as she requested.

"I hope you enjoyed yourself today?" The duchess picked up a delicate cup decorated with roses and sipped her tea.

"Yes, Your Grace. I can't remember when I've had such a wonderful time. Thank you again for welcoming me into your home."

The duchess eyed Margaret over the rim of her cup. "What do you think of the organization Mrs. Anderson has formed? I hope you'll consider joining her and the other ladies when next they meet in my conservatory."

"I would like nothing more, Your Grace. And I am

committed to assisting Mrs. Anderson in any way I can." Margaret would have access to a great deal of wealth once she married, which made it *imperative* she wed a man who would allow her to do as she pleased. Because it would *please* Margaret to fund the Royal Society of Female Musicians.

"I thought as much. You and I are of like mind in that regard. I hope I don't shock you, Miss Lainscott, when I say I believe everyone, especially we women, must have a passion —something which is important and worthy of our time besides a husband and children. His Grace was not inclined to such an opinion when we first met." She took another sip of tea, her voice softening as she spoke of her husband. "Though I am certain he feels differently now."

"I agree, Your Grace," Margaret said.

"That is why I've encouraged my daughters in their artistic pursuits. It matters not whether they excel or become noted for their accomplishments, though such a thing would be wonderful. What is important is that your passion feeds your soul, the part of you shared with no one else." She smiled. "My family teases me about my obsession with Greek culture, but I find pleasure in seeking the truth hidden inside a Greek myth. I've studied the Iliad for years. Have you read it?" At Margaret's nod, she said, "I learned Greek so I could read the original text without translation."

The Duchess of Averell was not just a pampered, titled duchess. Margaret's respect grew for her hostess who was not only kind but obviously of high intelligence.

"I've two young, musically inclined girls who should be encouraged in their pursuits, and not because such talent means I can trot them out to perform for a recital and hope to prove their worth to a potential husband."

Margaret looked down at her hands, thinking of how Aunt Agnes had done such a thing to her.

A small sound of amusement left the duchess. "Only *two*,

Miss Lainscott. I've officially given up on Romy's musical talent." Her eyes met Margaret's. "Lucy tells me you compose as well as play the piano. What a magnificent gift."

"I dabble, Your Grace. My accomplishments are well beneath those of Mrs. Mounsey."

Margaret's dreams were small. She wished to encourage a love of music in others, help other musicians when she could, and possibly publish her own music one day. A husband who made demands on her would allow none of that. Winthrop certainly would not.

She *must* have her music.

"Forgive me, my dear, if I am overstepping, but I am well acquainted with Lady Dobson." A hint of dislike colored her words. "I feel certain you are not being encouraged and I doubt you've even a proper piano to practice on." The duchess set down the teacup and leaned forward. "I think we may be able to help each other, Miss Lainscott. Lucy is so very busy and cannot visit often enough to provide the encouragement I feel certain Phaedra and Olivia need. And Romy cannot continue to accompany them on the piano; quite frankly, Phaedra has begged me to allow her sister to do something else."

Margaret looked over to Phaedra and Olivia. The Duchess of Averell's daughter was waving the violin's bow about her head as she tried to make a point about something while Olivia nodded. She liked both girls very much.

"And you wish to compose, do you not? Wouldn't you rather use our piano in the comfort of my conservatory? My cook does make excellent scones," she added with a nod at the remains on Margaret's plate.

Margaret's eyes slid to the gorgeous piano in the corner. The sound had been sheer perfection.

The duchess noted the direction of her gaze. "It is a beautiful piece, is it not? I keep it regularly tuned. The piano was a gift to my stepson. A Broadwood. Wonderfully made. Certainly, the piano doesn't deserve Romy."

"Broadwood makes a very fine piano, Your Grace. The sound is like nothing I've ever heard. Even the piano I played at home." Her voice faltered. Her mother had possessed a piano which Margaret had inherited, but it, like everything else, had been sold at auction after her father's death.

"I have a proposal for you, Miss Lainscott. I would like you to visit twice weekly, more often if you wish. You will accompany Phaedra and Olivia and challenge them in their choice of music. Encourage them. You may also play and compose to your heart's content on that piano." The duchess nodded again to the Broadwood standing sentinel in the corner. "I may ask you to continue Romy's lessons. Infrequently," she said in a hurried tone. "Oh, I know she'll never be any good, mind you, music is not her passion. But Romy *did* promise her father to play a tune for him on his birthday, which is still some months away. She doesn't wish to disappoint him." Her eyes took on a faraway look for a moment. "My husband is in poor health, Miss Lainscott, and declines daily. Romy may need to find another way to please her father." She blinked and bestowed a smile on Margaret. "At any rate, I know I'm asking you for a lot, but I'm hopeful the lure of the Broadwood and the use of my conservatory will be enough to entice you to return?"

It would be no hardship to accompany the girls on the piano, nor to offer encouragement. And showing Romy how to play a simple tune would be her pleasure. The Duchess of Averell's proposal would benefit Margaret far more than her daughters. She snuck another look at the piano, knowing she would have to decline. It was doubtful Aunt Agnes would permit her to visit so often and for a reason other than being courted.

"I would love to do so, and your offer is incredibly generous, Your Grace. Unfortunately, my aunt —"

"You will leave Lady Dobson to me," the duchess said firmly. "I know she wishes you to marry; she makes such clear to nearly everyone she meets. I've only been back in London for a short time and even I have been apprised of her determination. Never fear, Miss Lainscott, I shall throw my weight around a bit. I am a duchess, after all." She gave Margaret a saucy wink. "You needn't worry. I'll settle everything."

"My goodness." The deep, husky baritone echoed from the entrance to the conservatory. "I expected to be greeted at the front door with some modicum of excitement. Instead, I was subjected to cooling my heels downstairs while a new footman who had no idea who I was went in search of Pith."

Margaret's eyes closed for a moment, reveling in the absolute beauty of his voice. What in the *world* was Lord Welles doing here?

The brilliant eyes scanned the room, landing on Margaret with a brief flash of surprise.

"Welles, darling." The duchess's face broke into an adoring smile. "I did wonder when you would appear."

"Tony!" Phaedra flew at him, wrapping her arms around his neck. Olivia came forward as well, and Welles wrapped an arm around her. "Did you bring me a present?" Phaedra grabbed at the lapels of his coat.

"Greedy chit. No, I didn't bring you anything. *I* am your present." He turned to the duchess. "What are you teaching these girls, Your Grace?" He kissed Phaedra's cheek then Olivia's. He whispered something in Olivia's ear, and she giggled. Welles sauntered over to the duchess, bowing low over her hand. "Your Grace," he greeted her properly.

The duchess offered her cheek for a kiss. "Have you brought Leo with you? Is he downstairs tormenting Pith?"

"No, Your Grace. But he sends his regards and eagerly

anticipates an invitation to dine." He reached across the table to snatch a tiny biscuit, popping it into his mouth with a satisfied sound. The rings of sapphire blue settled on Margaret though she couldn't tell whether he was amused or annoyed to find her visiting the Duchess of Averell. Certainly, he was curious. "And what have we here? Is that Miss Lainscott hiding behind a cushion?"

"My lord, what a surprise to see you." It was on the tip of her tongue to ask why he'd be at Averell House at all. A man known for inhabiting Elysium didn't seem the sort to stop by and have tea with a duchess.

Welles took her hand in greeting, sending a jolt of heat down the length of her arm. The long, tapered fingers gave hers a gentle, unexpected squeeze. "A pleasure, as always, Miss Lainscott."

Unsettled, Margaret pulled her hand away with a small jerk.

The wide mouth ticked up in amusement; he clearly enjoyed her discomfort.

"I wasn't aware you knew Miss Lainscott," the duchess said to Welles.

"We've been introduced." He sat down in a wing-backed chair directly across from Margaret, the length of his legs stretching beneath the table holding the tea tray. He was wearing a coat of deep indigo, a color that only served to enhance the beauty of his eyes. The material pulled against his broad shoulders as he reached for another biscuit, the sunlight catching across the brush of dark hair lining his jaw. He smiled at Margaret, his sensuous lips tilting in a way that made her stomach flutter. Welles was quite glorious, and he knew it. The females hovering about him in the conservatory only served to highlight his dark, masculine beauty.

And his *voice*. Margaret gave herself a mental shake. She

was close to mooning over Welles which she refused to allow herself to do.

"Tony! I wasn't sure you knew we had come." Romy, a wide smile of greeting on her lips, strolled back into the conservatory. "Oh, drat. I've missed tea."

"Welles has not yet eaten all the biscuits," the duchess said.

Romy had a band around her wrist filled with pins. Bits of fabric and feathers, of all things, were stuck to her skirts. Going directly to Welles, she kissed his cheek, before turning and grinning at her mother. "Thank goodness. The biscuits are my favorite."

Margaret stared, surprised at her own stupidity for not seeing what was right before her from the moment Welles had entered the conservatory.

The eyes. Welles's and Romy's eyes were identical, the same startling blue with the successively darker rings surrounding the iris.

This was *his* family. Romy, Phaedra, and the absent Theodosia were his *sisters*. The resemblance, now that they all stood together, was so obvious Margaret couldn't believe she'd missed it. The duchess was far too young to be his mother. She had to be his stepmother. Margaret had known Welles was an earl, but he was also the son of the Duke of Averell.

No wonder he's rather arrogant. He's to be a duke one day.

"Miss Lainscott, I can see the proper introductions aren't necessary as you've already met my stepson, Lord Welles." The duchess looked between them, a question in her eyes, obviously trying to ascertain how the roguishly handsome Welles had come in contact with the plain heiress, Margaret Lainscott.

"We were introduced by the Dowager Marchioness of Cambourne, were we not, Miss Lainscott?"

"Yes," Margaret assured the duchess. "At a house party given at Gray Covington last year."

"You hate house parties." Phaedra leaned over his shoulder and plucked at his shirt. She clearly adored her older brother.

"I do. Avoid them like the plague. But Gray Covington was on the way back to London. I was with Carstairs." He put a slight emphasis on his friend's name. "And Lady Cambourne invited me herself. No one disappoints the Dowager Marchioness of Cambourne. I thought it in my best interest not to be the first."

"Carstairs?" The duchess's lovely face wrinkled in confusion. "Oh, yes. I recall him. Your friend with the hunting lodge. I'm always concerned he'll shoot one of his toes off the way his mind wanders. Or worse, think you a deer and aim in your direction."

"That's mother's polite way of saying she doesn't find Carstairs to possess a keen mind," Phaedra piped up.

"Phaedra! I said no such thing. Pray, mind your tongue. We have a guest," the duchess said, glancing at Margaret.

"Oh, I think Miss Lainscott discerned all she needed to about Carstairs after meeting him at Gray Covington, didn't you, Miss Lainscott?"

Margaret choked on her bite of scone. "I find him very pleasant."

"He *is* incredibly pleasant." Welles slapped one hand against his thigh. "I've always said so. Doesn't remind one of a pear or any other fruit either, does he, Miss Lainscott?"

Lord Welles was a horrible man. She should never have confided such a thing to him. "Not at all, my lord." Margaret took another bite of what remained of her scone, hoping he didn't mean to inform Her Grace and the others of her request to become reacquainted with Carstairs, or of the reason.

"What an odd thing to say, Welles," the duchess said. "Comparing gentlemen to fruit. If I didn't know better, I would think you were foxed."

"Not in the least, Your Grace. I was only making conversation with Miss Lainscott. Have you ladies been practicing your music? God, don't tell me you've allowed Romy to torture my piano?"

Margaret momentarily stopped the chewing of the scone in her mouth. The Broadwood was *his* piano. And she'd spent the better part of the day with her hands on the gleaming keys, her fingertips caressing the beautiful ivory and wood. Almost like touching Welles himself.

The soft hum across her skin became more pronounced.

"No, I am thankfully relieved from duty," Romy informed him. "I shan't be distressing your piano any longer."

"I can almost hear it sigh with relief," he said.

"Mrs. Anderson visited and suggested Miss Lainscott might enjoy a day of music." The duchess nodded to Margaret.

"Ah, the Royal Society of Female Musicians." Welles tapped a finger to his lips, his eyes never leaving Margaret's face. "How is Mrs. Anderson?"

Warmth bloomed across Margaret's chest as Welles studied her. He made no disparaging remarks about the efforts of Mrs. Anderson and her friends, nor about Margaret's involvement.

"Quite well," the duchess replied. "She will be busy with her own commitments for the remainder of the year, but Miss Lainscott has agreed to accompany Phaedra and Olivia in her stead." She nodded at Margaret. "Relieving Romy and, indeed, all of us."

"How kind of Miss Lainscott." Welles popped another biscuit into his mouth.

Margaret hadn't actually *agreed* to Her Grace's suggestion

but from the look on the face of her hostess, the decision had been made for her.

"I haven't yet seen Lady Cambourne since arriving in London," the duchess said in a thoughtful tone. "I suppose I should pay her a call. She may be useful in garnering support for Romy."

"Why do I need support garnered?" Romy plucked what looked like a feather stuck to the lace of her sleeve and shot her mother an exasperated look. "I thought you said I could spend this season just enjoying myself."

"I wish to ensure your launch is successful," the duchess explained calmly.

"Much like any ship or more appropriately, an over-sized barge," Phaedra said innocently. "You aren't properly launched until someone whacks you with a bottle of champagne." She made the motion of cracking a bottle. "What do you think, Mama?"

Romy ran after her sister who skirted around the perimeter of the conservatory to finally return and hide behind Welles. Phaedra stuck out her tongue.

"Girls." The duchess clapped her hands. "Cease. Phaedra, we are not christening your sister with spirits. Romy, dearest, it never hurts to have Lady Cambourne in your corner."

Welles watched his sisters' antics with a great deal of affection. It was obvious he adored his half-siblings. He turned back to Margaret, his eyes shining in the light streaming through the room, and pierced her with a look. It was as if he could discern every curve of her body beneath the plain day dress she wore. The humming fell lower to nestle between her thighs, becoming more insistent the longer he stared at her.

Hastily, Margaret looked away. Welles had the most alarming effect on her; she could not let him distract her. She needed to be working on a way to have a private conversation with him about Carstairs.

The clock in the room struck the hour and Margaret looked up in alarm. Her aunt could not return and discover her gone.

"My apologies, Your Grace." Margaret set down her plate. "I must return home. The hour grows late, and my aunt will expect my return." Her chance to speak to Welles would have to wait, at least for today. She couldn't very well speak to him of Carstairs at the moment, not with the duchess and her daughters present. Perhaps she could send him a note.

"Oh, dear, where has the day gone? We've so enjoyed your company," the duchess said. "Please don't concern yourself over your aunt. I promised I will deal with Lady Dobson, and I shall. We'll see you on Tuesday."

Margaret stood, bobbing as she took her leave. "I would be delighted, Your Grace." She snuck one more look at the immense, lustrous piano, standing proudly in the corner of the room. No lover could be more seductive.

Her eyes slid over Welles. *Almost.*

Phaedra and Olivia came forward and bid her goodbye as did Romy, who stuck her unintentionally with a pin from the cushion attached to her wrist. Margaret liked the duchess and her daughters. Today had been the happiest she'd spent since her father's death and certainly the most fun she'd had since arriving in London.

Welles rose from his chair. "I fear I must take my leave as well, madam. I only stopped by on my way to attend to a business matter. I'll accompany Miss Lainscott out."

Margaret's pulse leapt wildly. It appeared fate was intervening. She became more certain of her plan for Carstairs, for surely the coincidence of Welles being here was a sign of sorts.

The duchess pouted prettily. "I expect you and your

brother to dine with us this week." The thread of steel returned to her voice. "Promptly at seven, two days hence."

Welles inclined his head. "We will both be here, madam. And I'll take you all for a ride in the park tomorrow," he said to Phaedra, Olivia and Romy. "And Theo if we can pull her away from her studio."

"Possibly a visit to DuPere's?" Romy asked, shooting a glance at her mother. "I wish only to look at the silks."

"Say yes, Mama." Phaedra came over and placed a hand on her mother's shoulder and squeezed.

"Of course." The duchess nodded. "But take a full purse, Tony. Your father says these girls are like to bankrupt us all."

The way Welles's face froze at the slight mention of the Duke of Averell was obvious, though he recovered quickly before taking the duchess's hand. "Until then." He pressed a kiss to her proffered cheek. "After you, Miss Lainscott."

5

Margaret marched to the door, every nerve in her body aware of Welles just behind her. She planned to broach the subject of Carstairs as soon as Margaret was assured she wouldn't be heard from the conservatory.

Welles's much larger form hovered dangerously close to Margaret's as they made their way down the stairs, making her feel much smaller than usual. Her senses were so inflamed, her body humming at an alarmingly high pitch, Margaret's attention wandered. Her heel caught on the hem of her skirts and she nearly toppled over.

Welles reached out and deftly caught her elbow. "I saw the look in your eye, Miss Lainscott. *Lust*."

Heat rushed up her cheeks. Had he guessed the direction of her thoughts? "Lust, my lord?"

"The *piano*, Miss Lainscott. I'm not certain any gentleman could compete with the Broadwood for your affection." His lips twitched. "What else would I possibly have meant?"

"Of course," she replied smoothly. "Was my admiration of your instrument so obvious?"

Welles paused for a moment, mischief swirling in the depths of blue, as he looked down at her. "Oh, Miss Lainscott, how lovely of you."

It took only a moment for Margaret to take his meaning. Her cheeks felt as if they'd been scorched by fire. "That isn't what I meant," she sputtered in mortification. "I would never—"

"Of course not, Miss Lainscott. Although you *are* given to rather improper suggestions."

Margaret caught a hint of his scent—leather and tobacco, mixed with wind and the outdoors. "About that, my lord. I consider it fortuitous we saw each other today. I wish to speak to you about Lord Carstairs."

"I was wondering if you would bring up your very unusual request. I'm not in the habit of playing matchmaker, Miss Lainscott. Furthermore, I consider the institution of marriage to be a form of entrapment. Why should I assist in landing my friend in such a circumstance?"

"Entrapment is a bit harsh, my lord. And I *do* apologize if I am presuming on our short acquaintance but I've no one else to ask." Margaret kept her voice low, lest the duchess's butler overhear. He stood beside the door as they passed through to the steps outside.

"What would you call such a thing?"

Margaret looked up to see him studying her intently. The deepening colors of sapphire in his eyes looked like the edge of the horizon, right as the sun had finally set but before the sky went completely dark. Perhaps the young lady who'd written an ode to Welles's eyes hadn't been as much of a peawit as Margaret had originally assumed. Being on the receiving end of the full force of Welles's attention was nothing short of *exhilarating*. Her skin buzzed deliciously, like a tuning fork.

"Miss Lainscott?"

"My cause is just," she said.

"In your estimation."

"My lord, most gentlemen choose their wives in such a way, do they not? Find a woman who is possessed of the qualities they seek and then set out to woo her? Possibly they enlist their friends and family to assist them. I am merely doing the same. I thought you more open-minded."

A lazy smile crossed his lips. "I am the very epitome of open-mindedness."

"Will you hear me out, my lord?" She tilted her chin, determined to keep her wits about her, and not allow Welles and his...*gorgeousness* to deter her from her task. It was *imperative*, especially with Winthrop circling her like a lion who intended to take down a wounded gazelle, that Lord Welles understand the *importance* of her request and agree to help her. Margaret had to get things quickly in hand which meant Carstairs.

She hopped down the steps to the sidewalk, stopping beside a luxurious carriage pulled by four perfectly matched bays. "Winthrop is pressing his suit most forcefully, Lord Welles. I've endured him twice already this week."

"An unfortunate occurrence. Are you certain it must be Carstairs? Is there no other gentleman who has your affection?

Just you. "No, my lord." Margaret shook her head.

"No one else who...*stirs* your emotions?" Another double meaning emphasized the word.

"My lord, not *every* sentence you utter must end in some sort of...improper innuendo."

A soft chuckle. "My apologies, Miss Lainscott, though I find it interesting you seem to pick up on all my indecent suggestions, *gently bred* young lady that you are. But I have my doubts about that. Do go on."

"I *am* gently bred. And no one could fail to notice

your...*nuances*. You aren't subtle in the least." Margaret looked away for a moment to compose herself. Now was not the time to argue needlessly over Welles's rakish behavior. "I truly see no other way out of my current situation. Believe me, if I could avoid marriage completely, I would. But since I am compelled to do so, I think Carstairs and I would be a good match. I wish to assure you I would be a good wife to your friend, Lord Welles. I won't infringe on his hunting or any other recreational activities. He can have as many mistresses as he wishes."

"How progressive of you." Welles regarded her seriously. "I see you've thought this through in a very logical fashion."

"Furthermore, I'm disgustingly wealthy." Her voice took on a pleading note. "My dowry isn't the largest this season but even so, the amount is obscene."

Welles nodded slowly. "All excellent points, Miss Lainscott. But I still—"

"I need you only to reintroduce us and possibly...help things along." She was pushing her luck and the boundaries of propriety in asking Lord Welles for such a thing, but Margaret knew her limits. She was no great beauty and older than most of the young ladies making the rounds this season. A high intellect wasn't valued in a wife. Margaret might require more than an introduction.

"Help things along?"

"You know what I mean, my lord." She waved about her hands. "Esteem me. Highly regard me. Perhaps mention your admiration for my talent on the piano."

"I do admire your talents."

"And I would ask your discretion in this matter." Surely a gentleman who adored his stepmother and sisters in such a way could be trusted.

"You have my promise I'll not speak a word of what

you've asked. But I'm not certain I am the right man to assist you. You could presume upon my stepmother, for instance."

"I've only met the Duchess of Averell today." Margaret's fingers curled into her skirts, tugging at the material in frustration. "Is there nothing I can do to convince you to help me? Another performance on the piano, perhaps?"

6

That was exactly what he'd been considering.

"Something like that."

Miss Lainscott was a tiny, petite thing. Delicate. Like a fine porcelain doll he'd once bought for Romy, except the doll's eyes hadn't sparkled with repressed fire as Miss Lainscott's did. There was an entire list of wicked things Tony wished to do to her, and each one involved her naked in a variety of positions.

He'd been shocked to see the object of his erotic fantasies taking tea with Amanda and the girls, though in hearing of Miss Lainscott's budding friendship with Mrs. Anderson, her presence in the conservatory made perfect sense. Tony wondered if Miss Lainscott would have hunted him down if they hadn't unexpectedly met today; he thought she would have.

Her dark eyes shone with urgency, hoping to convince him to help her. "A performance? Or something else? Does one of your mistresses require piano lessons?" A tiny smirk crossed her luscious mouth.

"Allow me to take you home. My carriage is much more

comfortable than a hack. We can speak further on the way." Poor Miss Lainscott. She was completely oblivious to his desire for her. If she had the slightest inkling, she wouldn't dare get in the carriage with him.

"My lord, if my aunt —"

"She'll never see you. I promise. I'll drop you in the back by the mews. You can make your way through the gardens."

Miss Lainscott frowned, considering his offer. "I don't think—"

"Carstairs has been out of town." Tony threw out the bit of knowledge like a carrot dangled before a mule. His friend had been fishing at the estate of Mr. Turnbull but was now returning to London. "I know which events he'll be attending in the upcoming weeks."

She looked between him and the carriage. "Fine. I would appreciate the ride home."

Miss Lainscott took his hand and climbed into the carriage, sliding gracefully across the seat, her features delicate and pale against the black leather squabs.

Tony settled across from her. Before he'd gone up to the conservatory, he'd noticed the pile of invitations by the door. Lady Masterson was having a garden party and she was a friend of the family. Her invitation had sat atop the stack. His stepmother would likely ask Tony to escort her to the party. He hadn't planned on attending but now he thought he would. Lady Masterson wouldn't mind if Miss Lainscott was also brought along.

The woman in question regarded him from beneath her lashes, pretending shyness, which he found absurd under the circumstances. Her deep chocolate eyes sparked and burned with intelligence, more enticing to him than an entire room of courtesans.

"My lord? What would you ask of me in return?"

"It does involve playing the piano," he finally said.

"Lessons?" she asked again. "Perhaps you need a refresher in technique? Or shall we play a duet?"

Tony kept his face bland. He was quite good on the piano, though not as talented as Miss Lainscott. "Not exactly. More of a private performance."

Her brows knit together. "Private performance? Are you having guests and I'm to be the entertainment? In Her Grace's conservatory? I suppose I could do such a thing but —"

"You misunderstand. I wish you to play for *me*. *Only me*. In a private room at Elysium."

Her eyes widened. "Elysium? The gambling hell? Why would I do such a thing?"

"Because you'll be clad only in your chemise and stockings." He sat back, waiting for her reaction. "I don't think my stepmother's home is appropriate for such a performance, do you?"

"Oh," she sputtered prettily. "I don't think—" Her mouth was open in shock, small breasts pushing furiously against her bodice as she tried to take a deep breath.

His cock, which had been aching since he spotted her eating a scone with his stepmother, thickened painfully at the very thought of her in his rooms at Elysium.

A squeak escaped her before she sat back with a whoosh, slapping her small fists to the squabs. A *giggle* escaped her. "Lord Welles," she said in a relieved voice. "You shouldn't tease me about such a thing." She wagged a finger at him. "You nearly had me with your 'improper' suggestion. I thought you were serious."

Tony sat transfixed. He'd seen her smile and look politely amused. But he'd never seen her genuinely laugh. Or *giggle* like a schoolgirl. Unable to look away from the pale line of her throat, he had the urge to press his lips to the spot where her pulse beat and shock them both.

Miss Lainscott giggled again, this time pressing a gloved hand to her stomach in her amusement.

Apparently, Tony's request to seduce her was incredibly humorous. Well, that was something he hadn't experienced before. He'd never made such a request to a virgin of good breeding and based on her reaction, he wasn't sure he'd ever do so again.

"I'm not teasing you. Or mocking you." He shrugged. "You *did* ask what I wanted."

Her head snapped back up in shock. She opened her mouth to speak then closed it, horrified by his outlandish request. And oddly fascinated. Her gaze flashed to his mouth for a brief second before a lovely rose color infused the skin of her cheeks.

"Dear God, you *are* serious. I can't imagine why."

"Humanitarian reasons, Miss Lainscott. Before you tie yourself to Carstairs, or, should you fail in bringing him to heel, Winthrop, wouldn't you wish to experience passion? I doubt you'll find it with either of your suitors. Think of your music, if nothing else. I am."

The delicious blush crept back into her cheeks, but she did not look away from him. "You, my lord, are *not* a gentleman."

"Alas, I've never claimed to be."

She shook her head and looked out the window, refusing to look at him until the carriage rolled to a stop.

"Never mind. I rescind my request for your assistance." Miss Lainscott placed a hand on the carriage door. "We've arrived at my aunt's. I bid you good day, Lord Welles."

7

Margaret paced back and forth across her bedroom floor, as she had most of last night and all of the morning. She hadn't slept a wink thinking of her conversation with Welles. She couldn't decide if he had been serious or not.

He had certainly seemed serious. The very idea sent a tremor of excitement up her spine.

Passion. He should have made a much more convincing argument. As if playing the piano for him in her underthings would inspire her musically or—

Arouse me.

Bollocks. The problem was, Margaret *did* find the thought of such a thing to be arousing, just as she did the improper innuendos he seemed determined to shock her with. The idea that Lord Welles *wanted* to see her in her stockings and chemise was nothing short of astonishing. And highly erotic.

Her pulse skipped a beat as she turned to view the invitation to Lady Masterson's garden party. It had arrived earlier that morning and Eliza had brought the note upstairs with Margaret's breakfast tray. Walking over to the invitation, she reread the words printed upon the fine vellum. A party to be held in the gardens of Lady Masterson's estate just outside of London. Nature-themed dress was encouraged.

She'd no idea what a "nature-themed" costume entailed; Margaret had no intention of dressing up like a bird or something equally ridiculous. The *ton* was often bored and looking for new and inventive opportunities to spend their money. Lavish, themed parties seemed an appropriate way for a pampered group of overindulged people to do so.

She looked again at the invitation knowing Welles must have had something to do with Margaret receiving the summons, because she didn't know Lady Masterson. The only other explanation was that Welles had told his stepmother of Margaret's interest in Carstairs and the Duchess of Averell had requested the invitation issued. Either way, she was certain Carstairs would be there; the invitation appearing at the same time as her interest in him was too coincidental.

The problem was in explaining the invitation to her aunt.

Elysium. He had wanted her to come to him at a notorious gambling hell, half-naked.

Margaret spun on her heel and walked the length of the rug again. She had always wanted to venture into such a place. Elysium was a notorious pleasure palace and gambling establishment where all manner of wicked things occurred. At least according to gossip. What would it be like to visit Elysium in the company of Lord Welles?

A slow burn of excitement coursed down her breasts to settle below.

She could never do such a thing. Ever. What if someone saw her?

Don't you want to know passion?

What if she walked into Elysium only to have Welles laugh uproariously at her appearance?

After tucking the invitation away, Margaret left her room

and soon found herself in front of her aunt's out-of-tune piano. Since playing the Broadwood, the ancient piano seemed even more decrepit than before.

Margaret ran her fingers over the keys, wincing at the sound. Clara, her mother, had been a pianist as well. She'd been playing for the amusement of her friends at a party when Walter Lainscott had seen her. The pair had fallen madly in love and eloped, despite the obvious differences in their stations. Her father had then brought Clara to Yorkshire where he bought her a gorgeous piano, specially crafted for her in Austria. But the piano hadn't kept his wife from withering away. She missed London and was plagued with repeated bouts of illness in her lungs. Her poor health had made her susceptible to the sickness which swept through the mines and eventually took her life.

Margaret's mother had always been fragile which strengthened Margaret's determination to *not* be.

The piano had been sold at auction, along with everything else that reminded Aunt Agnes of her younger, more beautiful sister. If it had been possible, she was certain Aunt Agnes would have sold Margaret off as well.

Her fingers flew over the keys, warming up the muscles in her hands before she launched into a complicated piece by Beethoven. Soon, the music filled her, allowing her mind to wander. She closed her eyes, envisioning herself sitting before the Broadwood with Welles at her side, his fingertips running over the backs of her hands. Warmth sank into her skin at the image of playing for him and only him.

"Miss."

Margaret's fingers slowed, disappointed to have been interrupted.

"Yes, Henderson?" She turned to see her aunt's butler watching her, disapproval deepening the grooves bracketing his mouth. Henderson found waiting on Margaret to be beneath him, as if the fact her father had been a tin miner before becoming wealthy was a severe violation of some butler code. Margaret had witnessed his injured pride when she'd heard him voicing his objections to her aunt. Since that time, she'd taken a more timid approach with Henderson because it made her life easier. Margaret had been tired of tepid tea and food which had grown cold. Henderson still detested her but at least now, the fire in her room was lit first thing in the morning.

But Margaret didn't feel shy or reserved today. Holding the butler's gaze, Margaret enjoyed the way he cleared his throat and shuffled at her directness, before looking down at his hands.

"Your aunt requests a word with you, miss."

"Of course."

Dutifully, Margaret rose and followed Henderson to the front parlor, a room Aunt Agnes typically reserved for answering correspondence or dictating people's lives over a chatty cup of tea. What a *burden* her aunt carried, to be so superior that it was left to her to play judge and jury over everyone in the *ton*.

She kept her eyes lowered lest her aunt see the dislike for her gleaming in them.

Aunt Agnes was perched at the very edge of a cream-colored settee in one of her best day dresses, her head topped by a luxurious velvet turban sporting an enormous ostrich feather in the center. A rather extravagant outfit for writing letters.

"Sit, Margaret."

Her aunt's beady eyes, small and black like bits of coal, followed Margaret as she came around to the chair and sat. She clasped her hands, careful to keep her expression neutral. Early on, Margaret had learned if she wanted as little interaction with her aunt as possible, and to avoid having her privileges at the piano taken away, she'd best project a docile manner. The more reticent, the better. Aunt Agnes found little pleasure in berating the pathetic creature she considered Margaret to be.

How she longed to tell Aunt Agnes of Welles's suggestion to play for him at Elysium.

"I was invited, *unexpectedly*, to take tea with the Duchess of Averell." Her aunt's icy regard never moved from Margaret's face. "I was *thrilled*, of course."

Aunt Agnes's voice had a horrible, gurgling quality to it, as if a piece of wet toast was caught in her throat. It was one of many things she didn't care for in regard to her aunt.

"The Duchess of Averell, though not a fixture in the *ton,* is still quite influential. Imagine my *delight* at being summoned."

Margaret bit the inside of her cheek to keep from smiling at her aunt's discomfort. Aunt Agnes typically did the summoning. She stayed still. Silent. The slightest word or twitch and Margaret would be pounced on, torn to shreds within the confines of her aunt's parlor.

The coal-black eyes narrowed into slits as the ostrich feather atop her aunt's turban quivered in accusation at Margaret. "Her Grace was so very pleased to make your acquaintance."

This was a favorite tactic of her aunt's. Throw out leading questions when unsure of how a particular situation had come about in hopes that the person being interrogated, in this case, Margaret, would stop and correct her or interject into the conversation, thus giving themselves away. Her aunt would then determine the punishment for her own lack of knowledge. Margaret had learned the hard way when she had first come to London. Her eyes remained on her lap. She had no intention of satisfying her aunt's curiosity.

"I was surprised, to say the least, that you'd made her acquaintance, as well as that of her daughters," Aunt Agnes continued. "Only the eldest has made her debut. Quite recently and somewhat quietly. I did wonder if there was something wrong with the girl. Is she lame? Scarred in some way? Has she already been ruined?" Her aunt watched Margaret's face for any sign Margaret would collapse under her regard and tell her everything.

Margaret focused her attention on a stray thread where she'd mended the pocket in her skirt.

"I don't recall the girl's name." Aunt Agnes rolled her eyes toward the ceiling as if trying to remember. Another ploy. Her aunt likely had all three of the duchess's daughters and Miss Nelson already catalogued in her mind along with their character deficits.

Margaret said nothing.

"She thinks quite highly of you."

"How kind of the duchess." Margaret finally spoke lest their meeting go on for hours.

"Apparently, Her Grace grew enamored of your playing when you accompanied Lady Patson's daughter at a party given some time ago. At least, according to *her*."

Lady Patson was a close acquaintance of her aunt's, another overly critical matron of the *ton* who doled out expectations and ruined those who didn't meet them. Margaret had been forced to accompany Lady Patson's daughter, Gertrude, as she sang during a small event in hopes the girl could impress Lord Thackery. Margaret had reluctantly agreed. She'd heard Gertrude 'warming up her voice,' and she'd sounded little better than a squawking crow. Gertrude sang, to the horror of Lady Patson's guests and Lord Thackery, for nearly an hour. Aunt Agnes had chastised Margaret during the entire ride home as 'deliberately playing too well' in order to eclipse poor Gertrude.

"I am pleased she enjoyed hearing me play," Margaret said.

Aunt Agnes leaned forward, turban wobbling as if about

to snap her aunt's thin neck. "I don't *recall* the duchess's presence at Lady Patson's. I can't *imagine* how she escaped my notice at such a small affair. Her eldest daughter—"

"Lady Andromeda." Margaret finally lifted her chin. She was growing weary of this game. Lady Masterson's garden party was on the horizon and Margaret not only needed to explain how she came to be invited, but she also had to find something appropriate to wear. Difficult when her aunt allowed her only the barest minimum of pin money. And there was the matter of attending the garden party, preferably without her aunt.

She looked at the tendrils of the ostrich feather which seemed to be drifting toward her. Poor ostrich, to give up a feather only to have it land on her aunt's head.

"Not only has the duchess requested your presence on Tuesdays and Thursdays to play piano and accompany her younger daughter, but she is insisting you attend a garden party with her and Lady Andromeda."

"I see," Margaret said quietly, as if awaiting further instruction. She became certain Welles was behind his stepmother's request. Hope stirred in her heart. Did it mean he'd agreed to help her with Carstairs after all?

"*Lady Masterson's* garden party. I assured Her Grace," Aunt Agnes shook her head, "you'd not been invited because I would *also* have received an invitation, but she *insisted* you had been and grew concerned your invitation had been lost." Her aunt drew her sticklike figure up, boney shoulders pointing toward the ceiling. "Imagine my *surprise* when Henderson informed me an invitation for you had indeed been delivered only this morning." Her aunt said nothing more for several long moments, waiting for Margaret to speak, her lips thin and tight.

Margaret wasn't certain what she *could* say. Clearly, her aunt smelled a rat. Margaret had to force her lips from forming a smile. She doubted Lord Welles had *ever* been compared to a rat.

"How did you make the acquaintance of Lady Masterson? And please, don't tell me she was also in attendance at Lady Patson's. Lady Patson wouldn't have such a scandalous woman in her home."

Margaret shrugged. "Perhaps I was included because the duchess wished me to be. I do not know Lady Andromeda but possibly she wishes us to become acquainted. Do you not *wish* me to be friends with the daughter of a duke? I would think it would be looked well upon." She schooled her features into one of tentative confusion.

Her aunt's face flushed an alarming shade of purple as her eyes searched Margaret for any sign of insubordination.

"I would not like to refuse a duchess, Aunt. But I will attend only if you give your permission." Margaret lowered her gaze and remained still.

A noise of displeasure escaped her aunt. The ostrich feather bobbed about her turban in agitation as if guessing Margaret had lied. But Margaret knew she'd won. Aunt Agnes, regardless of her suspicions, would never defy a duchess. Finally, she said, "I would not dream of disappointing the duchess by forbidding you to accompany her. But I am *not* pleased, Margaret. You are excused."

Margaret stood and bobbed before her aunt then calmly walked out of the parlor, forcing herself not to skip, though she dearly wanted to. She paused, making sure her aunt hadn't followed, before continuing to Lord Dobson's study.

Margaret had never known the man her aunt had been married to, but from references Aunt Agnes made, Lord Dobson had been a sportsman. He had particularly enjoyed fishing. She knew she had her work cut out for her in wooing Carstairs. Her knowledge of outdoor sport was limited to admiring the trees when she took a walk or perhaps throwing bread crust to the birds. But hopefully, Lord Dobson would inadvertently help her cause.

Coughing at the dusty smell as she opened the door, Margaret went to the first bookcase. Her eyes searched the titles, fingers running over the spines, determined to find a book on the basics of hunting.

8

"Oh, do stay still, Miss Lainscott. I only have this last stitch." Romy looked up at her, voice muffled by a mouth full of pins.

"Stop sticking her, Romy," Theodosia said, looking up from the tiny miniature she painted with painstaking care. "She isn't a pincushion. Poor Miss Lainscott will be full of holes by the time you're finished turning her into..." She looked to Margaret for help. "A tree nymph?"

Margaret knew she was a flower of some sort, though she couldn't remember which one. The name escaped her, as names often did. And what she was dressed as hadn't seemed as crucial as Lord Carstairs finding her attractive. She gave Theo a slight, almost invisible shrug.

"Iris," Romy said in frustration, pulling the pins from her mouth. "Goodness, she's a *flower*. Can't you tell?" She continued to fuss at the hem of the dress. "The gown is *green* like a flower *stem*."

Theo shrugged with an apologetic look in Margaret's direction and went back to her painting.

The garden party gown, as Margaret thought of it in

her head, was exactly the shade of new leaves, the sort that sprouted from tree branches just as spring was beginning. The skirt was cut and sewn to represent the stem while the sleeves, made from a lovely diaphanous lavender, floated about Margaret's arms in an imitation of petals. Now that she took notice, Margaret could see Romy's vision.

"I think she looks smashing." Phaedra strolled in, apple in hand.

"Thank you, Phaedra." Margaret smiled in her direction.

"You're welcome. What are you going as, Romy?" Phaedra took a large crunch of the apple, munching away as she crossed the room.

Theo looked up. "Are you a horse? You sound like my mare, Calliope. Pray keep your mouth closed as you chew."

"*I'm* the tree nymph," Romy replied. "There." She smiled up at Margaret. "Perfect."

"It's lovely, Romy. I've never felt so beautiful. Nor so floral." Margaret looked at Theo. "Calliope? Another Greek name?"

Theo looked up from her work, paintbrush hovering in the air. "Mother's habit extends to all our animals at Cherry Hill. She once had a parrot named Zeus."

"Zeus was a marvelous bird." Phaedra darted behind Theo, crunching the apple deliberately in her sister's ear. "Father taught him how to swear properly. Mama was horrified."

"Oh, go away, horse." Theo went back to her work. "Where is Olivia?"

Phaedra sauntered over to a chair, flopped down, and threw one leg over the arm. "Olivia is with Mama. It is their 'lady's day' together."

Margaret raised a brow.

"My mother insists on spending time with each of us

alone so we always feel special," Romy said as she fussed with the hem.

"How lovely," Margaret said. In the short time she'd known the duchess, Margaret had received more love and kindness than she ever had at the hands of Aunt Agnes.

"I'm sure Olivia will come home with all sorts of fripperies. She's a flutist who loves fripperies." A dramatic sigh followed a crunch and several loud chews. "I wish I could go to Lady Masterson's party. It sounds positively *splendid*."

Theo took off the small spectacles she wore and observed Phaedra's sprawl across the chair. "Your posture is exactly why you aren't permitted to go, not to mention your *chewing*. Look at you."

Phaedra defiantly wiggled one slippered foot.

Margaret shot Phaedra an affectionate look. Never having had any siblings of her own, she was envious of the easy way the sisters talked and tormented each other. They had all embraced Margaret with smiles, asking to be addressed by their Christian names even after such short acquaintance. Including the mysterious Theo who had decided to leave her studio and join them in the large parlor today. It was as if the duchess and the girls were *her* family. She'd been so busy enjoying their company, she'd almost forgotten all about Welles and the thoughts he'd put in her head.

Almost.

Last week, Margaret had appeared promptly to accompany Olivia and Phaedra on a new piece the three were going to learn and surprise the duchess with. But an hour or so into practice, Romy had interrupted, measuring tape in hand, insisting Margaret come with her *immediately*. Her friend had the perfect costume in mind for Margaret to wear to Lady Masterson's. Romy had already put some of the pieces together, but the gown had to be properly fitted.

Since Margaret hadn't had a clue what she would wear to

such an event and was pleased Romy had gone to so much trouble on her behalf, she'd followed her friend out, much to the dismay of Phaedra and Olivia.

Romy had whisked Margaret to the parlor where a dressmaker's dummy sat swathed in the green silk Margaret now wore. After whipping about the measuring tape, taking notes, and sticking pins everywhere, the gown had begun to take shape. Today was the final fitting before Lady Masterson's party. Romy was definitely talented, as the gown was beautiful. Margaret doubted she could have conceived of anything half as lovely.

"What made you decide on an iris, Romy?" Margaret had been meaning to ask her why she'd chosen that particular flower. "Why not a peony? Or an orchid?"

Romy tilted her head, her eyes the same startling blue as her brother's. The sight brought Welles to mind again and Margaret stubbornly pushed him aside.

"I suppose," Romy said, "because Mother and I were walking through the garden when she told me you would be accompanying us. We stopped right before a patch of miniature irises. Fate, I suppose. I was looking at all those tiny, delicate flowers and thought how you reminded me of one."

"I hardly consider myself delicate. I did grow up in Yorkshire."

"Yes, but the iris is also *hardy*, Margaret. And blooms wherever it is planted. You must promise to come here the day of the party and we'll get ready together in case your gown needs a last-minute adjustment. I'm sure your aunt won't mind."

Margaret agreed. Her aunt had barely spoken ten words to her since the discussion over how Margaret had come to be acquainted with the Duchess of Averell. She was sure by now Aunt Agnes had confirmed with Lady Patson that the duchess *hadn't* been in attendance at the party, but she would not be inclined to contradict the duchess. Her aunt would sit on her suspicions until she could spring them on Margaret at an appropriate time.

"I'll be here right after breakfast; will that suit?"

"Yes. We'll have tea and get dressed together. And Mother's lady's maid is a marvel with hair. I'm thinking fresh cut flowers from our gardens should do the trick."

"You've gone to so much trouble on my account," Margaret said.

"Nonsense. It's what I love to do," she said in a wistful tone. "Just as you love music and composing. Now look, what do you think?"

Margaret turned to face the large oval mirror one of the footmen had brought in. She *did* look smashing. The cut of the gown highlighted her small waist and made her bosom seem larger. Romy was truly a wizard to accomplish such a thing. She moved back and forth, watching the way the silk moved about her body.

"I like the way the sleeves flutter about. Very pretty."

Margaret jumped with a squeak at the words and turned to the door.

Welles leaned against the wall, eyes hooded as his gaze ran slowly down the length of her body, as if he were touching each bone beneath her skin.

Her palm fell over her madly fluttering heart, begging it to cease such foolishness at the sight of him.

"Tony, do knock before you enter when I'm ...doing things," Romy chastised him. "What if Miss Lainscott," her tone became formal in front of her brother, "had been...in a state of *undress*?"

Phaedra rolled her eyes and shot Welles a look. "She means Miss Lainscott may have been in her underthings."

"Thank you for the clarification." Tony winked at his youngest sister.

Phaedra gave him a roguish wink back.

"Hello, Tony." Theo looked up with a frown. "Don't encourage her." She nodded to Phaedra.

"My apologies to Miss Lainscott." Welles didn't sound at all contrite as he strolled further into the parlor. His eyes never left her as Romy continued to fluff the hem.

This would be the moment she should throw a witty quip his way, or better yet, ignore his presence completely. He deserved no less after the scandalous request he'd made of her. But instead, all she could say was, "Good day, Lord Welles."

He'd been out riding, she surmised, viewing the fawn-colored leather breeches topped by yet another jacket of indigo, cut sharply over his broad shoulders. She was quickly coming to realize he rarely wore anything other than dark colors. Margaret's eyes fell away from him, afraid her attraction to Welles would not go unnoticed by the others in the room. She took in the black Hessian boots, her gaze moving up to the muscle lining his thighs, so apparent beneath the snug fit of his riding breeches.

Indecently tight.

Heat curled low inside Margaret at his approach, something that happened with increasing regularity whenever he appeared. It made her feel unbalanced. Unsettled.

"Hello, demon." He walked over and pressed an affectionate kiss to the top of Phaedra's head. "I've been informed that I must serve as escort to Lady Masterson's garden party." He was speaking to Romy, but his eyes never strayed from Margaret.

"I wondered if you would attend," Romy said.

"Your mother is very persistent when she wishes to be."

Margaret pretended to adjust one of the sleeves, not wishing to dwell on the fact Welles would not only be in attendance, which she'd expected, but he would be escorting them.

"Lady Masterson had pressured me to attend, though I refuse to dress as a twig or a rabbit." Welles's eyes pressed into Margaret. "Besides, my friend Carstairs will be there, and I've not seen him in some time. He is intent on dressing as a stag, complete with antlers, making it easy for any *hunter* to spot him."

Margaret's lips tightened, refusing to be drawn into his teasing. "What a clever costume Lord Carstairs has decided on."

The humming in Margaret's blood increased to a dull roar as Welles tilted his head, pretending to admire his sister's handiwork. "Nicely done, Romy. I believe Miss Lainscott makes a lovely iris."

Warm honey wrapped around Margaret's spine.

"*Finally*, someone sees my vision." Romy bestowed a smile on her brother, pins sticking from her mouth, before she bent again to the hem.

Welles was so close to Margaret she caught a whiff of the soap he'd used to shave, along with tobacco and leather. The combination of the three created a wholly masculine scent which was all Welles. It filled her nostrils, calling to Margaret on some primal level, making her knees weak. She wobbled on the small box she stood on, nearly falling off.

Romy gave a puff of exasperation and tugged back on the hem. "One more moment. I beg you. Don't move."

"If you should fall, Miss Lainscott, I'll catch you." Welles circled her like a big cat, purring and begging to be stroked, eyes sparkling like the rarest of sapphires. "I do apologize." His voice lowered. "I didn't mean to startle you. Do be still." The words were completely innocent, but to Margaret's ears, they were imbued with the slightest hint of wickedness.

Good Lord, he's right. I assume everything he says to me is improper.

His face was very near hers. Gold flecks floated in the depths of his eyes like tiny bits of the sun or the stars. Dark lashes brushed against his cheeks as his eyes fell first to her mouth, then the tops of her breasts. One elegant fingertip skimmed lightly over the silk of her skirts.

Margaret inhaled sharply as heat curled between her thighs.

"There." Romy came to her feet. "I'll finish the hem and the work on the bodice in plenty of time before Lady Masterson's." She waved Welles in the direction of the door. "Tony, Miss Lainscott needs to change. Shut the door behind you."

Welles held Margaret's eyes a moment longer before he bowed and moved in the direction of the door. Mortified at her body's response when all Welles had done was come near her, Margaret looked away from him. He hadn't even touched her. Not really.

Phaedra popped up in the chair, apple core in hand, to tug at his coat sleeve. "Tony, come up to the conservatory. I've been practicing a new piece I would love for you to hear. Olivia is out with Mama so you can't hear the flute, but even so, I think you'll like it. Miss Lainscott says I'm quite good."

"I should like nothing better, demon," he replied with affection.

Phaedra fairly skipped out of the parlor. "I'll have Pith bring us refreshments."

Margaret avoided looking at him until the humming in her skin halted and the door clicked shut. Hopping off the ottoman, she lifted her skirts, careful not to dislodge any of Romy's carefully placed pins, and tiptoed to the decorated screen in the corner to change.

Romy was talking to herself as she picked up some discarded pins and bits of thread from the floor. She never once glanced toward the screen; she was too busy debating with herself on whether to add lace to the edge of the gown's bodice.

Margaret breathed a small sigh of relief. Romy hadn't picked up on the tension floating in the air between Margaret and her brother. Phaedra had been too absorbed in her apple. Satisfied no one had noticed, she dipped behind the screen only to catch sight of Theo.

Welles's mysterious middle sister had lowered her paintbrush and was watching Margaret, a smile tugging at her lips.

9

The streets of London faded from view to be replaced with countryside as the ducal carriage neared Lady Masterson's small estate outside the city. Dressed again in a coat of indigo, Welles had arrived on time to escort the duchess, Romy, and Margaret. Romy had protested her brother's lack of a costume, but Welles only shrugged and said again that he'd no interest in appearing in public as a woodland animal.

Margaret took in the dark blue of his coat, the buff trousers and boots, everything elegantly cut and exquisitely tailored, but free from any sort of embellishment. He could have easily been a barrister or a wealthy merchant rather than a future duke. But no one would ever mistake him for either of those. Ordinary gentlemen didn't look like Welles. Nor did most of the titled ones.

Romy and the duchess kept up a steady stream of conversation, requiring Welles to interject occasionally while Margaret listened. Every so often he would glance in her direction, but he'd not spoken to her directly, not beyond the polite greeting he'd murmured as he'd handed her into the coach.

Margaret told herself she didn't miss his teasing.

The duchess looked out the window and clapped her hands in pleasure. "I'd no idea Lady Masterson was hiding such a treasure only an hour's ride from London," she exclaimed as the carriage pulled onto a winding drive. A lawn stretched out from a lovely stone two-story house sporting profusions of blooms hanging from every window.

Margaret wasn't certain what she'd been expecting as she exited the carriage behind Romy and the duchess. Her vision of a garden party was limited to the few she'd attended in Yorkshire where elderly women showcased their hothouse orchids and won a ribbon for a splendid tasting pie.

Lady Masterson's garden party was quite different.

Several gentlemen and ladies were bowling on the lawn while liveried servants ran to and fro. The grass further down the rise had been cut to resemble a large chessboard. A dozen guests, sporting either a black hat or a white hat as they were "moved" about by the two teams played a friendly game of chess. Cards were being played under one tent. Everywhere, servants circulated carrying trays heavy with refreshments.

The hostess, golden and beautiful, was far younger than the Yorkshire matrons by several decades. Lady Masterson was closer in age to Margaret and already a widow, as the late Lord Masterson had died several years ago. She stood boldly at the entrance to her lavish gardens, daring anyone to remark on the bright fuchsia gown hugging her voluptuous curves with its scandalously low-cut bodice. Fat, golden curls, woven with tiny rosebuds, fell about Lady Masterson's shoulders in artful disarray as she greeted her guests, the flat American accent drawing looks of disdain.

Lady Masterson was quite something.

At their approach, she gave a little wave with one gloved

hand and excused herself from the group of guests she'd been speaking to.

Welles, a smile crossing his wide mouth, bowed and took her hand, brushing his lips across the knuckles.

"Lord Welles, how kind of you and the rest of the *Beautiful Barringtons*," she arched one plucked eyebrow, "to grace my little party." Lady Masterson dropped his hand and executed a perfect curtsy before the duchess. "Your Grace, I'm so pleased you could come. Lady Andromeda."

The duchess took her arm and pressed a kiss to her cheek. "Georgina, the name is likely to stick if you keep referring to us as the Beautiful Barringtons, and you know how little I care for notoriety."

"Your Grace, every single Barrington is a sight to behold, even Theodosia who lives beneath the eaves."

"Or Leo?" Margaret heard Welles say under his breath.

The only sign Lady Masterson heard him was a slight tightening of the smile on her lips.

The duchess laughed. "There are some who grow concerned I've locked Theo in her room as some sort of punishment. I need no more gossip directed at us." She gave a discreet nod in Welles's direction.

"Better a nickname extolling your family's beauty than the alternative. I speak from experience. I've several nicknames myself." Lady Masterson smiled. "Though I won't repeat them."

"Oh, do tell, Lady Masterson," Welles said.

Lady Masterson swatted him affectionately with her fan.

Margaret watched the interplay between the three. It was clear Lady Masterson was a friend of the family from the affectionate way the duchess spoke to her. But what of the beautiful widow's relationship with Welles?

Jealously pricked her, unexpected and sharp.

"You must be Miss Lainscott." Lady Masterson turned and greeted her.

Margaret bobbed. "Lady Masterson. Your gardens are lovely."

"How kind of you to come to my party." She leaned closer and Margaret was enveloped in a cloud of something floral. "And kinder *still* for not bringing your aunt."

"The pleasure is mine." It was impossible not to like Lady Masterson.

After conversing with the duchess and Romy for a few more minutes, Lady Masterson looked up at a pair coming up the lawn. Her expression became coldly polite before she excused herself to greet them.

The gentleman was tall and gaunt, almost stork like. Thick salt and pepper hair was combed back from a broad forehead and he sported a neatly trimmed beard and mustache. The lady clutching his arm reminded Margaret unpleasantly of her aunt. She had the same judgmental look in her eyes as she scanned the lawn full of guests. The moment she spotted Lady Masterson, her lips curled in a sneer.

"What a sour pair," the duchess said under her breath. "Why did she invite them? More importantly, why attend?"

"A perverse sense of self-punishment perhaps? The new Lord Masterson doesn't care for his uncle's widow and makes no effort to hide it," Welles said.

"No, he does not." The duchess's lips pursed into a grimace. "He should be grateful Georgina's dowry saved the earldom for him. Otherwise he'd have nothing but a debt-ridden title."

"Yes, but he didn't get *everything*," Welles said with a tic of his lips. "For instance, this estate. What he can never have, displayed so beautifully under the guise of a party. I think perhaps that was Georgina's purpose all along."

The duchess didn't take her eyes off the new Lord Masterson. "Do not expect him to attend my upcoming ball. He won't receive an invitation."

Welles nodded in the direction of one large, striped tent where servants were entering and leaving with flutes of champagne. "If you ladies will excuse me, I believe I'll see if Georgina is serving anything other than champagne."

He took his leave without another glance at Margaret.

She watched his broad-shouldered form disappear in the direction of the tent, missing his presence immediately.

Lifting her chin, Margaret reminded herself sternly she wasn't at the garden party for Welles. And his relationship with Lady Masterson, no matter what it may be, was none of her affair. Margaret was *here* to entice Lord Carstairs. She'd been up half the night concocting various anecdotes on hunting based on the book she'd filched from Lord Dobson's study and her observances of what little grouse hunting her father had done. At least she wouldn't have to fabricate Walter Lainscott's two dogs, Andy and Jake.

"Come, Miss Lainscott." The duchess touched her arm. "Let us see and be seen."

Romy linked her arm with Margaret's as they followed in the duchess's wake. Welles's sister was especially lovely today in a shimmering gown the color of charred toast which she'd cleverly stitched with irregular folds to resemble the bark of a tree. Her sleeves, in contrast to Margaret's, were tailored to fit her slender arms with strategically placed fabric leaves, acorns, and even a small bird sewn into the silk.

"You are masterful with a needle, Romy." Margaret squeezed her friend's hand. "A true artist."

"Thank you," Romy said. "But unfortunately, I doubt I'll be able to practice my art, as you call it. Perhaps, if I never marry, I could set up my own modiste shop."

"You're a duke's daughter," Margaret said, bestowing a smile on the younger girl. "Isn't marriage a requirement?"

Romy shrugged, her attention taken by the gown of the woman before them. "Yes. More's the pity. I'll be expected to make an impeccable match, preferably to one of the few dukes floating about London. Most are at least three times my age, and the few that aren't elderly, I find distasteful."

She dropped Margaret's arm and took out a small notepad and pencil hidden in the pocket of her gown. The duchess had paused to speak to someone she knew which gave Romy a moment to sketch discreetly. She looked up and frowned, her pencil stilled, gaze focused.

Margaret followed her line of sight directly to a stilted looking gentleman with coal-black hair. A scowl marked his features, turning his lips down in an ugly manner.

"He'd be far more attractive were he not frowning," Margaret said. The man was striking in a wild sort of way, and coldly austere, possessing none of the elegance that imbued Welles so effortlessly.

She clenched her hands, resolutely pushing Welles aside and conjured up an image of Carstairs. Or at least as much of him as she could recall.

"Gloomy Granby." Romy nodded in the gentleman's direction. "There's one of the last unwed dukes in all of England. I pity the woman who attracts his attention. An iceberg possesses more warmth." Romy tugged at Margaret's hand. The duchess was on the move.

Margaret took in the beauty of Lady Masterson's garden party, wondering at the young widow's vision in planning the event. The women attending were dressed in every color under the rainbow, drifting about the lawn like a mass of peonies, roses, and daisies all having escaped the confines of their carefully maintained flower beds. The duchess was much sought after, many of those present wishing to renew their acquaintance with her and ask after the duke. It was clear the duchess hadn't left her country estate for some time due to the ill health of her husband. Romy and her mother both spoke in glowing terms of the duke and with much affection, in sharp contrast to Welles. The mere mention of his father brought a scowl to his face.

She wondered what had happened between Welles and the duke to cause his sentiments to be so different.

Margaret smiled so much in the next several hours, her cheeks began to ache. Few of those she met recognized or remembered her until she mentioned her aunt's name. She supposed that was fair; to be honest, Margaret didn't remember any of their names either.

Scanning the gardens, she struggled to remember what Carstairs looked like. All she could recall was light brown hair and a vacant expression. Finally, thanks to Welles's previous description of his friend's costume, she spotted him. It was impossible to miss the antlers rising above the shoulders of the small group surrounding him. Excusing herself from Romy's side, Margaret struck out for Carstairs intent on reintroducing herself. It was bold, true, but they *had* met previously.

Margaret halted halfway across the lawn, spying a familiar indigo coat and set of broad shoulders. She nearly turned around but pressed on. She thought of Winthrop taking her hand the last time he had called, recalling the squeeze of his sweaty fingers against hers. The memory steeled her resolve. Margaret strode forward, confident she looked her best, and with a mountain of determination. It would have to be Carstairs

Time was running out, and she'd no time to find a better candidate.

10

Tony saw Miss Lainscott's approach far before she faltered in her steps after catching sight of him. He'd been watching her, albeit discreetly, since he'd left the side of his stepmother and sister. Her small, determined form, costumed so fetchingly as an iris, filled him with intense longing. Desire was an emotion Tony was well-acquainted with, but his feelings for Miss Lainscott were bordering on obsession.

The idea that Miss Lainscott, a woman of unique, untapped sensuality and above-average intelligence, would waste herself on someone of Carstairs's limited abilities was nothing short of shameful. It bothered him far more than it should have.

Carstairs was speaking, but Tony didn't hear him; all his attention was focused on the delicate woman dressed as an iris who rapidly approached the group, her dark eyes full of purpose. Carstairs didn't stand a chance against Miss Lainscott.

"Don't you think so, Welles?" Carstairs clapped him on

the back, nearly putting out one of Tony's eyes with the antlers strapped atop his head.

"In complete agreement," Tony replied, having no idea what Carstairs was talking about. Probably something to do with a gun. Or hunting. Maybe the bass he'd caught on his last fishing trip.

Regardless of his friend's lack of brilliance, Carstairs was a good man. An *honorable* man—far more so than Tony. He wasn't especially close to Carstairs and they had little in common outside of shooting or hunting, but Carstairs was uncomplicated and so bloody nice you couldn't help but like him.

But that didn't mean Tony wanted to just hand over Miss Lainscott.

Miss Rebecca Turnbull batted her eyelashes at Carstairs while Tony took in her coiffure. He assumed the young lady was attempting to be a tree or a giant bird's nest, Tony wasn't certain. Miss Turnbull's hair was a mass of golden ringlets woven through with twigs, leaves, and small blue ovals which he took to be robin's eggs.

He felt the brush of Miss Lainscott's skirts against his legs as she wedged herself next to him. "Miss Lainscott, I wondered where you'd gotten off to."

"Did you?" She smiled prettily, mostly for the benefit of Carstairs and the others in the group.

Carstairs turned sharply at Miss Lainscott's arrival, neatly snagging Miss Turnbull's hair in one of the antlers and pulling free a large portion of the young woman's coiffure. "Oh, dear." He gamely attempted to unravel her hair while the young lady struggled at his side.

"Dear God," Miss Lainscott uttered under her breath. She gamely stepped forward to assist in sorting out the melee of Miss Turnbull's hair. Her lips remained tight. Tony was fairly certain she was trying not to laugh out loud at the absurdity of the moment.

Carstairs swung his head back to Miss Lainscott, who deftly sidestepped the threat of his antlers. "Many thanks for your assistance." He looked at her with a wrinkled brow as if trying to place her. Carstairs looked at everyone that way. God bless him.

"Carstairs," Tony said. "You recall Miss Lainscott, do you not? We made her acquaintance at Gray Covington last year."

His friend's face remained devoid of any recognition.

Tony often wondered what went on behind those vacant eyes. Nothing, probably. "While we were on our way back from your hunting lodge," he gently reminded Carstairs. "The trip in which you shot that enormous grouse. Don't you recall?"

Carstairs's eyes lit up. He only ever recalled a person or a place if it related to his outdoor pursuits. The man never forgot any small animal or fowl he'd dispatched. "Yes, of course. Miss Lainscott." He took her hand. "Lovely to see you again."

Miss Turnbull frowned. Her hair was a mess. One of the pretend robin eggs fell from her hair, bounced off one cheek, and landed in the valley between her breasts. Worse, Carstairs didn't seem to notice.

Miss Lainscott stepped closer, risking life and limb with Carstairs whipping his antlers about.

Brave girl.

She seemed determined to ignore Tony, not even bothering to acknowledge his help in reintroducing her to Carstairs. He discreetly studied the slender lines of her arms and the way the sunlight glinted off the warm brown of her hair turning some of the strands to amber. He had the strangest urge to pull her to him and ask her to cease this folly.

"How large was the grouse you managed to snag, if you don't mind me asking?" Miss Lainscott gave Carstairs a pretty smile. She listened in rapt attention as Carstairs regaled her with a description of the bird in question much to the dismay of Miss Turnbull, who was forced to retreat and make extensive repairs to her coiffure.

Miss Lainscott, clever little thing she was, followed up Carstairs's tale of grouse hunting with one of her own. Apparently, she'd begged her father to take her grouse hunting on the moors and, much to his surprise, had snagged her own bird.

Carstairs was enraptured.

Tony nearly burst into laughter. If Miss Lainscott had ever toted about a rifle in the early morning hours to shoot a grouse, Tony would eat his boots. The fact that her tale was peppered with references to her unknown excellent shooting ability only made the entire story more absurd. She was a very convincing liar.

Just as she was about to launch into what he assumed was an equally fabricated tale concerning trout fishing, Miss Turnbull returned to stake her claim on Carstairs. She cooed in his ear, carefully this time, as her hair could not survive another swipe of the antlers. Her gloved hand floated over his forearm as she entertained them all with a story of a fox hunt, laying claim to Carstairs while her eyes surveyed the rival for his affections.

A furrow appeared between Miss Lainscott's eyes. She hadn't been expecting anyone to challenge her over Carstairs.

Miss Turnbull, after her lengthy story of the fox hunt, declared herself to be parched. She dragged Carstairs off in the direction of the refreshment table, pausing only to throw Miss Lainscott a look of challenge. Guests and servants alike scattered at Carstairs's approach to the tent, giving him a wide berth, horrified at the possibility of being stabbed while drinking—or serving—lemonade.

Tony watched his friend and Miss Turnbull disappear into the tent before bending down until his nose brushed the top of Miss Lainscott's head.

"Round one to Miss Turnbull."

"Not at all." She took a step back and gave him a defiant look, but he already saw her mind working behind her dark eyes to solve the problem of Miss Turnbull. "I think our first meeting went rather well."

"Not from where I stood."

"He liked my story of the grouse hunt," she snapped back and started to walk away from him in the direction of Lady Masterson's folly. "We've much in common."

Tony snorted in disbelief and followed at a slower pace behind her, enjoying the way her hips twitched in agitation as she walked. "Poor little iris."

Lady Masterson's folly, an octagonal white-washed structure, was set against the beauty of a man-made pond surrounded by cattails and tall grass. Several large lily pads floated as a chorus of frogs croaked at their approach.

Miss Lainscott steadfastly ignored him and picked up her pace.

In two steps, Tony caught up to her before slowing to match his larger strides to her smaller ones. He studied the graceful slope of her neck, thinking of how sweet her skin would taste beneath his tongue. She was worrying her bottom lip, something that made him want to kiss her *and* offer her comfort. "I think you're put out because now you know you need my help. Miss Turnbull is a worthy adversary, don't you think?"

"Not in the least." Miss Lainscott gave him a blinding and insincere smile as she wandered to the edge of the pond, absently pausing to flick a plump cattail with her fingers. The lavender sleeves fluttered prettily along her upper arms as the skirts of her gown blended in with the tall grass surrounding the lake. Her profile was firm. Undeterred. So bloody earnest and determined to marry the dim-witted Carstairs, all so she could have control over her future. He was surprised by the ache he felt as he looked at her, not between his legs, but somewhere in the region of his heart.

"I didn't realize you also possessed a talent for storytelling," Tony finally said. A stray bit of hair fell from the perfect nest of pins and peonies atop her head. "I quite liked the dogs in your story."

"The dogs were real," she said, turning to face him. "My father's." A sad smile touched her lips. "Andy and Jake were sold at auction when he died, along with everything else that belonged to him." A resigned shrug lifted her shoulders. "Which, I suppose included me, in a way."

Another contraction in his chest followed her words. He'd never cared for Lady Dobson and found he was liking her less as time went on.

"And my mother's piano," she continued in a quiet voice. "The one my father gave her. He sent all the way to Austria for it. I feel certain it would have challenged even the Broadwood."

A fierce sense of protectiveness came over Tony at the sadness lighting Miss Lainscott's eyes. He wished to pull her into his arms and assure her all would be well, a wholly foreign emotion, and one usually only reserved for one of his sisters when they were distressed. But his feelings toward this small woman were anything but brotherly.

"My mother played the piano as well," he said before he could stop himself. "She taught me to play. Then my father insisted I receive proper instruction."

"You became too skilled for her to teach you more?" Miss Lainscott's eyes were soft as they took him in. Like a pot of hot chocolate on a cold winter's day, silky and dark. "I think you've downplayed your musical abilities, my lord."

"No," Tony said. The pain when he thought of his mother had dimmed over time, but it had never gone away. He used to dream of her, of how she'd tucked him close to her side while she taught him his scales. Mother had always smelled of lavender. "She died."

Miss Lainscott turned to him, sympathy written across the small oval of her face. "My mother perished of fever—a sickness sweeping the mines that my father unwittingly brought home with him. He and I didn't get sick. Not even so much as a sniffle. I was barely twelve."

"Her name was Katherine." Tony heard the longing in his own voice. "She fell down the stairs while heavy with child." There had been so much blood. On the stairs. All over her dress. It had covered Tony from head to toe when he'd tried to pick her up. His mother had been on her way to confront her *lecherous prick* of a husband over his audacity in thinking it within his rights to fuck both Tony's mother *and* her lady's maid. She'd seen the duke and Molly together in the gardens from her bedroom window. Careless of them. But his mother had been virtually bed-ridden and rarely left her rooms. "She died very soon after." His mother had whispered the truth of what she'd seen in his ear even as Tony had screamed for help. "The child was stillborn." The doctor had been summoned, but far too late.

Tony had adored his mother. He still did. She'd been brilliant and educated, well-bred, and musical. She'd refused to hand him over to a nursemaid as his father had wished and insisted on raising Tony herself. He'd promised his mother, as the life ebbed from her body, that he would make sure the Duke of Averell was punished.

Miss Lainscott's hand fell against the sleeve of his coat, plucking at the material with her fingers. "I am so very sorry, my lord. I, too, still miss my mother, no matter the years that have passed."

Tony looked down at those slender fingers gently squeezing his arm, and he found himself wishing to bury his head against the nape of her neck. There was no guile or pity in her gaze. No artifice. Miss Lainscott regarded him as if Tony was worthy of her concern. He'd spent so many years living without a care for anyone, taking women as he pleased, doing as he wished. Running a club barely a step above a bordello. He'd promised himself he'd never marry. Never have a child.

"Is that why you don't play the Broadwood?"

A tremor went through him as her arrow hit its mark with remarkably little effort. "Who told you that? Let me guess," he said before she could answer. "Phaedra?"

She said nothing, her eyes like brushed velvet, shrewd and knowing.

Miss Lainscott *bloody* terrified him.

"I choose not to play the Broadwood. I've no reason to." Why had he told her about his mother? He never spoke of Katherine, the late Duchess of Averell. It was awful and tragic, not at all appropriate for a discussion during a garden party, *especially* with the woman he was trying to seduce.

"The Broadwood was a gift from my father," he said. "And I want nothing from the Duke of Averell."

11

Margaret inhaled sharply at the rage tingeing his words. Had she not been certain before, she was now. Welles *hated* his father. This was no mere disagreement, but an estrangement born of something terrible between Welles and the Duke of Averell.

His brilliant eyes grew shadowed, closing as Welles turned his head. The humid day had brought out the waves in his thick hair, giving the strands a more tousled look than usual, as if he'd been standing at the prow of a ship at sea. His anguish over his mother's death was obvious. Margaret longed to smooth the heavy waves from his temples and hold him. She reminded herself, in the strictest of admonishments, that Welles was an unprincipled rogue. But that wasn't *all* he was.

"Is that why you haven't married?"

The blue eyes turned to chips of ice and Margaret could almost see the wall he raised around himself as protection.

There are ways to breach walls.

Heir to a duke, Welles should have been married years ago, but he remained unwed in complete defiance of his duty. Every gentleman, especially a superbly titled one like Welles, had a responsibility to produce an heir. She looked up into his handsome features, now glacial and remote. There was nothing playful or sensual about him now. If anything, the dangerous look on Welles's face should have given her pause.

Margaret reached out and gently clasped his larger hand in hers.

Welles inhaled sharply at her touch but did not pull away.

Her heart, the organ which she guarded so selfishly, beat loudly, drowning out even the sound of the frogs in Lady Masterson's pond. It was a terribly bold, forward thing to do to take his hand. The pieces of Welles, more complicated than Margaret had ever imagined, all fit together seamlessly in an instant.

He didn't speak again, though his features softened, and he squeezed her fingers.

Margaret squeezed back.

They stood silently, save for the frogs, hands joined, while the rest of the party continued below on the lawn. After a few minutes, Margaret felt the tension in his body ease and Welles released her hand. He turned to her, the breeze batting the waves of his hair against his jaw. Lifting his hand, Welles tucked a loose strand of her hair behind her ear. His touch lingered for a heartbeat before one finger gently caressed the delicate skin of her cheek.

Margaret's entire body arched in his direction, pulled by some unseen force.

"Welles." His name broke from her lips in a dark whisper. She should be down on the lawn, chasing Carstairs about, avoiding being stabbed by his ridiculous antlers. Possibly she should consider pushing Miss Turnbull into the pond. "I should go."

"Shh." The finger ran along the side of her face to the corner of her mouth.

Margaret's eyes fluttered closed, unable to meet his eyes

as he carefully traced her lower lip before the lightest touch of his mouth on hers took the breath from her body. She stayed in place, her eyes shut, listening to the frogs until his lips left hers.

She took a deep breath wanting to ask him why he'd done such a thing but when she opened her eyes, Welles was gone.

12

"Oh, Mama, did you see what Miss Howard was wearing? The fabric was so thin and sheer." Romy sighed wistfully.

"I believe she was an orchid." The duchess bestowed an indulgent smile on her eldest daughter as the coach pulled away from Lady Masterson's estate.

"I didn't have a chance to ask where she purchased it or the modiste responsible for the cut of her gown. I should like to see the design."

"I believe her mother uses Madame Fontaine. I ran into her on Bond Street the other day while shopping with Olivia. You could start there."

Romy took out her notebook and started writing something down.

The duchess shook her head at her daughter's obsession. "Did you enjoy yourself, Miss Lainscott? Were there any gowns that caught your eye?"

"It was a wonderful party, Your Grace. I found some of the costumes to be quite...unusual," she said, thinking of Miss Turnbull's hair. "I was introduced to Miss Turnbull—"

"Speaking of pea-wits," Romy interjected, not looking up. "I'm wondering what induced her to put a nest of robin eggs in her hair, though I was relieved to find the eggs were fake."

"Do not be unkind, Romy," the duchess cautioned, "though I'm in agreement. Miss Turnbull has set her cap for Lord Carstairs, and her father favors him as well."

The thought of Miss Turnbull securing Carstairs should have bothered Margaret more, but just now, with the rain pattering against the top of the coach, all she could think of was Welles. It had only been a brush of his lips, but he'd kissed her. Margaret could still feel the featherlight touch against her mouth and the warmth of his hand in hers. She looked out the window in the direction of the folly, feeling a relentless pull in Welles's direction.

Damn it.

Margaret pressed her nose against the window. *Carstairs* was who mattered. Thankfully she'd made a good impression today and piqued his interest. All her reading on grouse hunting and the handling of firearms had been beneficial, and she sent a silent prayer of thanks to Lord Dobson. Carstairs had found her before Margaret had made her way to join Romy and the duchess, asking if he could call on her.

Margaret had agreed immediately. There was no point in beating around the bush.

Through the rain streaming down the window, Margaret could just make out Welles's large form running across the lawn, his strides wide and graceful. He held the hand of Lady Masterson; even from a distance, it was impossible to mistake the bright fuchsia of her gown. They ran toward the folly, no doubt seeking shelter from the rain.

Margaret turned from the sight, hating how quickly the jealousy she'd experienced earlier had returned.

"I do wish Welles had decided to come back to London with us, but I suppose he'll find another way home. Or perhaps stay the night, as I'm sure some of the guests are doing." The duchess leaned back against the squabs with a sigh. "Good Lord, but I'm tired. I'd forgotten how exhausting it is to be out amongst the *ton* and pretending to like most of them."

"Papa would be very proud of you." Romy grinned at her mother. "You made an effort."

"I daresay he would be. Even more so since I managed to have Welles escort us." Sadness flitted across the duchess's lovely face. "I wish I was as successful in getting him to come to Cherry Hill."

Romy took her mother's hand. "I know. Maybe someday Welles will relent."

Based on her earlier conversation with Welles, Margaret thought it highly unlikely Welles would ever relent. The look on his face when speaking of his father had been one of loathing.

"Welles and his father do not get on," the duchess said as if sensing the direction of Margaret's thoughts. "An estrangement borne of a mistake my husband made long ago that he regrets to this day." Her fingers drummed upon her thigh for a moment before she turned to the window and fell silent.

The sky grew increasingly gray the closer they drew to London, a dismal finale to the bright sunny day and the garden party. Margaret closed her eyes, thinking again of her conversation with Welles. She had the sense he rarely spoke of his mother, and Margaret was deeply honored Welles had chosen to share such a private story with her. Again, her heart tugged strongly in his direction, wishing for something that could never be. He would forever be a rake. Unprincipled. Refusing to marry.

He kissed me.

Her hand came up as the words thundered in her mind, her palm flattening over her chest against her heart.

And I kissed him back.

13

The following day, Carstairs arrived to call on her as promised.

Margaret thoroughly enjoyed the shock on her aunt's typically sour countenance at the arrival of the Viscount Carstairs. He walked into the parlor, all smiles, with a small nosegay in hand for Margaret, bowing politely to Aunt Agnes.

While her aunt sipped her tea, darting looks of disbelief in their direction, Margaret and Carstairs discussed the merits of rabbit hunting. What was more appropriate? A snare? A rifle? A bow and arrow?

Aunt Agnes bit off the edge of a biscuit and munched loudly.

Lord Carstairs proceeded to spend the remainder of his visit describing in minute detail a hunting lodge he'd once visited. His observations were incredibly detailed, especially in regard to the animals he hunted, and were a trifle gruesome. While not incredibly bright, Carstairs was well-mannered, respectful and, most importantly, genuinely seemed to *like* Margaret. She could secure Carstairs all on her own with no help from anyone.

With a promise to call at the end of the week, Carstairs departed, bidding both her and Aunt Agnes goodbye.

"Lord Carstairs is a delightful young man," Aunt Agnes said after he left. "However, we aren't *certain* of his intentions and thus must continue to allow Winthrop his courtship as well. It would be best to have more than one suitor to choose from."

Margaret only nodded demurely.

As if anything would induce her to choose Winthrop over Carstairs.

Carstairs, bless him, called again two days later bearing more flowers, this time for her aunt as well.

Aunt Agnes pursed her lips, giving him a brittle smile, her disappointment Winthrop hadn't dropped by to call apparent.

Margaret rang for tea, delighted both by his visit and her aunt's displeasure.

"I confess, Miss Lainscott," Lord Carstairs said as he accepted a small watercress sandwich, "I had never thought to meet a young lady who enjoys grouse hunting as much as myself. Why, it rivals even Miss Turnbull's love of trout fishing."

Margaret's hand paused as she reached for a sugared biscuit. Miss Turnbull was proving to be troublesome. "I enjoy fishing as well," she assured him.

Aunt Agnes coughed, her hand pausing over her embroidery hoop. She'd mostly stayed silent at Margaret's sudden knowledge of the outdoors.

"Splendid. I have an outing in mind. A small stream runs just at the end of a park I know. You and Miss Turnbull can cast your lures." Carstairs smiled, his face completely devoid of any artifice. "It would be delightful. We'll make a small party of it, with a proper chaperone of course." He nodded in her aunt's direction. "And with your aunt's permission."

Aunt Agnes nodded. "My niece does adore fishing," she said. "Though I've never known her to catch anything."

Margaret went still, clasping her hands in her lap. "Perhaps I'll prove you wrong, Aunt."

Carstairs, bless him, seemed oblivious to the tension in the room. Margaret bid him goodbye with assurances she couldn't wait for the outing he'd proposed.

※

THE FOLLOWING AFTERNOON, MARGARET FOUND HERSELF sitting on a blanket, swatting at gnats while praying an unlikely fish would find its way to the hook on the end of her line so she could prove herself to Carstairs.

She, Carstairs, Miss Turnbull, a maid, two footmen, and Miss Turnbull's elderly and somewhat deaf aunt were all picnicking on the banks of a bubbling stream at the very edge of the park. The clop of horses and carriages on the path above them was muted, drowned out by the sound of the water running over the rocks. The elderly aunt, whose name Margaret had forgotten within a minute of meeting her, had dozed off in the sun. Every so often she would shake with a loud snort, startling Margaret.

Miss Rebecca Turnbull, blonde ringlets trembling coquettishly around her temples, giggled every so often at something Carstairs said, occasionally touching his forearm as if doing so was accidental.

It wasn't.

Wearing a striped dress of blue and cream, complete with a broadbrimmed hat of straw on her head, Miss Turnbull and Carstairs sat at the edge of the stream, lines tangled together in the water, while her skirts formed a perfect circle of silk, arranged in a fetching manner.

Margaret *wholeheartedly* wished the lovely Miss Turnbull would fall into the stream and perhaps float away like a tiny boat. She closed her eyes for a moment, listening to the gentle bubbling of the stream, smiling as the sound formed musical notes in her head along with splashes of color beneath her lids. The hand holding her fishing pole went lax as a melody began to take shape and the annoying giggles of Miss Turnbull faded.

"You need to tug the line on occasion if you wish to catch something," a deep voice said from behind her.

Margaret's skin prickled deliciously in surprise. *Welles.*

He'd been mostly absent in her life since Lady Masterson's garden party, and she sensed he was intentionally keeping his distance. He had visited the duchess while Margaret was playing with Miss Nelson and Phaedra, but she'd caught only brief glimpses of him. He'd never visited the conservatory when she was present, nor had they spoken.

She turned to him with a look of annoyance, slightly piqued he was here to see Miss Turnbull outwitting her for the moment. But Margaret was terribly happy to see him. He just didn't need to know it.

Welles sat down beside her, the seams of his leather riding breeches straining across his thighs.

Margaret couldn't help but look. She was sure he had his breeches tailored in such a way intentionally.

The afternoon sun sparked across the brush of dark hair lining his jaw, giving him a slightly disreputable look. It suited him. A lazy grin pulled at his lips, deepening the creases at the corner of his eyes. "Glad to see me, aren't you?"

Must he always look so bloody splendid?

"Not in the least," she said tartly.

He took off his hat and tossed it to the blanket, barely missing the elderly aunt's feet.

"Who's that?" He nodded at the snoring woman.

"Our chaperone. I don't recall her name. Miss Turnbull's aunt." Margaret nodded to Carstairs and Miss Turnbull.

"I can see she's doing an excellent job." His eyes twinkled down at her. "Here." He took the pole from her and lowered his voice. "Just a small tug to give the fish something to chase." Welles jerked back on the line. "Like this."

"I know how to fish," she hissed back at him. Margaret was feeling so much better now that Welles had arrived.

His wide mouth tilted up on one side. "I'm sure your fishing skills are as *incredible* as those you use for grouse hunting. Alas, *your lures* don't seem as attractive as Miss Turnbull's." He pressed a finger to his lips as if he'd made a faux pas. "I meant her *fishing* lures, of course, Miss Lainscott."

"I'm doing fine without your help." She wasn't and he knew it.

"Of course, you are."

Margaret looked up to see Miss Turnbull clinging to Carstairs's arms as she landed a fish, squealing in delight as he reeled it in. Their heads leaned into each other so close, Margaret thought the younger woman might throw caution to the wind and kiss Carstairs. Shouldn't her aunt be paying more attention? She glanced over at Aunt...*Bollocks*. She racked her mind for the elderly woman's name.

"If you have come to mock my effort to avoid a marriage that will make me miserable, please leave."

"I would never mock you, Maggie. Nor do I think this a lark for you." The smile left his face.

Margaret's hands stilled against the blanket. No one had called her Maggie in a very long time. Not since the only man who had ever loved her, her father, had died. A lump formed in her throat. "What are you doing here? Do you have another improper request to make of me?"

"I was out for a ride and happened to see the carriage and recognized it as belonging to Carstairs. I thought I'd see what he was up to. No need to be so suspicious," he answered.

She looked behind her to see a horse tethered some distance away.

Miss Turnbull's high-pitched giggle filled the air.

"Ho, Welles." Carstairs held up the tiny fish struggling on the line. "Fancy seeing you here."

Margaret looked up at Welles. "A remarkable coincidence."

Welles contemplated her for a moment before saying, "Don't you know, Miss Lainscott, there is no such thing as coincidence?" Welles stood as Miss Turnbull and Carstairs stumbled up the slight incline.

"Miss Turnbull." He charmed her with a smile. "How lovely you look with a fishing pole in your hand. And you've caught something."

Margaret grit her teeth, knowing Welles was referring to Carstairs and not the fish.

The younger woman *was* quite pretty with her wide blue eyes and broadbrimmed hat, tied with a large bow beneath her chin. She looked as if she'd stepped out of a bloody Gainsborough painting. Miss Turnbull's appearance only added to Margaret's irritation. She swatted at the cloud of gnats determined to bite her.

"Now that you are here, Welles, you must join us for our picnic." Carstairs nodded and the two footmen rushed forward, each carrying an enormous wicker basket. Two chickens, sliced apples, berries, fresh-baked rolls, an assortment of cheeses, and two bottles of chilled white wine appeared on a tablecloth spread out on the grass.

"I don't mean to intrude," Welles deferred.

"Yes, you do," Margaret said under her breath.

A smile tugged at his lips. He'd heard her.

"Oh, you wouldn't be intruding in the least." Miss Turnbull gazed at him with awe, dazzled that the glorious Lord Welles would picnic with them. "We've enough food to feed half of London, I'll warrant. Douglas," she blushed prettily and put a gloved hand to her mouth, "I mean, Lord Carstairs, has a robust appetite." She lifted her chin in challenge, eyes meeting Margaret's.

I really should have pushed her in the stream myself.

"Then I'd be delighted." Welles escorted the laughing young lady back to the blanket where Margaret sat. He bent and plucked the rod from Margaret's hands and she caught a whiff of clean male and sunshine. "I'll just brace this over here." He walked to the stream and made a small pile of rocks. "Perhaps you'll get lucky and your *lures*," he intentionally emphasized the word, "will do the trick. If not, I'm happy to help." He winked at her.

The audacity. Her insides shivered in response.

Welles's strides were as graceful as the rest of him and unconsciously sensual. She imagined he danced or sat a horse the same beautiful way. Her gaze flicked to Carstairs and back to Welles. There really was no comparison. Carstairs was attractive, but he wasn't Welles.

The four of them sat around the enormous mound of food while Miss Turnbull's aunt snored softly.

Carstairs, kind to a fault, asked if he should wake her.

"No. Auntie Louise likes a nap in the afternoon. Which is why I had Cook pack us this delicious wine."

Miss Rebecca Turnbull wasn't quite as innocent as she appeared. Nor as unintelligent. Margaret accepted the glass of wine from one of the footmen and assessed her competition with a keen eye.

Welles sat down next to her, stretching out his legs, and

munched on a chicken leg. Margaret watched in fascination as his teeth tore at the meat before he swallowed.

Blue eyes sparkled back at her. Welles was very aware of his effect on women. Even Miss Turnbull, as besotted by Carstairs as she was, watched him as if he were some exotic creature who'd wandered into their midst.

Carstairs, bless him, was oblivious to the fact he'd invited the fox into the hen house.

The meal passed pleasantly enough. Carstairs spoke of hunting a red deer in the Scottish Highlands. His description of the event, down to what he wore and the way he'd crouched in the undergrowth while rain battered him, held Miss Turnbull rapt with attention; Margaret, however, after two glasses of the excellent wine, was humming to herself while she listened with half an ear.

"What a beautiful song," Welles said from beside her. He wasn't listening to Carstairs either. "I don't recognize it."

"You wouldn't. It's a sonata I'm working on," she answered with a shrug.

"You mean composing?" He kept his voice low so Carstairs and Miss Turnbull wouldn't overhear. Elderly Aunt Louise had recently awoken and only cast a mild frown at the empty wine bottles as she munched on a slice of apple.

"Yes," Margaret answered him. The wine had given her a light, floating feeling. "I studied composition for a time with Mr. Strauss, our neighbor in Yorkshire. He was once part of the Bavarian court and composed for King Ludwig. I learned much from him."

"I see why you are so enamored of Mrs. Anderson," he said, referring to the pianist who was friends with the duchess and had become something of a mentor to Margaret. "And Mrs. Mounsey. Is it your hope to compose and perform as those ladies do?"

"I," she shrugged, "well, I think I would want to emulate

them in some way. I don't really like performing for large crowds, but I love playing."

"Why don't you like performing?" His brow wrinkled, honestly confused.

"I don't like all the attention. I tend to get carried away. You saw me play at Gray Covington."

Heat flared between them. "A most enjoyable performance."

"Only because you didn't have your music privileges rescinded afterward. My aunt forced me to embroider for the rest of our stay. I wasn't allowed near the piano." Margaret stuck out her tongue. "Embroidery is torture. Pure and simple." She looked down, feeling a tug on her skirts.

Welles was absently running one forefinger along the hem, pulling gently on the sprigged muslin. "I'm sorry she did such a thing to you. Cruel."

"Yes. The worst punishment anyone could give me. Music is," she gave a careless wave as he watched her intently, "a balm for my soul. I see a field of flowers, but I also *hear* the music each daisy or buttercup makes." She shrugged, embarrassed by her confession. "I suppose that sounds as if I'm daft. It doesn't really make sense."

"Of course it does. You and I might see only a sack of flour, but a baker sees a magnificent three-tiered cake. A bolt of shimmering green fabric stuck on a rack at one of the shops on Bond Street becomes a ballgown for a queen in Romy's eyes."

"You do understand," she whispered, her heart wishing to leap out of her chest to his.

"I *see* you, Maggie." Welles gave a careful tug on the tiny bit of her skirts he held between his forefinger and thumb. "No matter how you attempt to hide."

"I've not given you leave to address me in such a way," she whispered, wondering at the odd intimacy growing between them. The skin of her legs and arms grew warmer and Margaret knew it wasn't from the dappled sunlight coming through the trees surrounding them. It was Welles.

"I know." His fingers gave a sharp, noticeable tug before stilling.

Suddenly her rod, propped up on the small brace of rocks, tumbled free and slid in the direction of the stream.

"Ho there, Miss Lainscott. It appears you've caught a fish." Carstairs hopped up and hurried down the slight incline toward the rod.

Margaret looked away from Welles and stood. "It appears one of my lures worked," she said, delighted to have possibly caught a fish. Walking down carefully to Carstairs, she took the rod only to have the line pull and the reel unwind before she could bring in her catch.

In his excitement, Carstairs took hold of her hands, helping her reel the fish in, while Margaret laughed. Carstairs smelled pleasantly of mint, and his hands were warm on hers, but there was no prickling of her skin or unsettling of her stomach at his nearness. Determined, Margaret intentionally brushed herself against him.

Nothing. Not even so much as an ounce of the heat only the sound of Welles's voice instilled in her.

When Carstairs leaned over her to tug at the reel, the line snapped, sending them both to land on their bottoms on the grass in an awkward sprawl. Margaret's bonnet fell off her head and she heard a slight tearing sound in the region of her sleeve.

Carstairs laughed. "Goodness, Miss Lainscott, are you all right?"

Margaret giggled. The entire day had been ridiculous.

Miss Turnbull, ever the good sport, laughed as well and ran forward, struggling to help them both up. Even their chaperone, Aunt Louise had a hand pressed to her lips to stifle her amusement.

Margaret looked toward the stream. Her line was long gone as well as the old fishing lure she'd found in Lord Dobson's desk, stuck amidst several buttons and a lone cufflink. It had been a boon to find the lure. She'd claimed to Carstairs it had belonged to her father.

"Oh, dear, Miss Lainscott. You've lost your father's lucky fishing lure."

"My father had several, Lord Carstairs. I've others." She'd have to search through Lord Dobson's things again to find another. Or not. Carstairs wouldn't realize she'd no idea how to fish or hunt until after they were married.

"My lord, Lord Welles begs your apologies. He was late for an appointment and had to take his leave," Margaret heard one of the footmen utter. "The matter was quite urgent."

"Oh, too bad." Carstairs smiled his usual pleasant, empty smile, while Miss Turnbull looked at him in adoration.

Margaret stared at the empty spot on the blanket where Welles had been sitting. He'd left without telling her goodbye. It pained her more than it should have.

14

Nearly two weeks later, sitting before the Broadwood at Averell House, Margaret wondered if she'd mistaken Carstairs's interest. Or perhaps after their fishing excursion, Miss Turnbull had managed to truly sink her hooks into him. She went over their conversation repeatedly at the stream and there was nothing to indicate he wasn't interested in pursuing her further. Before entering the carriage to take them all home, Carstairs had made a point to pull her aside and ask if she would be present at the duchess's upcoming ball at the end of the month.

Margaret assured him she'd be there. But Carstairs hadn't called on her nor had she seen him at the few events she had attended with her aunt since. It was as if he'd simply disappeared.

The only gentleman who *did* call on her was Winthrop.

Margaret's fingers slowed. She refused to think of Winthrop.

She looked around the empty conservatory, glad for the solitude. Miss Nelson was suffering from a cold, and the duchess had taken Phaedra and Romy shopping. Theo was somewhere on the third floor behind the closed door of her studio, painting miniatures. Margaret supposed she should have gone home, but she'd no desire to hear her aunt mutter how grateful she was for Winthrop now that Margaret had 'scared off' Carstairs.

I didn't scare him off.

Her right hand pressed several keys in succession.

No, that wasn't right.

She tried another series of notes before pausing to write down the sequence in her composition book. Her sonata was beginning to take shape in bits and pieces, the melody accompanied by a swirl of purples, blues, and greens in her mind. But mostly a cacophony of blues, particularly sapphires and indigo. Which made sense because those shades were the colors Margaret most associated with *him*. She'd never before considered a *person* when music came to her; usually, it was a place or a series of noises, like the clopping of horses making their way down the street. Not even in the throes of grief over her father had Margaret written music specifically in his memory.

Only Welles.

"I guess that stands to reason," she said out loud to the empty conservatory. "I'm playing his piano."

"Indeed, you are." The lovely baritone echoed in the stark silence of the room.

Margaret's hands stilled on the keys as footsteps drew closer to her place on the bench. The air around her suddenly came to life, the hairs along her arms rippling in anticipation. Her body arched back unconsciously, wanting to be touched. "Lord Welles."

A bare fingertip, devoid of gloves, gently traced the outline of her collarbone. The touch was so brief, she wondered if it was only her imagination.

Welles came around the bench to lean against the piano.

"That's the tune you were humming at the stream the other day." His voice lowered to an intimate rumble. "Your sonata."

Margaret's entire core grew taut as a slow, languorous ache started to hum low in her belly. "Yes. You find such a thing odd? My writing music?"

"Never. I have a theory that while there are a select number of those who are gifted enough to play the piano beautifully, finding a pianist who also *creates* is far more rare."

Margaret's heart tugged again in his direction, this time more firmly and with purpose.

"I think that is more of a statement of your opinion than a theory, Welles."

"Perhaps." A wave of dark hair fell into one eye and he absently pushed it away. Welles was dressed in riding clothes, something he wore often and to great effect. Her eyes ran down the length of his legs. He looked smashing in leather breeches and boots. Not to mention he was looking at her in a way that caused Margaret's insides to twist and tighten pleasurably.

"What are you thinking about?"

"Riding," Margaret blurted out. Welles's ability to make her lose her train of thought was unsettling, particularly for a woman who prided herself on being level-headed.

"Ah." The heat in his eyes was unmistakable.

Margaret blinked, reddening at the thinly veiled innuendo. "I meant *you* were doing the riding."

"Yes. You are making yourself abundantly clear, Miss Lainscott."

"A *horse*." She looked away. "Why must you do that? Turn the most innocent of words into something—"

"Improper?" He shrugged. "I suppose I can't help myself, especially when I have the proper inducement. Why do you seem to notice it so often?"

Margaret narrowed her eyes. "I can't imagine everyone doesn't hear such—"

His wide mouth twitched. "How *are* things going with Carstairs?" he said, cutting her off.

"Very well, thank you." She'd no intention of telling Welles that she hadn't seen Carstairs in two weeks. Or that he'd virtually disappeared with no note to her, despite her best efforts.

"Then you probably won't need this." He produced a rectangular package wrapped in brown paper and tied with a green ribbon from his coat and set it atop the piano. "A gift to help you strengthen your lead over the fair Miss Turnbull. Poor Carstairs. He has no idea of the scheming going on behind his back."

Margaret didn't want to discuss Miss Turnbull. Or Carstairs. "That's very thoughtful but—"

"Hopefully this," he tapped the package, "will help your cause." He leaned in her direction, so close his lips were mere inches from hers.

For the briefest moment, Margaret was convinced he meant to kiss her, but when he didn't, she said, "I have things well in hand and have no need of your assistance with Carstairs. Or anything else, for that matter," she murmured, her eyes lowering to his mouth before she caught herself. "Thank you, my lord."

"Not even for the sake of your art? And you, composing a sonata? A pity." His gaze ran up the length of her, lighting fire along her skin.

God, he was flirtatious. *Charming.* "Lady Masterson might have an objection to you proposing something so outlandish to me."

"Doubtful."

She'd been curious as to his relationship to the beautiful

American for some time, even jealous though she hated to admit it. "Aren't you—"

"God, no." A choked laugh escaped him. "Nor is she my mistress if that is your next question."

Margaret felt the heat nip at her cheeks. "I would never ask such a thing."

"Of course not; you're so terribly mild-mannered, you wouldn't dare."

"Perhaps you don't know me as well as you think you do, Welles." She snapped the words at him like a whip.

"Ah. There *she* is."

Margaret's lips tightened into a line. He was very good at pulling away the cloak of timid invisibility she liked to wear.

Welles drummed his fingers lightly on the Broadwood. "In answer to your implied question, even if I *had* the inclination to wed, which I do not, Lady Masterson would not be a candidate."

"Why?"

"The lady in question is already spoken for."

"No, why won't *you* ever wed? You're the son of a duke." He was not the only one who could find chinks in a person's carefully constructed armor. "A duke must have heirs." She'd been considering his reasons since their conversation at the pond but wanted to hear him admit it. "Even if that duke is you."

The handsome features clouded over and a snarl lifted one side of his wide mouth. "Bearing children merely to perpetuate the lineage of a title which should die out is not something I'm interested in. *Ever.* And marriage holds no appeal for me." Something like regret flashed in his eyes as he looked down at her before he abruptly pushed away from the Broadwood.

Away from her. Margaret had touched a nerve. Intentionally. "Welles—"

"I'll take my leave now." He leaned close until she could feel his breath against her neck. "Miss Turnbull can be a formidable opponent. She's been after Carstairs for some time and is well known for her *passion* for trout and bass fishing. Perhaps this will help even the odds." He tapped the package with one knuckle. "Good day, Miss Lainscott."

His steps echoed in the empty conservatory, but Margaret did not turn around. As soon as the sound of the door closing met her ears, she took her hands from the keys and looked at the package he'd left. The idea of more studying to capture Lord Carstairs held little appeal. The thought of marrying Winthrop even less so.

Don't you want to experience passion?

She did; that was the problem. Margaret shut her legs tightly against the sudden fluttering between them at the mere thought of playing the piano half-naked for Welles. He'd deliberately not mentioned such a thing to her again. She knew Welles wanted Margaret to come to him.

Margaret didn't consider herself completely innocent, only *inexperienced*. Her plan, before her father's death, had been to stay unmarried but *not* celibate. She had planned to take lovers, though her choices in the small village where her father's estate lay were slim, to say the least. But in preparation, she'd purchased a copy of the Memoirs of Harriette Wilson. Margaret rarely decided to do anything unless she educated herself first. Sex was no different.

Harriette Wilson had been a courtesan of some renown and her recollections of her lovers were exceptionally detailed. Welles was wrong. Margaret knew *something* of passion, just not firsthand. She knew what sex entailed at the very least. Would it be so terrible if it were Welles who introduced her to such things? According to the gossips of London, he was incredibly skilled.

Her fingers banged against the keys.

Margaret liked Carstairs. He was a *decent* man. Honorable. She would have a comfortable life at his side though she doubted he would ever inspire the feelings within her that Welles did. But Carstairs was a far better alternative than Winthrop.

Her fingers flew to her lips, remembering the touch of Welles's mouth, no matter how fleeting it had been. "I can't believe I'm considering such a thing," she said, standing up from the bench and gathering her things. "I've set my cap for his friend."

She reached out, picking up the package Welles had left for her. The size and weight suggested a book. Wondering what sort of book Welles would bring her, she undid the ribbon and the brown wrapping paper fell away.

The Flyfisher's Entomology by Alfred Ronalds

Margaret opened the book but there was no inscription, only page after page of fish and instructions on fly fishing. She shut the book with a snap, her hand lingering over the fine leather binding. He'd said he wouldn't help her woo Carstairs, and yet Welles kept doing small things to ensure she would have what she wanted. Making certain she was at Lady Masterson's where Carstairs was. Re-introducing them. Buying her a book on fishing.

Offering to show her passion.

The clock struck the hour and Margaret stood to gather her things, praying fervently that Carstairs had called while she was gone.

15

"Miss." Henderson greeted her at the door with his usual mild dislike. "Lady Dobson awaits you in the drawing room."

The drawing room? Alarm bells immediately sounded for Margaret. Her aunt only ever used the room for meetings of importance. Or intimidation. She handed over her cloak to Henderson but held on to her composition notebook and Ronald's fly fishing treatise which she'd re-wrapped in the brown paper.

Henderson gave her a bland look, but his eyes darted to her hands as he clearly tried to discern what she carried.

"I'll just put these away," she said in a rush, hurrying to her room before the butler could stop her. "Please let my aunt know I will join her promptly."

She didn't want Henderson touching her things, especially not her composition book where she kept her music, and it would be unwise if he saw the book Welles had gifted her. Questions would be raised as to why Margaret was carrying around a book on fishing, and she didn't want to add to what she assumed would be an interrogation or a lecture from her aunt.

Upon reaching her room, Margaret locked the door, thankful Eliza, her lady's maid, wasn't waiting for her return. She had suspicions Eliza was reporting back to her aunt, though Margaret couldn't prove it. Margaret got down on her knees and slid partially beneath the bed, wedging both books between the frame and mattress. Satisfied the books were hidden and wouldn't be discovered, Margaret smoothed her skirts and made her way to the drawing room.

Of all the rooms in her aunt's home, Margaret hated the formal drawing room the most. She'd been berated in the lavishly decorated crimson and gold chamber more than once since arriving in London. The tasseled pillows and paisley damask covering of the sofa were stark reminders of Margaret being given over to her aunt's care. Grief-stricken over her father's death and devastated at being unceremoniously wrenched from her home, Margaret had been dumped into the drawing room to await the pleasure of Aunt Agnes. Seated on the sofa, the blood-red walls closing in on her, Margaret had faced the chilly reception of her aunt, a woman she'd met only once before. There had been no warm embrace. No condolence on the death of Walter Lainscott. Not a bit of affection was spared on Margaret. Instead, Aunt Agnes berated her for nearly an hour at the *stain* Margaret represented on the perfect lineage of her mother's family. A shameful secret Lady Dobson had kept from the *ton* she now had to acknowledge.

"There you are, my dear."

Margaret halted briefly in the doorway at the uncharacteristic cheery greeting, the hair on the back of her neck raising. Her aunt was never pleasant, at least not to Margaret.

Aunt Agnes sat perched on her favorite chair, an uncomfortable piece of furniture with little padding and a hand-embroidered silk covering. The stitching on the chair was so delicate and fine, one risked tearing the fragile depiction of roses climbing up the cushions with only the slightest movement.

Margaret avoided the chair as if it carried a disease.

Oddly enough, her aunt was smiling, a startling toothy grin which frightened Margaret nearly as much as the cordial greeting. Dressed all in blue, today's turban held a large peacock feather sprouting from the center.

"Come and sit, Margaret. You look especially lovely today. The dress suits you."

Margaret glanced down at the light brown day dress with its motif of acorns carefully stitched into the skirt and along the bodice. It was one of her favorites but had never elicited any compliments from her aunt.

Oh, God.

Instantly she knew why she'd been summoned to the formal drawing room. She should have guessed. The season wasn't over yet but apparently, Aunt Agnes didn't have any intention of waiting to see if Lord Carstairs would call again. Margaret swayed ever so slightly as she made her way to the sofa, her foot catching on the wooden leg so that she fell with a whoosh into the cushions.

I thought I had more time.

Aunt Agnes gave her a gleeful stare, the small, beady eyes snapping in triumph. A fresh pot of tea sat before her on the table, along with a selection of sandwiches.

Horrid woman. She can hardly contain herself.

A sharp rap sounded at the door of the drawing room. "Lord Winthrop." Henderson, her aunt's butler intoned, a hint of satisfaction coloring his announcement.

Aunt Agnes brought up her chin. The peacock feather waved at Margaret, tendrils fluttering with mockery.

The dreadful clomp of too large feet clad in ridiculous

shoes sounded in the hall seconds before the twin odors of sweat and talc permeated the drawing room. Winthrop was dressed in burgundy velvet, far too rich and heavy for the warmth of the day. Moisture had gathered between his brows and atop his upper lip, glistening in the sunlight streaming through the windows.

A giant, moist pear. Margaret kept herself perfectly still, determined not to shirk from him in disgust. Such a thing would delight her aunt and would not halt the proceedings.

Winthrop waddled forward, greeting her aunt politely. "Lady Dobson."

"Lord Winthrop, what a surprise to have you call," Aunt Agnes said. "Margaret and I were just about to have tea. Please join us."

"Miss Lainscott." He took Margaret's hand. "You are looking especially lovely today."

Margaret could do little more than stare at Winthrop and try to rein in her mounting horror at what was about to occur. She thought briefly about suddenly developing a headache, but Aunt Agnes would see through such a ploy. Could she faint? Perhaps collapse over the tea tray?

Winthrop settled his heaving form next to Margaret, making his appearance here even more glaringly apparent.

No. No. No.

She told herself to remain perfectly still and to keep her eyes trained on her lap. She managed not to cringe as he leaned in her direction.

"Would you like tea, Lord Winthrop?" Aunt Agnes was practically dancing a jig she was so pleased.

"Yes, thank you."

"Margaret, please pour." Her aunt was still smiling, almost daring Margaret to defy her or attempt to escape her fate.

Margaret nodded, her manner docile, and poured tea, pausing only when Winthrop instructed her on the amount of milk he liked in his. Taking a deep breath, Margaret composed herself while her mind ran through a series of excuses she could use to leave the room and never return.

Perhaps she was wrong, and Winthrop was only here to pay one of his annoying and awkward calls upon her. She took in his elaborate coat and carefully styled hair. He wasn't paying a casual call. Winthrop was about to pounce.

Winthrop and Aunt Agnes exchanged pleasantries while Margaret poured her aunt's tea and tried to make herself as invisible as possible. Maybe they would forget she was there. Her aunt claimed Margaret to be so unmemorable, barely anyone recalled her presence. Wishful thinking in this case.

Panic roiled her stomach. Winthrop's smell only contributed to her mounting nausea.

After demolishing two plates of tiny sandwiches, Winthrop put down the delicate porcelain plate he had clasped in one sweating paw. His eyes ran over Margaret with resignation.

"Miss Lainscott, would you care for a walk about the gardens? There is something I wish to discuss with you." He inclined his head in the direction of her aunt. "With your permission, of course, Lady Dobson."

No. No. No.

Margaret glanced at him from beneath her lashes, not trusting herself to raise her head. There was a crumb dangling at the corner of his mouth, stuck to the dampness that was Lord Winthrop. Margaret felt very light-headed. Perhaps she really would faint and land atop Winthrop's hideous shoes. The pair he wore today were burgundy, to match his coat, with ornate silver buckles sporting tiny burgundy bows.

Oh, dear God.

"My gardens are lovely especially this time of year. And it is a perfect day for a walk. Margaret would be happy to take a turn with you. My roses are in bloom." Aunt Agnes motioned for her to rise, eyes gleaming in anticipation.

Standing, Margaret forced herself to keep still as Winthrop took her hand, tucking her fingers into the fleshy meat of his forearm. The velvet he wore was already damp. What would it be like to be trapped beneath this...*monstrosity?* She could barely stand to be near him. The horror of the future her aunt planned for Margaret nearly made her faint.

Blinking at the sunshine as they moved outside, Margaret took in the garden. Birds were singing. The smell of roses filled the air. A perfect day and place for a marriage proposal.

Her stomach, already unsettled by the smell of Winthrop, lurched and pitched. She'd had nothing to eat since breakfast and the moment the sweating pear had appeared, Margaret had lost all interest in the tea tray. She placed a hand against her mouth. A hysterical scream was threatening to bubble up her throat as well as her breakfast.

"Miss Lainscott, I have come to know you quite well in the short time we've been acquainted. I feel we would get on well enough." A beaded drop of sweat ran down the side of his nose.

At least he has the decency not to drag this horrifying situation out with a romantic declaration.

"I have come to the conclusion we suit, despite your background."

I'm in desperate need of your dowry, though you are the daughter of a tin miner.

"I admire your maturity."

A bit long in the tooth, nearly on the shelf, so I feel certain you'll get no other proposal.

"Your aunt is in agreement."

She doesn't wish to fund another season nor wait to see if Carstairs reappears.

"I see," was all Margaret managed to choke out. The

aroma of the roses mixed with the smell of Winthrop's talc invaded her nostrils and pores.

Oh, God, I'll be smelling him the rest of my days.

"Miss Lainscott." He mopped his brow with a hastily procured handkerchief already stained with sweat.

A bitter taste filled her mouth.

"I would be pleased if you would consent to be my wife."

"I—" She swallowed and removed the hand at her mouth to press her fingers against her stomach. Margaret had one glance at Winthrop's horrified face before she turned to the rose bushes lining the path. Leaning over the pale pink buds about to bloom, Margaret tossed up her breakfast right into Aunt Agnes's prized rose bushes.

16

"I should die from embarrassment." Aunt Agnes shut her eyes tightly as if to block out the sight of her unfortunate niece. Her painfully thin form stalked back and forth over the Persian rug in Margaret's room, fingers curled into her skirts, like an agitated scarecrow.

Margaret shot her aunt a baleful glare from the comfort of her bed. It would be far too much to hope Aunt Agnes would perish from mortification.

"Breakfast didn't settle well this morning. Perhaps the butter had spoiled, for I only had toast. I can't imagine what else could have caused such a reaction." Margaret congratulated herself for saying such a thing with a straight face.

"Apparently, your *unsettled* breakfast did not keep you from visiting the duchess earlier today. Henderson claims you seemed well enough when you arrived home."

"At least I didn't cast up my accounts *on* Lord Winthrop." The rose bushes had paid the price for her dislike of the pear-shaped lord and her utter horror at his marriage proposal. Thank goodness she'd had the foresight to become ill in the rose bush instead of all over Winthrop's expensive, silly shoes.

Winthrop had sputtered, his pear-shaped form jumping back in horror at her distasteful display. He'd barely had the presence of mind to toss his well-used, sweaty handkerchief in her direction, the smell of which had caused Margaret to retch again into the roses. The bit of linen was still stuck among the thorns in her aunt's garden.

Margaret had murmured an apology of sorts, while Winthrop made sounds of disgust, and rushed up the stairs to her room. After washing her face and rinsing her mouth, Margaret felt somewhat better as Eliza had helped her to bed. She lay, staring at the ceiling, dread slowly seeping into her core. A short time later, Aunt Agnes had appeared, turban tilting dangerously and peacock feather quivering with indignation.

"Winthrop was *horrified*, Margaret." She stopped and put her hands against her hips, the bones of her knuckles poking through her skin. "As am I. Thankfully, he is an understanding gentleman. Much more than you deserve." Aunt Agnes scuttled about Margaret's bedroom like a tiny beetle, peering at the space as if expecting to find something else to chastise her niece for.

Margaret had been right to secret away her things earlier.

"I assured Winthrop his suit is welcome. The contracts will be sent over from his solicitor to mine. There are a few more points to be agreed upon. Minor things. But once I sign, you'll belong to Winthrop."

She swallowed back the bile hovering in her throat. "But I haven't accepted him. I have another suitor, Aunt. I am expecting Lord Carstairs—"

Her aunt's head snapped around so swiftly, the ridiculous turban nearly slid from her head. "*Your* agreement to Winthrop's suit isn't necessary. His proposal was only a formality. Lord Carstairs hasn't called in *two* weeks. I'll admit, I was overjoyed when he seemed to pursue you, but as with most other gentlemen who come to know you, you've alienated him in some way." She threw up her hands. "No one wants you but Winthrop, Margaret."

Margaret knew that to be somewhat true, but it was still hurtful to hear the words aloud.

"You fail to acknowledge *I* am your legal guardian."

"Surely my father—"

"Meant for me to guide you. He knew I would save you from the same mistake your mother made in marrying him. Your future is mine to do with as I please and it *pleases me* to give you in marriage to Winthrop."

Margaret took a sharp inhale of air. If she had to plead with her aunt, so be it. "But why him? Why are you so set on Winthrop? Please, I only ask for a bit more time. Once I see Carstairs at the Duchess of Averell's—"

"Carstairs is *gone*, Margaret, without offering for you. The only way you would garner another wedding proposal this late in the season would be if you were compromised." Aunt Agnes gave a short, bitter laugh. "And we both know *I* have a greater chance of being compromised than you."

Margaret didn't think her chances were all that terrible; after all, she'd been propositioned by Lord Welles. "But—"

"The only wise thing Walter Lainscott *ever* did, besides marrying my sister to further his lot in life, was to entrust your future into my capable hands."

Margaret often wondered why he had done so. She had been barely twenty-three when her father had died. Perhaps her father had thought he was doing the right thing. He'd wished her to marry and had never been comfortable with the idea of his only child becoming a spinster. While he'd not liked Aunt Agnes, her father had appreciated her fine breeding and connections.

Oh, Papa. Your intentions were honest but misguided. Margaret felt tears well behind her eyes and hastily blinked them away.

She refused to weep in front of her aunt, who would seize upon any weakness and use it to her advantage.

"You are too much like my sister, Clara. Flighty and empty-headed."

"I am not empty-headed."

"So timid you can barely meet a gentleman's eye, let alone garner his attention. So lacking in distinction one forgets you in a moment." Aunt Agnes continued. "The only thing you care for is playing the piano. No wonder no one wants you."

Resentment boiled up within her. Margaret had played the shy, reserved young woman in order to avoid marriage to a man like Winthrop and not antagonize her aunt into taking her music away. It was a means to survive until she could figure out a way to escape her situation. Margaret could now see doing so had been a mistake. Aunt Agnes thought her to be weak-willed and docile, much like Clara. But the only thing Margaret had had in common with her mother was music.

"I'm nothing like my mother," she said, her tone glacial. Clara Lainscott *had* been flighty. Easily distracted. A beautiful woman who *needed* someone to care for her and make difficult decisions. She *needed* servants. A maid.

Margaret needed none of those things. Only her music and a modest income to live on.

Her aunt's head snapped back, surprised at the vehemence in Margaret's words.

"My father was wrong."

Aunt Agnes skewered her with a hostile look. "Really? Is that why he left you to me?"

Margaret looked down at her hands, hating her father for his betrayal. How could he have left this woman in control of Margaret's future?

"I gave you an entire season to make your own choice and what did you do? *Wasted it.* You sat in this house, incessantly playing the piano. Scribbling in that leather-bound book as if anyone would ever even look at anything you composed." A nasty chuckle left her. "Your head has been in the clouds instead of paying attention to what is around you." She snorted. "This season I took a more active role in ensuring you would find a suitable match. But once again you frittered away your time, playing the piano for the Duchess of Averell like some paid entertainer. Meeting with those women. Mrs. Anderson."

Margaret's fingers tightened on the sheet at the mention of the Royal Society of Female Musicians. "I'm not sure what you mean."

Aunt Agnes gave a derisive snort. "Did you think I didn't know about your *little* club? No doubt you plan to give them a large donation once you are married. Those women are nothing but a bunch of parasites who wish to bleed you dry. You stupid girl. Luckily, Winthrop has assured me he will manage your funds."

"That isn't true." Margaret raised her voice. "There are female musicians who are in need of assistance. I wish to help. It is a noble cause. And there is money set aside for me *alone* once I marry."

"You can't be trusted with such a sum else you'd give it all away. What next? Will you roam Covent Garden and toss coins to the jugglers and fortune tellers? The only reason such women would curry your friendship is for your *money*, Margaret. Are you so blind? Winthrop will *ensure* not one penny goes to fund such a ridiculous cause. As his wife, you will be expected to support a charity much more meaningful. Orphans, for example."

No. This could not be happening. Her stomach heaved again.

"You know that isn't true, Aunt. The duchess is a supporter. Mrs. Anderson is an eminent pianist and teacher in her own right. She has encouraged me to compose and nurture my talent."

"What you mean is she encourages you to behave like a *harlot*. Anyone who has seen you play bears witness of your base nature. I wonder that the duchess has allowed you around her daughters."

"I play with passion," she choked out, her throat thick with emotion. "I have talent."

"Your mother was *exactly* the same. Her *passion* for music resulted in *you*. I can still see your father groping her at the piano. Touching her. Debasing her. A *miner*." Her aunt's chest heaved with fury, her bitterness toward her late sister and Walter Lainscott all too apparent. "Clara was the daughter of a viscount. A noble title that was *tainted* by your father. After their marriage your mother was not received, did you know that? She was shunned by all her former friends and acquaintances. My own prospects were dimmed by her selfish decision to marry Lainscott. Our mother's heart was broken. My father was devastated that she would elope with such a man. But I will *not* allow the same to happen to you." Spittle had formed at the corners of her aunt's mouth as she hissed her venom at Margaret.

"Aunt Agnes, please." This was why her aunt disparaged Margaret's passion for music. This was why Margaret's talent was only trotted out for special recitals when Aunt Agnes was pressured by her friends to do so. Or when she wished to impress someone. No wonder her aunt detested her. She blamed Margaret for all of Clara's mistakes. "I am *not* Clara. Please give me a chance to find another suitor."

"You cannot be trusted, Margaret. One day you will be carried away by music and find yourself seduced. I won't *stand* for such a thing." Her aunt's eyes had become wild, her breathing ragged and full of rage. "I will *not* suffer the humiliation of another scandal."

"Please don't marry me to Winthrop," Margaret pleaded, cringing at having to debase herself before her aunt. *"Please."*

Margaret sat up, hands reaching toward her aunt. "I find him to be repulsive, Aunt. He disgusts me. I would have some affection in my marriage."

"Affection? I had *none* in my marriage. Your mother's impetuous decision saw to that. But in hindsight, wedding Lord Dobson was all for the best. We were partners, combining our contacts and wealth to improve our status. A much more logical way to determine one's future spouse than affection. Look where *love* got your mother. Your father wished for something better for you. A title." Aunt Agnes shook her head in disbelief at what she clearly considered to be Margaret's idiocy.

"You'll be the wife of an earl, a countess, and will rise above your mother's station in life. You'll have a place in the *ton*. I know what is best for you, Margaret. And it's Winthrop." The turban nodded at Margaret. "He is in agreement that music will be a waste of your time as Lady Winthrop. You won't even have so much as an out-of-tune piano in his household to take your attention away from your husband and children. Or the care of his sickly mother." A thin, ugly smile crossed her lips. "One day you'll thank me." With a final look, Aunt Agnes disappeared from the room in a swirl of indignant skirts, slamming the door behind her.

"I'll never thank you," Margaret whispered as she stared into the canopy above her bed, wishing a hole would appear to swallow her up. After seeing her aunt rage about the bedroom, spitting out her vitriol against Margaret's parents, Margaret knew there wouldn't be any swaying her aunt's decision. Her mind was set. If her aunt had her way, Margaret would never have her music, nor would she be able to help her fellow musicians.

Both situations were intolerable. Winthrop was intolerable.

She allowed herself exactly two hours to wallow in a

horrific bout of self-pity, sobbing out her fear and anger into her pillow before resolving to find a way out of this mess. There was absolutely *no way* she could marry Winthrop. She would flee from this house and live on the streets before she did so.

Several hours later, Eliza brought a dinner tray to her room. Broth and two slices of bread. Apparently, her aunt didn't care for Margaret's outburst earlier and meant to starve her into obedience. It didn't matter. Margaret wasn't hungry.

"Is there anything else, miss?" Eliza set down the tray.

"No." Margaret had held suspicions earlier about trusting Eliza, but in light of her aunt's comments about Mrs. Anderson, she knew she'd been correct in hiding her composition book beneath the bed. Mrs. Anderson had sent Margaret several notes, as had the duchess, all of which she'd stupidly left on her desk. Eliza couldn't read, but that hadn't stopped her from sharing the contents with someone who could. Probably Oakes, her aunt's maid.

Bloody traitor.

"My stomach is still unsettled." Margaret made a great show of rubbing her stomach and appearing weak as she flopped back against the bed. "I'll try a bit of the bread to see if it suits me. But I really wish to sleep. I won't need you again tonight." A weak smile crossed her lips as she looked up at Eliza. "You may seek your own bed."

The maid's face was devoid of friendliness. "Your aunt wishes me to let you know if you aren't well in the morning, she will send for the physician."

Margaret wanted to snarl at the maid; instead, she said in a quiet voice, "I'm sure that won't be necessary. All I need is a good night's sleep to put me to rights, but if not, I believe a doctor is warranted." Margaret should have assumed sooner that her aunt had the entire household watching her every move. Especially Eliza.

Margaret closed her eyes. "Goodnight, Eliza."

"Goodnight, miss." The maid left, taking the broth, and shut the door behind her with a soft click.

Margaret counted to ten before her eyes popped open. She turned to look at the clock on her nightstand. She must wait.

When her aunt opened Margaret's door a few hours later to check on her, Margaret lay very still and kept her breathing even and slow. Aunt Agnes was on her way out. She'd been asked to join Lady Patson at a ball tonight. Margaret couldn't remember which one, nor did she care. She'd caught a glance at the invitation sitting on a tray in the hall. She could smell her aunt's freshly applied perfume and hear the swish of her silk gown. If she rolled over, Margaret would catch sight of a hideous turban perched on her head.

She didn't move until she heard the front door close and her aunt's carriage pull away.

Margaret threw back the blanket. She positioned the pillows from her bed to resemble a person sleeping and then drew up the coverlet. In the darkness, no one would know the difference. After all, Aunt Agnes always said Margaret left so little impression on a person she was nearly invisible. Tonight, she'd put her aunt's philosophy to the test.

Eliza was a traitor, but she was also stupid.

Clad only in her shift and stockings, she made her way to her wardrobe and grabbed her worn half-boots, ignoring the neat row of dresses and gowns. Where she was going, a dress wasn't required.

An old wool cloak hung in the back of the wardrobe, one she hadn't worn since leaving Yorkshire. The wool was gray, slightly moth-eaten, and patched in places. If any of the servants caught sight of Margaret, they would assume her to be one of them. She threw the cloak over her shoulders and paused at the mirror.

A thick braid of hair hung over one shoulder. As she pulled the cloak around her, Margaret was relieved to see the old wool covered every inch of her from chin to ankles. Her eyes were dark against the stark oval of her face, but she didn't look the least bit afraid.

Not at all like a woman who was about to perform a private concert, half-naked, for a gentleman at Elysium.

17

Tony leapt from his carriage and walked into Elysium, shrugging out of his velvet-lined cloak before handing it to the waiting attendant.

"A pleasure to see you this evening, my lord."

"Thank you, Johnson. How are your wife and little girl? Was the physician I sent to tend them sufficient?"

Johnson's eyes widened at Tony's words. "More than sufficient, my lord."

"I am glad to hear it." Tony and Leo had a habit of collecting strays. Men and women whom life had tossed to the winds, in dire need of someone in their corner. Like Johnson. Johnson lacked a right arm, the limb having been caught beneath a cart while filching food from a baker's stall one day to feed his small family. He'd barely survived the loss of his arm, and would not have if the cart and the driver involved hadn't worked for Elysium. Johnson had been brought to the club where Leo immediately had him tended and cared for. Hearing the man's story, Leo had hired Johnson, who had now been the doorman at Elysium for several years.

"Ida is much improved?"

Johnson beamed, showing an uneven row of teeth, flattered Tony remembered the name of his daughter. "She's much better, my lord. The fever is gone and she's mending fine. I thank you again for sending the doctor to us. My wife keeps you in her prayers for doing so."

"I am pleased to hear little Ida is better." Tony patted him on the shoulder. "And my thanks to Mrs. Johnson. Though I fear her prayers are wasted on me."

Johnson nodded. "Doesn't hurt none, though, my lord."

"No, indeed not."

Tony and his brother believed, strongly, that treating their employees with respect fostered loyalty. As a result, the employees of Elysium rarely left their employment and couldn't be poached by competing establishments. The club and its employees were a family. They took care of their own.

As he walked into the plush interior of Elysium, a rush of pride filled his chest. Technically, Leo was the proprietor of Elysium, but the *ton* knew Tony was his brother's partner in the club. Society's main objection to Tony's involvement seemed to be centered on Leo's status as the bastard son of the Duke of Averell. Not that such a thing hurt business. Elysium was packed day and night with patrons, and the waiting list for membership stretched into next year.

Leo handled the day to day operations while Tony often used his cache in the *ton* to draw patrons from their old haunts to Elysium. At least he had in the beginning. What had started as a way to piss off their father, the duke, had made Tony and Leo incredibly wealthy. When the duke had threatened to cut Tony off without a cent if he didn't marry, Tony had ignored him. He didn't need the duke's money or anything else his father peddled.

Elysium, from top to bottom, was as elegant and luxurious as Tony's velvet-lined cloak. He'd picked out many of the furnishings himself by raiding the homes of the impoverished nobility. It was amazing the things a titled gentleman would part with when he needed to pay a gambling debt. The club was housed in the former home of a rather eccentric merchant. The merchant, long dead, had built the home at the very edge of one of the most respectable neighborhoods in London, as close as he could get to society without marrying into it, though he'd tried. At the time, the construction of the mansion had caused an uproar. The *ton* had been outraged a man of such low breeding would live so near their own fine homes or worse, his equally low bred family would be walking their streets or stealing into their gardens.

But the merchant had prevailed. He *had* been horribly wealthy.

What he'd left behind was a monstrosity. A mansion so large and haphazard many had called for the building to be torn down. Parts of the home had been added at different times, depending on when the previous occupant had been flush with money or between wives; he'd had three. The result was a warren of rooms that led into each other and three floors with more false endings than the maze of the Minotaur.

Tony loved every winding curve. Leo had won the mansion from the man's son in a card game, but it was Tony who had suggested turning it into Elysium. A place where paradise could be found. At least for a few hours and with enough money. The first floor housed the gaming tables. On the second floor, pleasures were offered which catered to a variety of tastes. The third floor was reserved for Leo and Tony exclusively. Leo lived at Elysium, but Tony only spent some of his nights upstairs, mostly for convenience's sake.

Taking a turn in the direction of the faro tables, Tony caught the scent of feminine perfume and the rustle of skirts from his left side.

"Lord Welles, how lovely to see you this evening." Lady

Masterson stood in a shimmering gown of sapphire blue, cut so low the tops of her breasts pushed out over the silver thread lining her bodice. The gown would create a stir, as she'd meant it to. Georgina adored thumbing her nose at London society; she had since arriving on England's shores as a terrified seventeen-year-old girl, destined for marriage to an earl more than twice her age.

"You're looking stunning," he said in greeting, taking her hand. "As always."

She settled herself in the chair next to him and winked, gesturing to the dealer.

"Please tell me you didn't come unescorted." It was obvious she had, though she'd been expressly asked *not* to. Although if anything were to happen to Georgina, it wouldn't be at Elysium. She was probably safer here than anywhere else in England, even her own home.

"I don't need an escort." She smiled brightly. "I do as I please."

"Think of the talk it will cause for the *ton* to see the merry widow out and about. You'll be butchered in the press tomorrow." He inclined his head. "Especially in that dress. Christ, even I can't help looking."

"Don't tease, Welles. The *ton* doesn't give a fig about me nor I, them. Did you enjoy my party? I thought it was quite a wonderful way to spend an afternoon, though the cost was staggering. Lord Masterson and his wife were *beside* themselves at the expense. I heard him muttering about the cost of the champagne and spirits I served."

Tony was sure Lord Masterson did more than complain of the expense. "You should be careful with him. He means you ill."

"I reminded him that *my* money paid for the party, not his or my late husband's estate, which he now controls. You'd think Harold would find it in his cruel little heart to thank me for not leaving him and his wife with a bankrupt earldom. Did you notice he didn't even bother to *try* and dress appropriately?" She gave him a pointed look. "Nor did you. Spoilsport."

"I had no inclination to dress as a tree or a rock to please you, Georgina. Wherever did you get such an idea?"

"I felt like doing something frivolous."

She'd done it to tweak Masterson's nose. "It was a lovely party."

"Anyway, I shall spend my fortune as I see fit."

It was *her* fortune, not Masterson's, which only added to Masterson's dislike of his uncle's young widow. Georgina's husband, thumbing his nose at tradition, had left a large portion of his fortune to her alone, the bulk of which was the remainder of the dowry she'd provided upon their marriage. Masterson was furious to have only inherited what was the entailed portion of his uncle's estate. Georgina's husband had provided his heir a decent annual income as well and the estate was no longer in debt, thanks to Georgina's money. But Harold was greedy.

"I've no intention of staying in London, at any rate." She studied the cards in her hand. "I may even sell my pretty little house when I leave. Then the *ton* can all gossip about me to their heart's content." The flat nasal sound of her words drew the attention of two gentlemen across the table dressed in evening clothes. The man on the left whispered quietly to his friend as both openly admired Georgina's neckline.

She stared back and pushed her chest forward. "Yes, I'm *that* Lady Masterson, gentlemen. The American one."

Both gentlemen pretended to ignore her little outburst but continued to shoot her furtive looks over their cards.

"So, you *do* intend to return to New York?" Tony wondered if Leo had been apprised of her plans.

"Yes. I never thought I'd find weather that made me long

for Newport in the winter and yet I have." Her eyes sparkled in the light. "The *chill* in London is quite noticeable." She laughed softly at her little joke.

"Why now? You've finally managed to throw a proper English garden party."

Georgina laid down her cards, taking the next trick. "Who is Miss Lainscott?" She gave him a cheeky look.

Tony's smile froze. "No one of any import." The lie left him easily. He wasn't certain he could explain what Miss Lainscott was to *himself*, let alone anyone else.

"And yet you requested I send her an invitation to my party."

"My stepmother has taken an interest in her. I assumed she'd want Miss Lainscott to accompany her and Romy. I knew it would slip Amanda's mind, so I asked for her."

"Beautiful liar." Georgina motioned to the dealer for another card.

"I appreciate the compliment." He pretended to study his hand. Georgina was too perceptive by half. That she'd guessed at his interest in Miss Lainscott put him on guard.

"I thought you preferred blondes."

"Like yourself?"

"No." She shook her head as if desolate. "I'm much to well-rounded for you." She patted a hip. "Some might even call me plump."

Georgina *was* curvy and deliciously voluptuous. She was also beautiful, intelligent, and witty, none of which served her well in London.

Tony wasn't the least bit attracted to her. He looked down at Georgina's hands. Her fingers were perfectly graceful in her gloves as she wielded her cards. But she didn't play the piano with incredible abandon.

Nor expose bits of my heart to sunlight.

Tony's jaw tightened. Because Miss Lainscott had

managed to accomplish such a feat as making him feel something, Tony had reacted in a way he wasn't especially proud of. The gnawing possessiveness he felt toward her finally erupted and had caused him to send Carstairs on a make-believe errand to inspect a hunting lodge Tony pretended he wished to purchase. Removing Carstairs from London temporarily had eased the jealous ache Tony had recently developed over Miss Lainscott and had provided the added benefit of not having to watch her fawn over his friend.

Tony didn't deal with jealously very well.

The small piece of property was three days' ride from London. Tony had merely asked Carstairs to give his opinion of the estate and report back on its potential use as a hunting retreat. Carstairs had jumped at the excuse to stalk rabbits and other furry creatures through the woods. He'd never even questioned why Tony wouldn't be going with him.

Carstairs would return in a day or two, in time for the ball Tony's stepmother was hosting. Miss Lainscott could continue her pursuit of his friend then.

The scotch turned bitter in his mouth at the thought of Carstairs and Miss Lainscott.

It isn't as though you could have her.

"What's wrong, Welles?" Georgina said from beside him. "You're frowning. A poor hand?"

Jealousy was such an ugly emotion. He didn't care for it.

"Something like that."

18

Margaret hopped out of the hack she'd ridden in and stared at the entrance to Elysium. Part of her wanted to run after the driver and beg him to take her back to the relative safety of her aunt's home. She gave herself a little shake remembering why she was here.

Best to see this through.

A boisterous group of young men sailed past her, drunk and laughing.

Cautiously, she pulled the hood close around her face to hide her features and kept her eyes lowered. Elysium, surprisingly, was located at the very edge of one of the toniest neighborhoods in London. She'd thought the driver hadn't understood her destination until he'd taken a sharp turn up a winding driveway and through a cluster of trees before halting in front of an immense, red door. A discreet gold-lettered sign to the right of the door proclaimed the establishment was, indeed, Elysium.

A doorman with one arm stood guard before the entrance, watching the laughing group of gentlemen with hooded eyes. He inclined his head and greeted each by name. The giant next to him only grunted, the muscles of his immense arms and shoulders rippling beneath the fabric of his coat. The material parted revealing a pistol tucked into his waistband as he waived the young men forward.

The gentlemen's laughter quieted as they stepped around the giant and into the club.

Margaret briefly reconsidered the wisdom of what she was about to do. She wanted Welles's help with Carstairs, but that wasn't why she'd come. At least it wasn't the only reason. She pulled the cloak tighter and took a step forward.

After the group of gentlemen passed through the door, Margaret cautiously approached the doorman. He looked frightening with his broad forehead and barrel chest, but he smiled easily, watching her with curiosity.

The giant glanced her way then dismissed her.

Taking a deep breath, Margaret walked forward, meaning to enter the door. She wasn't sure what she would do once she was inside. Ask for Welles, she supposed.

"Here now. What's this?" The man with one arm stopped her with a frown. "You can't go in this way, miss. Surely you were told?"

Margaret's cheeks puffed. "Why ever not? You allowed those gentlemen before me to do so."

"They're *members*. Are you a member?" He gave her a skeptical look. "I thought not. I've never seen you before." He peered at her, his eyes narrowing. "You here at someone's request?"

"A...request?" She supposed she was, in a manner of speaking. Her presence had been requested. "Yes, I am."

"Then you should know to go around back." He jerked his thumb. "They'll check to see if your name is on the list. If not, then you can catch a hack."

"But—"

The giant rolled his eyes and took her arm, dragging her along with him before she could object.

Margaret had to run on her tiptoes to avoid being dragged, all while struggling to keep the cloak closed. Torches lit a gravel path winding around the side of the building to another door, this one not nearly as grand as in front; this door, too, was painted red.

Two ladies stood awaiting entrance while another man, equally as large as the one in front, checked a ledger. The women turned at her approach, their faces each covered with an ornate silk mask sufficiently hiding their identities. The sound of their laughter reached Margaret's ears as they were waved inside.

The giant moved her forward to stand before the door.

"Who are you here for?" The man looked her over with little interest.

"I'm not on your list," Margaret said. "I had an open invitation and I'm not certain—"

"Your name and who you're to see."

Margaret lifted her chin. What difference did it make if these two men knew who she was or why she was here? She doubted Elysium would still be in business if the employees were less than discreet.

"Margaret to see Lord Welles."

"Margaret?"

"Just Margaret. I'm here for Lord Welles."

The brute holding her arm cursed softly. "I'll let Johnson know."

The man at the door shrugged and put down the ledger. "Inside with you then, miss." He took her arm and led her through the doorway.

Margaret swallowed. "Would it be possible to wait outside for him?" The cloak slipped revealing her naked collarbone and she pulled it tighter around her.

He shook his head. "No. You wait inside."

Her escort barely took notice of the fact she was half-dressed under the cloak. She supposed in his line of work he'd seen things much more interesting than the exposed collarbone of a plain-faced spinster.

Taking her by the elbow, he opened the door. A gangly youth leaned against the wall just inside, reading a book of all things. Her escort motioned for the young man to go outside. "I've got a package for Lord Welles I need to deal with."

The youth took one look at Margaret and then went outside.

"Is Lord Welles here?" Belatedly it had occurred to her that he might *not* be here tonight. Margaret rarely made rash decisions, but in her panic about Winthrop and the horribly revealing discussion she'd had with her aunt, she'd chosen to come to Elysium without a second thought. She should have sent him word she was coming.

"He's here," the guard assured her before opening the door to a small parlor. A fire burned in the hearth; shivering, Margaret immediately went to stand before the flames to warm herself. She turned to ask another question but saw only the door closing behind him.

Margaret circled the room, taking in her surroundings. The furnishings were understated and elegant, the rug expensive and plush beneath her feet. A silver tray on a sideboard held a collection of crystal decanters, each filled with amber liquid. Walter Lainscott had liked scotch and Irish whisky, and the parlor at her home in Yorkshire had been filled with the stuff. Eyeing one decanter, she lifted the crystal stopper and sniffed.

Scotch. Margaret smiled to herself.

If there was ever a moment for her to have scotch, it was tonight when she desperately needed a bit of courage. Margaret picked up a glass and poured herself two fingers.

She took a cautious sip and immediately started to cough and sputter.

The burn down her throat left her gasping for breath but once her eyes stopped watering, a pleasant warmth spread across her chest. After a moment, she took another swallow and didn't cough once.

The door to the parlor opened and Margaret swung around, expecting to see Welles.

The man who'd escorted her to the room, the guard, had returned.

Margaret's heart sank. Welles was here but didn't want to see her. She cursed softly. How utterly humiliating. She would now have to go down to the street and call a hack.

He looked at the almost empty glass of scotch in her hand. "This way, miss. You can pour a bit more and take it with you." His tone and manner were much more deferential now that he'd returned. "Lord Welles has asked me to escort you upstairs."

Relief filled her. He was here and would see her. Margaret poured another finger of scotch into her glass. "Shall we?"

"I'm Peckam," he said, introducing himself as he led her up a narrow flight of stairs to the second floor where a door opened into a narrow hall. Loud conversation, cursing, laughter, and the sound of a piano met her ears as they approached a wide landing. Margaret stopped to look over the side. The entire gaming floor of Elysium was spread out before her. Gentlemen milled around the tables in groups, occasionally escorting a well-dressed lady. Other women, clearly courtesans, fluttered about the tables, recognizable by their scandalous gowns and flirtatious manner. A tall, dark-haired man strolled nonchalantly about the tables, stopping here and there to speak to someone. She leaned over the rail to get a better look, certain it was Welles below her. Her eyes widened, taking in his waistcoat which was a dizzying swirl of crimson and green with an exorbitant amount of gold thread. She'd never seen him wear something so...outlandish.

Her escort tapped her politely on the arm. "Come, miss."

"I believe Lord Welles is downstairs." She pointed down to the man on the gaming floor.

Peckam followed the direction of her finger and shook his head. "No, miss. That's Mr. Murphy, *not* Lord Welles. This way, please."

So that's Leo. Margaret's eyes lingered on Welles's mysterious half-brother. She couldn't see his face clearly, but from a distance, he looked remarkably like Welles. The duchess and her daughters spoke of Leo often and with great affection, though if he visited, it hadn't been when Margaret was there. She watched him for a moment longer, wishing he would turn her way.

"Miss?" Peckam was waving her down the hall. The second floor was quiet once they walked past the landing. Muffled sounds came from behind the row of doors as she passed. Each door was painted a different color and numbered.

The two ladies who'd preceded her into Elysium earlier came down the hall from the opposite direction. Giggling, with wine glasses dangling from their fingers, they stopped before one of the rooms and opened the door without knocking.

As Peckam ushered her by, Margaret caught sight of a man, lying on his side, facing the door.

The man was naked save for the mask covering his face and was quite...well endowed.

The two women entered the room with another giggle and closed the door behind them.

Margaret looked away, her cheeks flaming. Again, she questioned her wisdom in coming to Elysium. But after

Winthrop's proposal and Carstairs's sudden disinterest, Margaret needed to see Welles.

It was madness to be here, Margaret knew that. Scandalous. But she could still feel the warmth of Welles's larger hand in hers at Lady Masterson's party. How he'd told her about his mother. The press of his lips. The look of understanding on his face when she'd told him she heard music in the flowers.

I want to be here. Her heart beat louder in her chest.

As sure as she was that she would marry Carstairs, Margaret took no joy in it. He was only better than Winthrop.

I want Welles.

She and Peckam walked the entire length of the second floor to yet another set of stairs with a velvet cord strung across the steps. Two thuggish looking men stood guard before the barrier. The brute on the left, with a shock of red curls falling across his forehead, nodded at Peckam and lifted the cord for Margaret to step under.

"Have a good night, miss." Peckam made a short bow. "At the landing, take a right. Lord Welles's rooms are at the far end of the hall."

Rooms? Welles lived here?

Margaret climbed the stairs to the top, reaching a small landing. Two narrow halls led from the junction of the landing, with an enormous set of double doors at the end of each. She turned right, as instructed. One of the doors stood ajar as the notes of a Chopin nocturne floated out to wrap around her.

Welles was playing the piano.

Margaret stepped through the doorway and stopped.

The room wasn't overly large and was sparsely furnished, though even in the candlelight she could see the rugs and furniture were all expensive. A large, overstuffed chaise, the size of a small bed, faced the piano. Two leather wing-back chairs sat at angles before a fire blazing on the hearth; a small table sat between them. A sideboard filled with various bottles and decanters took up one corner. There was also a washbasin and a stack of towels. A bookcase lined one wall and was packed full of bits of paper, books, and ledgers. Above the fireplace, a painting hung—a landscape of a pond surrounded by thick woods.

But it was the piano, and the man playing Chopin which commanded Margaret's attention.

Another Broadwood, she could tell by the lines and the sound even without seeing the gold lettering across the front. Welles had discarded his coat and the sleeves of his shirt had been rolled up to reveal muscular forearms. The thick waves of his hair curled in disarray around the edge of his collar and the stark lines of his jaw. His hands floated gracefully over the keys as he bent forward in concentration. The Chopin piece was as beautiful as it was difficult. It was one Margaret played often.

A bolt of longing struck her. For the piano. For him.

Sensing her presence, his fingers slowed on the keys, the gold signet ring he wore on his pinky finger winking at her in the light. The top of his shirt was unbuttoned, revealing the hollow of his throat along with a light dusting of hair. Welles turned in her direction, a small lazy smile gracing the corner of his wide mouth. He was so beautiful sitting at the Broadwood, like Hades playing Chopin in the underworld.

A delicious hum began beneath her skin as she approached the piano. Margaret felt dizzy, intoxicated by the sight of him. Or perhaps it was only the scotch. She set the glass down on the table.

"Hello, Maggie."

Her nickname. He'd called her Maggie the day he'd interrupted her fishing with Carstairs. The ache inside her grew more pronounced. Her skin always hummed in his presence, the blood rippling with urgency through her body the closer she got. Her trepidation at coming to him dissipated, and the sight of Winthrop sweating in her aunt's garden faded away to nothing.

"Lord Welles."

"I was surprised when they told me you were asking for me at the door. Why are you here?"

The deep baritone seduced her, skimming across the surface of her skin. Welles was one of those rare human beings who possessed an innate sensuality. She'd noticed that about him the very first time she'd seen him at Gray Covington. Every smile or careless gesture was imbued with subtle hints of his sexual nature, every movement of his body graceful and tinted with something erotic. The attraction Margaret had for Welles far outweighed everything else in her life, even eclipsing her passion for music.

"I wanted to see you," she whispered.

A small wrinkle appeared between the dark brows. "What's happened, Maggie?"

She ignored his question. "You were playing Chopin." Her fingers ran lightly along the top of the piano. "And you purchased another Broadwood."

"Technically I only bought this one. The piano which you play so often was a gift."

"I stand corrected." Margaret found herself looking at his mouth. Like the rest of Welles, it was beautifully made.

"I met him once, have I ever told you? Chopin. He visited London shortly before I met you at Gray Covington. I attended a soiree given for him at the home of James Broadwood."

"James Broadwood? *The* Broadwood? The piano maker?" If it were possible, Margaret was more intrigued by Welles than before. Tiny flutters swirled deep in her belly.

He nodded, lips tilted. "I've finally managed to impress you. It's been bloody difficult." His fingers ran over the keys and the hint of the earlier piece came out. "All it took was a little Chopin. I suppose the book on fly fishing didn't suffice?"

"I haven't cracked open the fly fishing book as of yet, but I'm certain it will make for riveting reading. And you lied. You do still play and very well, I might add."

A soft chuckle. "I hope it helps your cause. The book. And I never said I *didn't* play any more," he said. "I believe I declined to answer. But my talent is not like yours. *You* become the piano. I can only play it."

A memory flashed before her: Welles watching her perform at Gray Covington when she'd so horrified her aunt and everyone else with her passionate performance. He hadn't been impressed with her playing.

He'd been aroused.

The realization surprised her. This gorgeous creature, one of the most beautiful men she'd ever seen, wanted *her*. Her joy was eclipsed by the knowledge that he also didn't *want* to feel so strongly about her. The thought was painful, but not unexpected after his remarks about his mother and the Duke of Averell.

"Why are you here?" he asked again.

"I've come to play for you." She undid the clasp of her cloak, letting it fall to the floor, and lifted her chin. Her chemise was only a thin barrier of cotton between her body and Welles; she was certain he could see her naked form beneath. Her nipples hardened at the low growl of satisfaction coming from deep in his chest.

"As you requested, my lord. Stockings. Chemise. Piano."

19

Tony's eyes trailed over every inch of the delicate, slender body barely hidden beneath the thin cotton of her chemise. He wondered if she had any idea of how...*magnificent* he found her. How he *thirsted* for her. His cock had hardened to marble in his trousers the moment Johnson had informed him Maggie was at the door asking for him.

I sent Carstairs away. He wasn't proud of himself for doing so. His friend's abrupt disappearance had probably caused Maggie a great deal of anxiety. Is that why she was here? "The request I made of you was improper."

"It was."

Her eyes were huge and dark. Unfathomable. Maggie wore nothing but chemise, stockings, and a hideous pair of old half-boots, as he'd asked of her. Her breasts were small and exquisitely shaped, the tiny buds of her nipples pushing up against the worn cotton. The dark shadow at the apex of her thighs beckoned for his touch.

"What will you have me play?" Maggie's voice had gone low and husky. "More Chopin?"

My cock. "Whatever you wish."

He stood and waved her toward the seat, struggling to keep from touching her.

"You're barefoot." Maggie stared at his feet for a moment before seating herself on the bench.

"I am." He didn't even bother to hide the heavy outline of his erection from her.

"You have lovely feet," she said before running her fingers over the keys to warm up her hands. "I didn't know men possessed such beautiful toes." A soft heartfelt sigh. "Much like the rest of you."

It was one of the most erotic things anyone had ever said to him, having his toes admired. It was all he could do not to simply toss her on the chaise and ravish her.

The first notes floated up into the air as Maggie started to play.

※

HER MIND WENT BLANK. WHAT SORT OF MUSICAL composition was deemed appropriate for a seduction? Margaret knew full well she wasn't here to play a song and then have Peckam escort her out.

The hum beneath her skin threatened to drown out everything else and her thoughts became lazy. Sensual. Every brush of the chemise against her breasts teased the hardened peaks of her nipples. Even the bench beneath her seemed to chafe at the backs of her legs and buttocks.

The piece she would play came to her in a moment, accompanied by an insistent ache between her thighs. It was for him, after all.

Two frail notes echoed in the room before she bent forward, allowing the music to flow into her veins, moving through her slender body as if a match had been struck to set her aflame. Greens and purples swirled before her along with great bursts of sapphire blue. The same color as his glorious eyes.

All she heard was the music, the low vibration of the strings bursting through the keys to her fingertips. She could feel his eyes on her, sensed he was mentally stripping the chemise from her body, and exploring the curve of her spine. When she arched back, Margaret wasn't surprised at the firm wall of muscle circling her. Welles straddled her on the bench while she played, his strong thighs trapping Margaret's smaller body. His breath stirred the hair at her temples, his larger form curling around hers.

When she bent forward, Welles matched each movement, his fingers running over the length of her arms, sending flames down through her fingertips. The burn of his lips pressed against her neck as Margaret struggled to focus on the music. His arm snaked around her waist, holding her pressed tight to the hardness at the juncture of his thighs. A warm hand cupped one breast, stroking the underside as if memorizing each curve before rolling the peak of her nipple between his fingers.

Margaret whimpered as sensation shot from her breast down between her legs. Teeth grazed the side of her neck and she missed a note. The arm holding her loosened as the other hand trailed down the length of her hip gently tugging at the hem of her chemise. Another whimper left her at the touch of his fingers against the bare skin of her inner thigh. When he finally touched the swollen folds at the core of her, Margaret was already shamefully wet.

A rumble came from deep in his chest. He bent her back slightly, like a bowstring, forcing her legs further apart. When his fingers traveled over her, teasing and stroking, Margaret hit several wrong notes in a row. When he spread her further and pressed two fingers inside, she gasped, struggling to remind her hands to move.

"Don't stop," he whispered.

Welles was everywhere, above her, around her, inside her. Each intimate press of his fingers drove her mad with need. He became part of the music because he *was* the music.

Her music.

His thumb searched and found the engorged bit of flesh hidden in her folds, a place Margaret had only herself tentatively touched. Stroking lightly, he nuzzled beneath her ear, the wide mouth whispering of his desire for her. When he pushed a third finger inside her and gently flicked against the small nub with his thumb, Margaret's hands left the keys with a clang. She moaned, flailing against him while pushing her hips up to meet every stroke of his fingers against her flesh.

"*Jesus*, Maggie." Welles's voice was rough against her throat. He pulled her back against his chest with a groan, lifting her thighs up until she was in his lap. His fingers continued caressing her until Maggie panted, begging him for relief.

"Please," she sobbed. Margaret's entire body throbbed. The fire Welles had stoked within her burned beneath her flesh. His fingers left their ministrations and she heard herself cry out in disappointment. Perhaps Aunt Agnes had been correct, for the combination of Welles and the music had made Margaret a wild, wanton thing. She heard herself beg. "Please."

"Shush." Welles took her in his arms and carried her to the chaise. Gently, he laid her down, his hands running along her hips and legs. He lifted one foot and pressed a kiss to the inside of her calf before he removed her half-boot.

Margaret watched the graceful movement of his hands as the other boot fell to the floor. He paused, rubbing his thumb against the bottom of her foot. He pressed another kiss to her ankle. Then up her calves, lifting the hem of her chemise in slow increments. Each time a piece of her was exposed by his fingers, his lips followed. When he nibbled at the hollow of her knee, Margaret's head fell back against the cushions, her legs splaying wide of their own accord.

Inch by inch he tugged the hem of the chemise further. She gasped at the nip of her skin above her navel. Whimpered his name as his tongue traced the outline of her ribs. Every bit of Margaret was worshipped. Adored. When the cooler air of the room drifted across her breasts, she raised her arms to allow him to pull her chemise free without a qualm.

"Welles." She breathed his name like a prayer as his teeth grazed one nipple. His fingers once more caressed the spot between her thighs, stoking the fire that burned within her. He suckled one breast while his fingers explored and teased until Margaret's hips writhed against his hand.

He cupped the base of her skull with one large hand, leaving her breast as his lips brushed over her cheeks, before claiming her mouth. The kiss was slow and deep, asking for her surrender which Margaret would gladly provide. When he nipped at her bottom lip, she opened her mouth without hesitation to allow his tongue to search out hers. Margaret reached up, threading her fingers through the thick waves of his hair, before moving her thumb to graze the lobe of his ear. Her fingers floated over the rough brush of hair along his jaw before gliding down his neck to press her palm against his heart.

He finally pulled away, kneeling back on his heels between her legs. Without breaking eye contact, Welles continued to touch her and tease her swollen flesh. Gently. Insistently. Drawing out her arousal to a careful peak before retreating.

"I wish to do everything to you." The heat in his gaze was unmistakable.

"Yes," she sighed as his fingers thrust gently inside Margaret before he bent to take her in his mouth.

She cried out at the feel of his tongue flicking against her sensitive flesh.

He nudged her legs apart, cupping one buttock, holding her still. The sight of Welles, still clothed, his dark head between her thighs was so erotic, every nerve in her body sparked adding to the sensations building at her core. His fingers curled inside her as he sucked the small bit of flesh between his lips.

Margaret's head fell back, breath stopping, before falling through the night into a dazzling array of colors and music, like the twinkling of a thousand stars. Intense pleasure rolled over her in great waves, lapping at her skin until her toes curled. When he finally released her, Margaret lay boneless beneath him.

Harriette Wilson's description of this act did not do it justice.

A puff of air blew through the soft hair covering her mound, tickling her. Welles was kissing his way up her naked body again, whispering against her skin, stopping every so often to nip or press a kiss to a particular spot, claiming each piece of Margaret for himself. He sat back with a hiss and looked down at her. Even in the candlelight, she could see the hard, raised ridge against his thigh.

"You should leave." His baritone was raspy. *Pained*.

She shook her head and opened her arms to him. Didn't he understand? She wanted all of this. All of *him*. Even if it was only tonight. "And before you ask, I'm sure."

He looked so conflicted, so anguished by her decision.

Margaret's fingers grabbed his forearm. She sat up trying to pull him to her.

Welles took her hand and pressed a kiss to the pulse beating in her wrist before he nodded, making his decision. "Undress me." He slid off the chaise and stood before her.

Margaret moved until she was kneeling before him. Her fingers trailed over his chest, plucking lightly at the fabric, uncertain how to proceed.

"Buttons first," he growled in a dark tone laced with amusement.

Margaret had never undressed another human being in her life and the current task seemed a bit daunting. Deciding imitation was the sincerest form of flattery, she stretched up as far as she could and boldly pressed a kiss to his neck.

"A good start."

She undid another button, pressing her mouth to his shoulder. When she slid her hands beneath the shirt and pressed against his chest, Welles's eyes fluttered shut and a low sound of pleasure rumbled from deep within him.

Encouraged, Margaret continued, unbuttoning and kissing until his shirt hung open.

He leaned forward with a smile.

Grabbing the edge, her fingers shaking, she pulled it up and over his head.

Welles impeccably clothed in his uniform of indigo coat and buff riding breeches was a stunning creature, but nothing prepared Margaret for his appearance *without* clothing. His body was a thing of masculine beauty, as if he'd been carved and sculpted by the finest craftsman. Margaret's fingertip traced the curvature of one pectoral muscle, firm and sleek, to the line of his ribs. Welles bore not an ounce of fat on his body; every bit of him was solid. Powerful. A dusting of dark hair spread out over his torso, tapering down into a thin line before disappearing into his waistband.

He took her hand, pressing an opened-mouthed kiss to her palm. "Now the rest just as you did the shirt." The nipple of one breast tingled as he brushed the tip with his thumb, stoking the flames simmering between her legs back to life.

She took hold of his waistband, allowing her fingers to

slide between the material and his skin, reaching down until she could touch the hardened length of him with her fingertips.

Welles sucked in his breath.

Margaret ran her finger along the velvety length smiling at the sounds coming from his chest. He smelled delicious, like the wind before a storm. She inhaled deeply before urging her fingers to finish the buttons, nuzzling her chin to his stomach.

"Tease," he growled out.

Margaret had never felt so powerful. So seductive. When she laid her head on the ridges of his abdomen and took hold of both sides of his trousers, Welles trembled beneath her cheek. Tugging as hard as she could, they fell from his hips.

Welles moved back and stepped gracefully out of his trousers, kicking them aside. He stood before her, his hands tugging at the braid of her hair until the dark strands fell over her shoulders.

Margaret was intimately aware of a piece of his anatomy directly in front of her. Without thinking she reached out and wrapped her fingers around the hard length, wondering how she should proceed.

"Maggie," he breathed, placing one hand over hers, "are you very sure?"

"Yes. I've never been more sure of anything in my life."

He pushed her back against the cushions and nudged her legs apart before settling between them, claiming her mouth for another kiss. His lips held an urgency, a possessive heat that sent her heart racing. Where before he had asked for her surrender, now Welles demanded it, running his tongue along her bottom lip before moving his mouth to trail down the slope of her neck.

Margaret welcomed his possession. She rocked her hips up against him, her fingers clutching at the muscles of his back. When his hips shifted and the heavy thick heat of him pressed into her, Margaret's legs instinctively wrapped around his waist.

"Slow, Maggie. I don't want to hurt you." His voice was strained.

She whimpered and lifted her knees forcing him deeper. Welles was being infinitely patient and careful in destroying her virtue, making her heart yearn for him even more, if that were possible. Margaret pushed her hips up again, begging him to take her.

In response, Welles pulled back. His hand cupped her cheek, eyes full of heat and desire mixed with worry over the physical pain of their joining. "I'm sorry." He captured her mouth in a deep kiss, stealing the cry from her lips as he thrust forward, imbedding himself.

Margaret's eyes widened at the sudden invasion. Her body, so much smaller, struggled to accommodate his. The sensation of being stretched and full was *different*, but she otherwise felt little pain at the destruction of her maidenhead. The loss of her virtue amounted to little more than a sting, no worse than a pinch on her arm from her aunt. And having Welles inside of her was...*wonderful*.

His breathing was ragged as he kissed the slope of her neck, his body taut and still.

He's afraid to hurt me. Margaret's heart thudded dully in her chest.

And Welles was repeating something, like a poem or a prayer, the words low and muffled.

"What are you saying?" her fingers cupped his chin.

In response, Welles smiled and laced her fingers with his, raising her arms above her head. He started to move, each stroke bringing him deeper inside her as if he was trying to merge his much larger form with hers.

Margaret found the feeling pleasurable, although not as lovely as what he'd done before.

He hooked one of her legs over his shoulder, angling the lower half of his body.

"Oh." A sharp prick of heat rolled up inside her again. Perhaps she'd been mistaken.

"There?"

"Yes, I—" The rest of her words dissolved into a moan. Each thrust brought her closer to the pleasure she'd experienced before, but this time it was different. The music of Welles sank into her bones echoing through the surface of her skin. Their bodies moved together in a beautiful duet, a perfect harmony of her and Welles. The muscles in the lower half of her body tightened as her release approached, urging him deeper.

He grunted in satisfaction and increased his pace. When his teeth sunk gently into her shoulder, the sting of his bite mixing with the intense pleasure, Margaret shattered, the music of Welles the only thing she could hear. She arched against him, marveling at the stars as her eyes closed. A cacophony of every shade of blue sparkled beneath her eyelids.

Welles thrust into her twice more, swearing softly before pulling out. A spray of hot liquid ran across her belly and between her legs. His breathing was uneven and heavy as he fell against her to press a kiss to her forehead. "Maggie."

Margaret knew what he'd done. Harriette Wilson's book had covered withdrawal as a way to prevent conceiving a child. Welles didn't want children. Her arms tightened around him. She should have been glad of his consideration, but instead, his actions pained her. A tear ran down her cheek though she tried to blink it away. She had come to Elysium with no illusions regarding Welles, nor any expectations. Welles bore her some affection, as evidenced by his tender regard tonight, and for that, Margaret was grateful. But their physical relationship couldn't progress past this one night, not when Margaret had to secure her future.

Welles kissed her and got up, padding naked to the other side of the room.

She closed her eyes, listening to the crackle of the fire and Welles moving about. In a moment the chaise dipped as he sat next to her. A wet cloth gently wiped at her stomach before pressing between her legs. Her eyes fluttered open to see him watching her, a tender expression on his handsome face as he carefully cleaned her.

Another tear escaped her eyes and she brushed it away lest Welles see it. Was this how all rakes behaved when deflowering virgins? Her heart beat hard within her chest.

"Don't worry, my Maggie. You are safe for the time being from my lecherous advances. Did I hurt you?" His brow wrinkled in concern. "You're so much smaller than me, and I—"

"No," she assured him, placing a hand on his stomach. "You didn't hurt me."

He nodded, running the cloth along the inside of her thighs, more gentle than she could have imagined a notorious despoiler of women would be. "So beautiful." He pressed his mouth to her stomach.

"I'm not," she said quietly, soaking in his praise, no matter how exaggerated she found it.

"More intelligent than most men and yet you fail to realize your own appeal." His tongue flicked out to the tip of her breast.

Margaret shivered, his touch already stirring her own passions again.

"You're cold." Placing the cloth aside he picked up her naked body and stretched her out on top of him. Strong arms wrapped around her back and lower body as warmth seeped from his larger form to hers.

Margaret placed her cheek to Welles, the hair covering his chest tickling her nose. She listened to his heart, wishing it beat for her.

Stop it.

Margaret shut her eyes, wanting just a few more minutes of Welles before returning to her aunt's. Now was not the time to feel sorry for herself. Practical to a fault, Margaret knew she still had to secure Carstairs, no matter her feeling for Welles. *Especially* because of Welles. Mooning over a man she couldn't have would only end with her married to Winthrop.

"Welles," she said quietly, knowing the hour grew late. "I should go." It would be more difficult for her the longer she stayed. It was bad enough she meant to ask for his help. She scuttled off his chest before he could stop her. Stepping out of his reach, she picked up her chemise from the floor.

A hand stretched out to her. "Come back to me." The deep baritone caressed her still throbbing body, making her unsteady.

She took a deep breath, ready to recite the speech she'd prepared. An idea had come to her during her earlier conversation with her aunt. One she'd mulled over in the hack on the way to Elysium. "You must know, Welles, I wanted to be with you tonight. My honor has not been infringed upon. I have *no* expectations of you."

"Maybe you should," he said softly.

"Later, if you feel even a shred of guilt, I beg you do not on my account."

"Why did you come to me tonight, Maggie?" His voice was rough, almost irritated.

Because I'm in love with you.

Blinking, she turned her head because at that moment, it hurt to look at him. She was afraid he'd see the truth in her eyes. He would pity her, something Margaret didn't want. Welles would *never* marry. He'd made his feelings abundantly clear and his reasons were deeply entrenched in every fiber of his being. Margaret, on the other hand, *had* to marry. Preferably Carstairs. She hoped someday Welles would forgive his father and let go of the bitterness he held on to. The thought of him anguished and alone for the remainder of his life broke Margaret's heart.

Steeling herself and her emotions, she turned to face him again. Margaret couldn't allow her compromised heart to stop what must be done. And her heart *was* compromised, much more thoroughly than her body had been. Lifting her chin, she looked him in the eye.

"Winthrop has offered for me and my aunt has accepted, though the contracts have not yet been signed. I no longer have the luxury of convincing Carstairs to court me. I need to be compromised."

The wide mouth drew into a grim, hard line. "You've *been* compromised, in case you haven't noticed." The words flung at her like chips of ice. "*Come. Here.*"

Margaret shook her head. "Why are you so bloody angry?"

"Was this your way of bribing me to help you trap my friend?" The words came out angry and cold. "How mercenary of you."

Why was he being so awful? "No, of course not. One has nothing to do with the other. Besides," she felt her own ire rising, "you were the one who originally made such an improper suggestion."

"I only asked you to play the fucking piano." He sat up on the chaise, clearly furious with her.

"There is no need for vulgarity, Welles." Margaret pulled her cloak up over her shoulders, jerking to secure the garment around her neck. "I don't blame you for what happened tonight. Please be assured I don't expect anything from you."

"Stop saying that."

"Fine. Don't help me avoid Winthrop. I'll compromise Carstairs on my own."

He shot her another angry scowl and stood. Walking naked to an armoire hiding in a dark corner, Welles pulled out a clean shirt. Grabbing his trousers, he jerked his legs through and then pulled on his boots.

"Carstairs is honorable," she said needlessly. "If he compromised me, he'll do the right thing."

"As opposed to me who is dishonorable and will not?"

Margaret lifted her chin. "I didn't say that."

"Carstairs will be at my stepmother's little ball. A close gathering of the *ton* to which I'm certain you've already received an invitation," he said in a chilly tone. "He's already promised to attend."

"Thank you for telling me," she said. His irritation at her, his coldness after what they'd shared, was unwarranted. He should be happy she didn't want anything from him.

Welles took her hand. "I'll escort you out. My carriage is downstairs."

"I can take a hack, my lord." She tried to wrench her hand from his. The longer she spent in Welles's company, the more unsettled Margaret became with the thought of trapping Carstairs. But what choice did she have? Her aunt was only waiting to receive the final contracts from Winthrop's solicitors. If Carstairs did not compromise her, she would be married to Winthrop in less than a month if not sooner. Trapped forever beneath a giant, sweating pear with no music.

I couldn't bear it.

"You *can* take a hack, but you aren't going to." He grabbed her fingers, ignoring her efforts to pull free again. Gently, he laced their fingers together and some of the chill left his words. "I'll make sure you get home safely. Pull your cloak tightly around your face."

Nothing more was said between them as Welles led her out of his rooms and down the hall to a door set so perfectly into the paneling you would miss it if you weren't looking. Opening the door, he grabbed a lamp sitting on a small shelf just inside the passageway and lit it. Holding the lamp high, he led her down three flights of steps.

When they reached what she assumed to be the bottom, Welles finally spoke.

"Almost there." Another door appeared, barely discernible in the arc of light from the lamp he held. Welles pushed the door with a hard shove of one shoulder to reveal a wrought iron gate opening into a lovely garden. A fountain bubbled before them and just on the other side sat a carriage and driver.

The moonlight cast Welles in shadow with only his profile visible. She held tightly to his hand, a part of her wanting never to let go. "Elysium has a garden?" she said to break the silence.

"Not open to our patrons. Only Leo and I use it." He led her through the carefully maintained beds to the carriage. He dropped her hand and spoke quietly to the driver before assisting her inside.

Margaret slid back against the leather. The carriage held Welles's scent and she inhaled deeply, taking comfort that a part of him would be with her as she returned to her aunt.

"No. You mustn't." She held out a hand as he tried to climb in beside her. "If I am caught, I'll be in enough trouble. Please instruct the driver he needs to drop me a block from the house. I'll walk the remainder of the way. You can't be seen with me, Welles, for both our sakes." She bit her lip, not knowing what more she could say. "Especially with my... upcoming plans."

He raked a hand through his hair, frowning at her.

"Please, Welles." Her voice broke. "If you care for me even a *little*—"

A disgruntled sound came from him as he looked away.

Margaret pressed her lips together. She shouldn't have said that. It sounded as if she were begging him to admit to feelings he didn't have. "What I mean to say is, I would appreciate it if you don't interfere with what I need to do." She gave a brittle laugh. "I should never have presumed upon our acquaintance in such a way nor asked for your help. I hope you can forgive me for having to be slightly dishonest in my dealings with Carstairs. I've little choice. All I wished was for my aunt to leave me in peace, allow me to become a spinster, and play the piano. But I threw up into my aunt's rose bushes as Winthrop proposed. I cannot go the rest of my days doing such." God, she sounded pathetic. Pitiful. Like the little mouse everyone thought she was. "And he doesn't even own a piano," she said with a small laugh. "Can you imagine?"

20

Tony *didn't* wish to imagine Maggie wed to either Winthrop or Carstairs.

He should be thrilled he'd barely had to crook a finger to entice the object of his obsession into his bed. Maggie had climbed in of her own accord, with very little persuasion on his part. She'd come to Elysium, titillated by his improper request, just as he'd originally wished. Better yet, she expected *nothing* from Tony because she was intent on marrying another man.

A pinch of pain crossed the region of his heart.

Carstairs was honorable. If she managed to compromise herself with him, which Tony had no doubt she would, Carstairs would marry her instantly. Hell, Carstairs would probably have offered for Maggie on his own if Tony hadn't interfered and sent his friend on a make-believe errand. Jealously had made him behave badly. The day he'd seen her with Carstairs at the stream had filled him with such an ugly, cloying jealously he'd had to leave abruptly to avoid doing Carstairs violence. Then he'd sent Carstairs to the country, inadvertently pushing Lady Dobson to betroth Maggie to Winthrop.

All Tony had wanted was Maggie away from Carstairs. He'd never even considered the cost to *her*.

What a selfish prick he was.

Just like your father, a voice whispered.

Another bite of pain crossed his chest.

As the carriage pulled Maggie away from Elysium *and* him, the awful tugging of his heart in her direction increased tenfold. He wasn't even aware of the damn thing most of the time and hadn't used it in years.

I'm bloody well aware of it tonight.

Surprising how much it hurt.

His cock hadn't been the only organ engaged in the ruination of Miss Margaret Lainscott. Tony himself was *compromised* in a way he'd never anticipated. His fingers fluttered, still feeling Maggie's slender hand in his, already missing her.

She wants Carstairs. His fingers curled into fists at his side. And it was just as well she did.

"Who is she?" The words floated in the night air along with the smell of a cheroot.

"No one," Tony said to his brother. Leo was almost invisible in the darkness. "You should have announced yourself."

"Why? And spoil your farewell? I also beg to differ. That was *someone*," Leo said as Tony walked to the stone bench where his brother sat and settled next to him.

"It doesn't matter." In the grand scheme of Tony's life, the virtue of an almost spinster who played the piano shouldn't be of any importance, especially when weighed against the rage and bitterness he wielded like a sword against the Duke of Averell.

"I think it matters quite a bit. I think *she* matters."

"Shut up, Leo." Tony didn't want Maggie to matter. That

was the problem. "She's just a young lady whom I was trying to entice into bed. I've decided she's not worth the effort. I'm sure she'll make someone an adequate wife." He lied smoothly, hating the way his heart rebelled at his own words.

"Just not yours."

"God, no." He snorted. "The line of the Duke of Averell ends with me. My final revenge on our father. Besides, I'm morally bankrupt, as all of London knows. What would I do with a wife?"

Smoke hovered in the air from the cheroot before Leo said in a quiet voice, "He'll be dead soon, Tony. When he is, will it matter that you denied yourself something you clearly desire?"

"Who said I wanted her? I've just told you—" Tony sat back. Sometimes Leo just needed to shut up. "I might say the same to you."

Leo said nothing for a few moments. "My situation is much more fraught with difficulty. Who is she?"

Tony turned, trying to make out his brother's features, so like his own in the dark stillness of the garden. For the first time, Tony had something he didn't want to share with Leo. He was confused. Wounded and raw as if he were bleeding. More unsure of everything with each passing day.

"A dalliance only," Tony heard himself say, nearly choking on the word. "I doubt I'll remember her name in another week."

"Who are you attempting to convince? Yourself or me?" Leo flicked his cheroot to the ground and tamped it with the heel of his boot. He stared at Tony for a moment, as if considering his words, before he said, "Nothing you do to the Duke of Averell will bring Katherine back."

Tony stiffened at the mention of his mother. "This discussion is over," he hissed. How could Leo bring her up?

Leo stood and made his way back inside Elysium, pausing

beside the door to look back at Tony. "In all the years we've owned this establishment you've never *once* entertained a woman in your private rooms. *Never* played the piano for any female you were trying to seduce. I think that makes her *someone* to you, whether you realize it or not."

21

Margaret shifted on her feet before the mirror as Eliza moved around her, putting the finishing touches on her coiffure. The pale gold silk had rows of tiered fabric, lined with brilliants, glittering in the light as the full skirts belled around Margaret's ankles. She even had matching slippers.

Eliza gave a final pat. "There, that should do it." The maid had arranged Margaret's hair in heavy coils, pinned up in the back and threaded with silk cord. "The dress brings out the gold in your hair. You look lovely, miss."

Margaret had to agree, for once not feeling the least plain or beneath notice. Tonight, she spun before the mirror like a fairytale princess. Or, more appropriately, a woman courting ruination.

I've already been ruined. Compromised. In the most beautiful way possible.

She pressed a hand to her stomach, whispering to her heart to be still. Her energies and focus needed to remain on the upcoming evening and maneuvering Carstairs into a compromising position, not on Welles.

She caught another glance of herself clothed in gold. The gown had arrived, swathed in mountains of tissue, from one of the most exclusive modistes in London. The note accompanying the box only stated the gown and matching slippers were a gift from the duchess, a gift she hoped Margaret would wear to her upcoming ball.

Margaret knew the moment she held the luxurious gown up to her shoulders that it would fit her perfectly. Romy already had her measurements and had probably shared them with her mother. The unexpected kindness of the gift touched Margaret deeply. She hoped after creating a small scandal with Carstairs tonight, the duchess and her daughters would still wish for her company.

Aunt Agnes was less than pleased that the duchess held Margaret in such affection that she'd sent her a gown but could hardly send it back without offending her. Instead, she satisfied herself with making disparaging remarks that Margaret's skin would appear sallow against the gold of the gown.

Margaret kept her features composed and docile while her aunt threw a host of barbs in her direction, enjoying her aunt's displeasure. Aunt Agnes would be even less happy after Margaret compromised Carstairs.

"Thank you, Eliza. That will be all. Please tell my aunt I will be down in a moment."

As the door clicked shut, Margaret took a deep breath, or as deep as she could. Eliza had laced her stays incredibly tight. She wished she could play the piano, if only for a short time. Music would calm her frayed nerves. Thankfully, Winthrop hadn't called today, although neither had Carstairs. Margaret's fingers clutched the silk of her skirts, wrinkling the fragile fabric as a bolt of longing for Welles struck her.

Calm yourself.

Carstairs *had* sent a note, apologizing for being detained;

he had left town on unexpected business. He begged her forgiveness for not sending word sooner and looked forward to seeing her this evening at the duchess's ball. Margaret had read his message twice just to reassure herself of his attendance. Now she only had to figure out how to get Carstairs alone, somewhere private, and then make sure they were discovered. She hated to repay the duchess's kindness to her with a scandal, but there was little help for it.

After returning to her aunt's house without incident after the night at Elysium, Margaret had avoided visiting the duchess and her daughters. It was cowardly of her, to be sure, but she thought it in the best interests of her own self-preservation to avoid Welles. Tonight would be difficult enough.

Last night, she'd dreamt of playing the piano again for Welles, this time in a field of wildflowers. She'd been completely naked. He'd been smiling down at her, the blue of his eyes so startling, her fingers had frozen on the keys. Welles had tickled her beneath the chin with a daisy before his mouth fell on hers.

The woman reflected in the mirror before her was blushing furiously.

She clasped her hands and took a deep breath, determined to regain her composure. It was either Carstairs or accept a marriage to Winthrop. Shakespeare himself couldn't have written a better tragedy. She would compromise herself with the friend of the man she was in love with, in order to avoid marriage to a gentleman Margaret abhorred. Aunt Agnes would be playing the part of the villain.

"Bollocks," she swore softly, stepping away from the mirror.

Guilt caused a slight tremble in her hands. Carstairs *would* be happy with her, even if she had to trudge through every bloody stream in England carrying a wicker basket full of fish. It was a solemn vow Margaret had made to herself. Carstairs would not regret marrying her for a moment. She meant to be the perfect wife and partner.

Winthrop would be furious at losing her dowry and probably sweat more profusely than usual. The betrothal to Margaret hadn't yet been announced nor the contracts finalized, so Winthrop would not suffer the shame of being jilted, though his feelings, if he had any, were the least of her concern. Miss Turnbull would not be pleased, but she would easily garner a score of other offers by the end of the season. Aunt Agnes would be fine as well, as she only wanted Margaret gone.

As Margaret made her way down the stairs to join her aunt, the sound of a male voice met her ears. Her slipper halted on the next step, refusing to move forward.

"There you are." Aunt Agnes looked up at her. "We've been waiting for nearly half an hour, though I see the time has been well spent." Her thin lips pulled back to show her teeth in a facsimile of an indulgent smile. "Doesn't she look appealing tonight, Lord Winthrop?"

I'm not a bloody iced biscuit.

Margaret pasted a polite look on her face and a shy smile on her lips. She only had to endure him a bit longer. "Lord Winthrop. I didn't realize you were joining us this evening."

This was an unexpected fly in the ointment or rather, in the case of Winthrop, a giant pear. She hadn't planned for Winthrop to be present for her little tableau tonight, but maybe it was for the best. Still, enduring his company when she was already so anxious didn't make Margaret happy.

Her stomach pitched and she pressed a hand to her midsection.

Winthrop held out a gloved hand. "We're to be married. Your aunt assured me it was proper for me to escort you both this evening."

Of course she did. Margaret had to keep herself from

knocking the blood-red turban from her aunt's head. Devious Aunt Agnes. Why did she find Winthrop to be so suitable?

"How kind of you." She kept her eyes downcast lest Winthrop see her distaste in them. Lately, Margaret was finding it harder to maintain her docile, timid manner.

Winthrop took her hand.

She swallowed in disgust at his moist touch.

"Margaret is quite recovered from her earlier illness. I believe it was the excitement over becoming your wife which led to her earlier distress," Aunt Agnes assured him.

"I'm certain of it." Winthrop flashed Margaret a bland smile, but anger tightened the lines around his mouth and eyes. She'd been correct. He *was* stupid and cruel, a combination found most often in wild pigs. He considered Margaret to have committed a grave offense by puking during his marriage proposal.

It was *intended as an insult. So is the assumption he thinks I'd be pleased to marry him.*

Winthrop waddled, girlish shoes turned outward so that he resembled more a duck than the pear he was, down the steps to his waiting carriage. He'd taken her aunt's arm, pointedly ignoring Margaret, leaving her to trail a few steps behind. She took in the bottle-green coat and matching trousers Winthrop wore along with the feminine shoes and wondered if his valet didn't burst into laughter when dressing his master. She thought the unknown valet's care of Winthrop to be a much greater sin than Margaret tossing up her breakfast at his marriage proposal.

Entering the carriage, Margaret seated herself next to her aunt while Winthrop settled opposite them. He mopped at his brow, pushing the stained handkerchief into an unseen pocket and plopped down, rocking the carriage with his weight. He stretched out his legs in her direction, crushing the edge of her gown. *Purposefully*.

Margaret dared a glance in his direction.

Winthrop's eyes ran over Margaret with unconcealed dislike, promising future punishment for all the ways she'd offended him. He couldn't wait to make her miserable; she could see the truth of it in every line of his sweating body.

He detests me.

She looked away, pretending to observe the view outside the window.

"I don't think a long engagement is necessary do you, Lord Winthrop? Given the age of the bride?"

Must Aunt Agnes sound so hopeful?

Winthrop gave a soft chuckle. "Margaret and I are mature adults. I'm sure a short engagement would suit us both." He shot her a pointed look, daring her to object.

He is already calculating how to spend my dowry.

"And I would like an heir before the end of the year."

The mere thought of Winthrop bedding her after she'd been with Welles was so repulsive Margaret's hand fell to her stomach to stop the sudden roll of nausea. She cautioned herself to remain perfectly still and keep her features composed.

"As well you should." Aunt Agnes concurred, searching Margaret's face for any reaction she might take issue with.

Margaret's eyes fell to her lap, reminding herself not to flinch as they continued to speak about her as if she were merely a broodmare for Winthrop to sweat on.

Her eyes fluttered closed, remembering Welles pulling up her chemise, pressing his mouth to her skin as he moved up her prone body, worshipping every inch of her. She doubted Winthrop would show any woman such care.

Focus, Margaret.

She forced her thoughts back to the matter at hand, opening her eyes to see Winthrop watching her. His escort presented a small problem in that he may stick to her side like an immense burr beneath a saddle, perspiring over everyone, especially Margaret. She would need to escape his attention and that of her aunt for a short period of time to be compromised properly. The duchess would have gaming tables set up. Winthrop liked cards, though according to rumor, he wasn't very good at faro or whist.

Hopefully, she wouldn't have to think of how to get rid of Winthrop. If she was lucky, her pear-shaped problem would take care of itself.

22

Tony stepped into the Averell mansion and immediately into the embrace of his stepmother. Amanda smelled of lilies and powder as she offered her cheek for his kiss. She was resplendent in an emerald-green gown, her wrists and ears dripping with Averell diamonds. She even had a tiny tiara atop her red-gold hair.

"Welles. I'm so glad to see you this evening. I became worried you wouldn't come."

He was a trifle late, but not overly so. "I would never miss your ball, madam." He took her hands. "You look stunning. I will have to keep an eye out for any rogues who may approach you."

She blushed and shrugged off his hands. "My son, ever the charmer."

A burst of affection filled him for his stepmother. She rarely referred to him or Leo as anything but her sons in public, ensuring the Barringtons all presented a united front to the *ton*. Despite his feelings about the duke, Tony's father had done something wonderful in marrying Amanda.

"And you've brought Lord Carstairs," she said with a smile. "I'm delighted to see you."

"Your Grace." Carstairs executed the required polite greetings with a vacant smile, perfectly happy to be attending a ball tonight and not out stalking a deer. He'd spoken adoringly of the estate he'd inspected for Tony, assuring him on the carriage ride over the property would do very well as a hunting retreat.

Tony pretended he gave a shit. He had a great many other things on his mind.

When Carstairs had casually mentioned Miss Lainscott, expressing his complete admiration for her, Tony had barely resisted seriously injuring his friend. The idea of giving Maggie to Carstairs was rapidly becoming intolerable to Tony. The idea of Winthrop pawing her was even more loathsome.

She belongs to you, a tiny voice whispered.

Despite visiting his sisters every day, much to the delight of Phaedra who pestered him to accompany her on the piano while she screeched away on the violin, Maggie had not appeared. The object of his desire seemed determined to avoid him, which was probably wise on her part. Tony didn't think he would have been able to refrain from touching her had she arrived to take tea with his stepmother. He'd thought of very little else but Maggie since she'd left Elysium.

After greeting the duchess, he and Carstairs walked into the warren of rooms leading to the ballroom. Tony looked around him, barely seeing the portraits of his ancestors, the cream-colored walls, or the carved wainscoting. He resented Carstairs's presence at his side, wanting nothing more than for his friend to leave him in peace.

Carstairs, for his part, chatted amiably about flushing out a group of rabbits and didn't Tony think rabbit, if seasoned properly, went well in a pie?

Tony cast him a bland look. Carstairs had no idea how

close he was to being strangled like the rabbits he was gushing over. He reminded himself that his friend was doing a service for Maggie, he just wasn't aware of it. Carstairs was the *honorable* one. A man who would marry her. Unlike Tony, who would not. All he had to do was imagine the Duke of Averell's happiness at hearing that Tony planned to wed, and a chill would fall over him along with a burst of resentment toward Maggie.

You could have her.

Besides, Maggie *wanted* Carstairs. A bloody dimwit she could control. She wanted marriage to an *honorable* man who wouldn't ask her to play the piano half-naked in a pleasure palace. A man who would welcome a wife and child. She wanted to avoid Winthrop. And *no one* should be subjected to Winthrop. It was normal, after what they'd shared, for Tony to feel protective of Maggie.

I want her.

Carstairs slapped him on the back, startling him out of his thoughts. "I see Miss Turnbull." He pointed to a far corner of the ballroom where the young lady was holding court amongst a small group of young gentlemen. "I would like to apologize to her for leaving town in such haste. It was terribly rude of me after our fishing trip."

"Are you always so fucking nice?"

Carstairs blinked his eyes at Tony, confused. "Why, yes. What good would it do for me not to be?" He nodded before going to the side of Miss Turnbull.

Tony cursed beneath his breath. Carstairs was undeserving of his foul mood. He was a good, if not-too-bright, friend. He'd left town to inspect an estate as a favor to Tony without a second thought, asking no questions, because he'd been asked to do so. Tony turned his attention from Carstairs to his stepmother's ballroom, taking in the glittering display of titled wealth before him. The room was full of beautiful women who were, even now, casting looks in his direction. In the not so distant past, Tony would have taken advantage of so much bounty, but not tonight.

Damn her.

"You look bloody angry at Carstairs. I can't imagine what he's done to provoke your ill-temper. Isn't being mad at him rather like kicking a puppy?"

Tony turned to Leo, who lurked in a dark alcove next to a statue of some Greek god.

Leo tilted his head toward the piece of marble he leaned against. "Who's this bloke?"

"Apollo, I think. They all look the same to me. I don't dare ask Amanda, or she'll bend my ear for the next hour. What are you doing, Leo, hiding? I hadn't expected you'd be here tonight." Tony knew Amanda had asked Leo to attend, as she did every other ball, dinner party, and fete held at Averell House, but he rarely did so.

"I promised Amanda." Leo grimaced. "Why couldn't she be like any other woman when confronted by her husband's bastard son and just dislike me? Keep me at arm's length? It's not right, I tell you."

Tony laughed at his brother's discomfort. Amanda had never treated Leo any differently despite Leo being born on the wrong side of the blanket. Most titled ladies would never even acknowledge Leo's existence, let alone welcome him with open arms. Her treatment of Leo and, indeed, Tony, was a testament to Amanda's generous and loving heart. She was far too good for the Duke of Averell. But she loved Tony's father, deeply and unconditionally. Amanda wasn't unintelligent. She knew of her husband's sins and loved him anyway. Tony thought his father underserving of such devotion.

"Christ. There's Winthrop. Don't let him see me," Leo said in a low tone, sinking back further into the shadows. "I've extended his credit again and he's already close to the new limit. Insists he'll pay me back the enormous sum he owes Elysium when he marries. Says the heiress has accepted his proposal and the contracts are to be signed as soon as the legalities are ironed out." Leo shrugged. "Apparently, the bulk of the girl's fortune doesn't become his upon marriage automatically, and he's seeking to have that overturned with the support of the girl's guardian. Still won't tell me who she is. He'd better be successful, though. All he has left, besides the entailed family seat, is a small, isolated estate and I've no desire to have that foisted upon me. Nor his mistress, though he's offered her up."

Maggie hadn't exaggerated. Her aunt had already auctioned her off just as she had Walter Lainscott's hunting dogs. "He has nothing else?" Tony could smell the desperation on Winthrop's sweating body from across the ballroom.

"No," Leo assured him. "Why *do* you dislike him so much?"

"I have my reasons." One very small, delicate reason.

When Winthrop moved aside, Tony saw Maggie, Lady Dobson clinging to her side. His foot actually took a step in her direction before he stopped himself. She looked beautiful. The gold silk had been an inspired choice. He'd never purchased so much as a decorated fan for a woman before, let alone such an expensive gown, but it had pleased Tony to do so for Maggie. The gold silk brought out the streaks of blonde in her otherwise dark hair, making her shimmer in the light of the chandeliers. Tony's only regret was in not purchasing her a pair of topaz earrings to complement the outfit. He'd paid the modiste handsomely to deliver the gown courtesy of his stepmother, knowing Maggie would never accept the gift from him.

Leo made a small sound of surprise, his head following Tony's gaze. "Christ, *she's* the heiress Winthrop's been bragging about bagging." Understanding suffused Leo's features.

"*She* was the girl at Elysium. Miss Margaret Lainscott, Lady Dobson's niece. No *wonder* you hate him."

Tony gave his brother a scathing look before returning his attention to Maggie. His eyes ran over her petite form again, remembering in detail every curve and hollow of her body. Her skin had felt like satin beneath his lips.

Misery shone from her eyes. When Winthrop moved in her direction, Tony could see her shrinking back from him, trying to make herself as small as possible.

Pear-shaped prick. A deep possessive rage pulsed through him as Winthrop took Maggie's hand, pulling her forward to stand next to him. Winthrop wasn't even remotely suitable for her, yet Lady Dobson was in favor of the match. Why?

"What do you know about the late Lord Dobson's finances?" Tony asked his brother in a chilly tone.

"Lord Dobson? You realize he's been dead for years?"

"I'm aware."

Pressing a finger to his lips Leo said thoughtfully, "he was *heavily* leveraged at Elysium. Owed me a small fortune for gambling and his *other* pleasures. I took pity on the man after meeting his wife." He nodded in the direction of Lady Dobson. "His debts were settled upon his death *by her*, which surprised me."

"Why were you surprised?"

"While he was alive, he couldn't pay me the sum he owed. He'd only the London house left. I'm not sure where Lady Dobson got the money, nor do I care. She paid off his other creditors as well, though not his mistress." Leo chuckled.

Tony suspected Walter Lainscott had given the money to Lady Dobson. And probably supported her lavish lifestyle during his lifetime. An immense scandal had erupted over her younger sister's hasty marriage to Walter Lainscott, nearly ruining the chances for Agnes to make a decent match. She'd had to settle for Dobson. Amanda had told Tony the entire sordid tale over tea one day. His stepmother didn't care for Lady Dobson in the least.

Now that Walter was dead, Tony surmised Lady Dobson had lost her source of income. There was probably an annual sum for Maggie's support, but the bulk of the money would be in her dowry. Maybe Lady Dobson had made a bargain of sorts with Winthrop in return for agreeing to the marriage.

"No wonder you're in a snit. Your Miss Lainscott is set to wed Winthrop." Leo shot him a sympathetic look and nodded in Maggie's direction. "She looks smashing, by the way. Pity the dress will be ruined once Winthrop paws her. I've never met a gentleman who sweats so much."

"I agree," Welles said, not wishing to give away the anger mounting with every look Winthrop bestowed on Maggie. "A shame to ruin the dress. Though it isn't any of my business whom she marries. Winthrop or anyone else."

"True," Leo said absently. "It isn't as though *you* could marry her."

Tony ignored his brother's baiting.

Lady Dobson stood smug next to Maggie, the massive crimson turban on her head tilting slightly as she greeted an acquaintance. Her angular features were made sharper by the light of the chandeliers. She said something to Maggie, a chastisement of some sort, if the sneer on Lady Dobson's face was any indication.

"Bitch," he cursed under his breath, his fists clenching.

"*Careful*, brother," Leo said softly. "You can't run across the ballroom floor and claim her."

The sight across the room made Tony angrier, fueling the ugly jealousy and possessiveness already circulating in his system.

A flurry of blue skirts appeared, surrounding Maggie. It was his sister, Romy. Maggie and Romy greeted each other warmly while Lady Dobson frowned in displeasure. She didn't care for the fact her niece had managed to garner the support of the Duchess of Averell and her daughters.

"Tony—"

"Oh, look, there's Lady Masterson and she's nearly falling out of her gown," Tony said, knowing his brother's questions about Maggie would be immediately forgotten. Leo's attention would be focused elsewhere. Tony turned back to his tiny pianist clothed in gold.

You want her.

So, take her.

23

If I don't remain calm, I'll soon be sweating like Winthrop.

Margaret cast a glance at the gentleman who assumed she'd marry him without a protest. Were he, at the very least, a kind man, or perhaps less prone to dousing himself with talc, she might not be taking such drastic measures this evening.

"I adore the dress." Romy took her hand. "Such a lovely gown. Where did you have it made?" She walked in a circle around Margaret, taking in every detail of the gold gown.

Surely Romy knew her mother had purchased it as a gift for Margaret. After all, she would have given the modiste Margaret's exact measurements. "Don't be silly; you know very well where this came from." She gave a small laugh, lest Aunt Agnes wonder what they were speaking of. "Please tell the duchess I am most grateful. My aunt," Margaret lowered her voice, "would never have allowed me something so exquisite. Or expensive."

Romy's lovely features wrinkled in confusion. "The dress was a gift from my mother? She never mentioned—oh, here comes Tony."

Margaret's breath stilled, her heart fluttering wildly in her chest at the appearance of Welles. A wave of dark hair fell against his cheek as the startling blue of his eyes caught hers. The light humming of her skin, her body's response to his nearness, floated deliciously up her arms.

"Lady Dobson." The deep baritone brushed over Margaret as he greeted her aunt politely, but he was looking at her.

Aunt Agnes bobbed politely.

He barely gave a nod to Winthrop before turning to his sister. "You look smashing, Romy. Did you design the dress?"

Romy twirled before her brother, powder blue skirts flowing around her like ripples in a pond. "What do you think?"

"Quite lovely. How nice to see you, Miss Lainscott."

Margaret looked up at the touch of his hand on hers, unsurprised at the shocking trickle of warmth sliding between her thighs. She had ceased to wonder why she only responded in such a way to him. It was just part of Welles. Like the music she heard in her heart when he was near. Or the bits of gold floating in the deep blue of his eyes.

"It seems I have perfect timing," Welles said, neglecting to release her hand as the musicians struck up a waltz. "Lady Dobson, with your permission." He didn't wait for her aunt's reply, whisking Margaret out to the ballroom floor without a care for her chaperone. Or Winthrop, who was staring at both of them with disapproval. Margaret couldn't risk angering her aunt lest she be sent home early before Carstairs would compromise her.

"What are you doing?" she hissed, though her body bent eagerly to his.

"I'm the son of the hostess. And a future duke. You're a close friend of my sister's." He nodded in Romy's direction. "It's perfectly acceptable for me to whisk you onto the dance floor. It may even improve your standing amongst the *ton*." His gaze roamed the ballroom, "Though considering my reputation, probably not."

"But this is a waltz."

"I've never been too concerned with what others think of me. You shouldn't be either. Besides, do you really think Winthrop has the gumption to stop me?"

Margaret turned to see Winthrop's face puffing with distress. Aunt Agnes spoke to him, one spindly hand clutching his forearm like an oversized spider.

"I don't care what Winthrop thinks." She pressed her lips together, trying not to tremble as Welles pulled her closer. A large hand settled on the small of her back, sending a tingle along her spine. "But I shouldn't like to cause a scene. Nor put Carstairs off."

He gave her an expert twirl and leaned in. "Have you a plan?" Welles was smiling again but she sensed he wasn't truly amused. "For the intended ruination of Lord Carstairs?"

Margaret hadn't quite figured out how to lure Carstairs away. "I suppose I'll ask him to take me for a walk in the gardens."

"A tried and true method." His cheek grazed her temple. "I adore the sounds you make as you climax, by the way," Welles purred into her ear.

Margaret missed a step. "Don't say or speak of it again." She bit her lip. "I beg you."

"It's a very fond memory. There are so many other things I wish to do to you. *Delicious* things." The baritone lowered to a growl.

She missed another step.

"Cease. I do not want to discuss what transpired between us at Elysium."

"Why not?" His eyes flared with blue fire. Angry.

Margaret looked away.

Her aunt and Winthrop were sending her withering looks from their place against the wall, but no one else paid the least bit of attention to Lord Welles swinging Margaret about the dance floor. He'd been right that no one would think it out of place for him to dance with her. The duchess had made it clear at Lady Masterson's garden party she considered Margaret to be a friend of the family. Margaret and Romy had been seen together walking in the park along with Theo. It *was* perfectly natural for Welles to grant her a dance.

"Very well. Let's discuss your agenda for the evening." His wide mouth held the barest hint of a smile. A dark line of hair stretching along his jaw begged for her touch. Or the press of her lips.

"You should speak to your valet," she finally said, flustered to be studying him so openly. "He didn't shave you close enough."

"What a thing for you to notice, Miss Lainscott." He spun her, pulling Maggie close so her skirts wrapped around his legs. Welles took the opportunity to notch one muscled thigh between hers.

A lazy coil of warm honey twisted around her core at his actions. Heat flooded up her body, while her fingers tightened on his sleeve.

"You're blushing, Miss Lainscott."

She raised her chin to see him watching her, a knowing look in his eyes. He knew exactly what he'd done to her and relished her reaction. She supposed this was how casual lovers behaved, as if their joining was merely amusement, and not fraught with emotional consequence.

"The ballroom is warm."

"Such *wantonness* sits contained within you, Miss Lainscott. It begs to be set free. It's a shame only the Broadwood has seen it. And me." His teasing was tinged with something sharp. She had come to know the timbre of his voice, and though it was well hidden, anger bled into his words.

"Is there a point to you tormenting me?"

His wide mouth pulled tight. "You are *certain*, Miss Lainscott, on your course of action? You wish to be compromised tonight, publicly? Forced to marry? Despite the scandal?"

Maggie nodded dully. When put in such a way, it didn't sound appealing at all. Then she caught sight of Winthrop along the wall. "Yes. Absolutely."

"Very well. The library has a large trout mounted on one wall."

"Excuse me?"

Welles turned her and his hand moved up her back, pulling her closer. His eyes fell to her bodice, taking in the swell of her small breasts against the gown. "I used to boast to Carstairs about the size of the trout, one my grandfather caught in the Scottish Highlands. He's been asking to see the damn thing for years. *You* are the trout."

"I see." Not a welcome comparison, but so be it.

"I'll bring Carstairs to the study at half past eleven and get him settled with a glass of brandy. He likes brandy. You should remember such a thing for the future."

"I've taken note," she said, detesting this conversation.

"I'll make an excuse to leave, and you'll arrive. A short time later, you'll be interrupted probably by my stepmother or someone equally prestigious, like myself."

Margaret looked down at the buttons of his coat, counting six in all. She thought of the hard, muscular chest she'd been pressed against while playing the piano, now hidden beneath the coat and the buttons. He'd been so beautiful standing over her, naked and unashamed. Her heart would carry Welles and their night at Elysium for the remainder of her days.

"Maggie." The baritone vibrated through the material of her gown. "Are you well?"

"I'm listening." She tilted her head at him, ignoring the ache in her chest. "I'm to throw myself at Lord Carstairs after dazzling him with my knowledge of fishing lures. Thank you again for the book, by the way."

He smiled, this time with warmth, as he took her in. "Good girl. Remember, half past eleven. Don't be late."

The music ended, and Welles led her off the floor to Aunt Agnes and a scowling Lord Winthrop. Winthrop claimed her for the next dance, a horrible experience in which she was much too close to his moist form, dancing about in his ridiculously feminine shoes. Any more of his attentions and the beautiful dress, her gift from the duchess, would be ruined.

One more hour and this would be over.

24

At exactly a quarter past eleven, Margaret excused herself. Winthrop had wandered off some time ago, likely put out by her nonexistent responses to his attempts to speak to her. The smell of talc and Winthrop's overuse of pomade had only served to unsettle her stomach further. Finally, he waddled in the direction of the gaming tables, probably to gamble away her dowry before he'd even wed her.

He'll never have my money.

Lifting her chin, Margaret once more reassured herself of the rightness of what she was doing and the fact that she had no real choice. Should she back down on her plans for this evening, she would find herself married to Winthrop. The conversation between Winthrop and her aunt in the carriage had left no doubt.

Spurred on by thoughts of Winthrop, Margaret quickened her pace.

Earlier, she'd danced with Carstairs and conversed with him at length on the merits of a particular type of fly used for fishing, knowledge all gleaned from the book Welles had given her. Carstairs had been enthralled with her description of an imaginary afternoon she'd spent fishing for bass with her father wearing wading boots. During their conversation, he had mentioned the trout residing in the library of the Averell mansion and his excitement in being able to view the trophy.

Margaret should have been relieved Welles was helping her but instead, the knowledge unsettled her further.

She had never ventured to the library on her previous visits, but Margaret knew the room lay a few doors beyond the conservatory. As she made her way down the hall to meet her fate, Margaret caught a few notes of music. She stopped, thinking at first it was the musicians below.

More notes floated out into the hall from the conservatory, a piece she didn't recognize immediately, though it sounded vaguely like Chopin. One of the duchess's guests was playing the Broadwood. Drawn by the beauty of the music, and overly possessive of the piano, Margaret stepped into the conservatory.

Welles was sitting at the Broadwood, an instrument he claimed he never played. His fingers ran in a fluid motion over the keys, drawing out the dark and melancholy notes of Chopin. She saw his fingers pause, and the last note hung in the air, the only sign he knew she was there.

Margaret told herself to take a step back and continue down the hall to the library where Carstairs would be admiring the trout, but instead, she walked silently into the conservatory, unable to resist the temptation of Welles.

Just once more before I compromise myself with Carstairs.

Without a word, Margaret sat next to him on the bench, basking in his presence and forgetting all about Carstairs. She could only see Welles. Only hear him.

One of his hands left the keyboard and took Margaret about the waist, tucking her in next to his side.

She snuggled against him, comforted for the first time since leaving Elysium. Her emotions quieted as she sunk into his warmth. "Welles, what are you doing here?"

"A lure much greater than any trout," he whispered, leaning over to press a kiss below the base of her ear.

Margaret's breath caught, unable to move as his lips trailed over the length of her neck before returning to her ear. His tongue traced around the curve, only stopping to suck the lobe between his teeth and nibble.

Her mind screamed to get *off the bench* and march into the library. *Immediately*. But her heart and body clung to Welles as if he were a life preserver.

Welles stopped playing and pulled her into his lap. The hard length of him rubbed against her backside as he pressed her against him. Fingers sunk deep into her hair, loosening the pins. She could still hear the music in her mind as his mouth, hot and demanding, took hers.

A sigh left her, one filled with surrender. Her body curled into Welles, seeking sanctuary even as her mind warned her of the danger of being here with him. When his tongue ran along the crease of her lips Margaret opened to him with a whimper. If she could just kiss him a moment longer. Just one more second with Welles, where her heart and soul wished to be, before a lifetime with Carstairs.

"Oh, dear." The duchess's voice sounded from the doorway.

I left the door open.

"Welles!"

Margaret struggled to break away, her mind fuzzy with desire, horrified at being discovered with the wrong man in the wrong room. One of her breasts was nearly out of her bodice. She looked up at the doorway, her fingers fumbling as she made a useless effort to fix her hair.

Oh, God.

At the doorway stood the duchess accompanied by Lord Carstairs and Miss Turnbull. All three stared at the sight of Margaret on Welles's lap.

Welles's hands tightened on her waist, his fingers digging into her flesh through the silk. He didn't appear the least bit upset. In fact, he looked oddly satisfied.

Miss Turnbull's mouth popped open in shock. "Miss Lainscott has been compromised."

"What have you done?" Margaret whispered under her breath, struggling to get off his lap and stand. Her hair fell in tangles around her shoulders, the pins littering the floor beneath her feet. Margaret was *utterly* compromised. Ruined. Caught in an indiscretion.

"Hello, Your Grace." Welles greeted his stepmother as if he hadn't just nearly ravished Margaret on the piano bench. "My apologies. Miss Lainscott should have shut the door."

The duchess immediately turned and pushed both Carstairs and Miss Turnbull forcefully down the hall. "Do not so much as breathe a word of this or you will regret it," she threatened. "It was merely a trick of the light. They were only playing the piano." As she shut the door, Margaret could hear Carstairs bemoaning the fact he'd not gotten to see the trout.

"You did this on purpose," Margaret said beneath her breath to Welles.

Welles gave her a stony, unapologetic look.

"You were playing bloody Chopin with the door open, knowing I would investigate." A small cry left her, and she pushed her fist against her mouth. "You've ruined it."

His jaw hardened at the accusation. "Have I?"

"Welles." The duchess's voice was imperious. "This is beyond the pale, even for you." Her gaze landed on Margaret, eyes full of pity and disappointment. "Ruining a young lady because you can."

"Amanda—"

The duchess took a step forward, piercing Welles with an icy stare. "Take the servants' stairs down and return to the ballroom from the direction of the terrace. I must try to mitigate the damage done to Miss Lainscott."

Welles stood from the bench. "I do not need to be reprimanded as if I were a schoolboy."

"Do you not?" The duchess whirled on him, clearly furious. "Congratulations, Anthony. *You* have succeeded in copying your father's previous selfish behavior. How *proud* you must be to have ruined Miss Lainscott at *my* ball. Yet another shot fired in your unending desire to further insult and shame the Duke of Averell. And *me*." Her voice shook with anger. "How *dare* you. Miss Lainscott is under my care. My patronage." She shook her head. "You have finally become the very thing you despise—the father you remember."

Welles fell back, eyes wide open in shock from her attack. "Amanda—"

"In the future, *Lord Welles*, you will address me as Your Grace." The duchess was fairly trembling with rage, her tone scathing and glacial, so unlike the easy affectionate way she usually addressed Welles.

Margaret flinched as well. She'd caused this. Why hadn't she just gone to the library? Taken one look at Welles and fled. *And to what end?* Looking down at her hands, Margaret could finally see the ridiculousness of her plan to force Carstairs into a compromising position. Her scheme had been flawed from the start, even more so now.

One of the duchess's statues wore more expression on their carved marble faces than Welles did. Pain radiated from his eyes as he regarded his stepmother. Abruptly, he bent in an exaggerated mockery of a bow. "Your Grace." His glance ran briefly to Margaret, but there was no warmth in his beautiful eyes.

The duchess shut her eyes as if she couldn't bear to look

at Welles a moment longer as he strode in the direction of the door. Once gone and the sound of his steps faded, her lids fluttered open. Pity, regret, and disappointment were thrown at Margaret in equal measure.

"What have you done, Margaret?" She came forward, fingers grazing over Margaret's shoulders. "Let us try to make you presentable again. We haven't much time."

Margaret choked back a sob. The duchess had never called her by her given name; that she did so now told Margaret just how distressed she was.

"I blame myself. I saw the way he looked at you. Wondered at his request for you to accompany us to Lady Masterson's party. He said it was for Romy's sake." Her hands flitted over Margaret's shoulders and neckline. "Theo mentioned his interest. I should have warned him off. He's *never* toyed with a young lady of good virtue so boldly. And now he's gone and *spoiled* you, my dear Margaret."

She wasn't a rotten piece of fruit someone forgot to toss. "No. It was *only* a kiss." Welles pressing his lips up her naked body flashed before her eyes and she pushed the image away. "Nothing more happened between us tonight." That at least was the truth. She'd been *spoiled* before ever setting foot in the conservatory.

The duchess wasn't listening, all her focus on gathering the pins that had fallen from Margaret's hair. "I worried he saw you as a challenge of some sort. Thank goodness Carstairs caught me and asked the way to the library, else there is no telling what would have occurred. Welles had promised Carstairs and Miss Turnbull a look at a stuffed trout mounted on the wall."

Margaret's breath caught. The last remnants of hope this debacle had been accidental fled with her words. Welles had told her he would leave Carstairs in the library. Alone.

Her knees buckled suddenly.

Oh, God. Winthrop.

The duchess caught her elbow.

"Now you musn't despair. We may yet be able to brave this out. We'll go down together. You've been with *me* this entire time," she instructed. "And I will *ensure* that this is made right." The duchess was steely-eyed. "You can count on my discretion but unfortunately not that of Miss Turnbull."

Margaret barely heard her.

Welles had lied. He'd never meant to help her at all.

25

The duchess had been right about one thing. Miss Turnbull's discretion could not be counted on because it didn't exist.

The whispers began the moment they returned to the ball. At first, the looks were discreet, merely quiet hisses behind fans that snapped shut in her direction. But as the hour grew late, more scandalized faces looked Margaret's way in pity and thinly veiled malice. Everyone in the *ton* adored good gossip and the ruination of plain Miss Lainscott by the rakish Lord Welles was simply too juicy not to repeat. All of London would know by tomorrow morning, if not sooner.

Romy, loyal to a fault, stood next to Margaret chattering away on a variety of topics, none of which Margaret really listened to. Discreetly, Romy leaned over and tugged a bit of hair out of Margaret's coiffure.

"To cover the bite mark," she whispered, her cheeks pinking.

Margaret nodded, horrified down to the tips of her slippered toes. Bad enough her lips were swollen and her coiffure a tangled mess, but there was also proof of Welles' ruination on her neck, for the entire room to see. As if he had taken a bite of the spoiled fruit Margaret now was and tossed her back into the bowl.

Carstairs circled the ballroom with Miss Turnbull clinging to his side like a silk-clad barnacle. He avoided eye contact with Margaret, never once turning in her direction. Miss Turnbull shot her a look of sympathy mixed with triumph while twirling her fan about. Every so often she would stop and whisper to another young lady. The listener's eyes would widen in distaste while listening to Miss Turnbull's recollection of the events in the conservatory.

Welles did not reappear. Margaret was certain he'd left.

The duchess circled the room, trying her best to contain the gossip, but by the looks thrown Margaret's way, it became a losing proposition. The duchess finally pulled Aunt Agnes aside and whispered furiously in her ear.

Aunt Agnes nodded grimly at the duchess, her eyes rising to Margaret who stood next to Romy.

Moments later, Winthrop emerged from the card tables, his sweaty face sour and full of muted horror. Aunt Agnes went to his side immediately, clasping his arm and speaking in a soothing tone. When both Winthrop and her aunt glanced in her direction, Romy reached out to take her hand.

"I will have a conversation with Miss Turnbull," Romy said under her breath. "And I will *not* desert you. Mother has told me what Tony has done. I am *ashamed* of my brother's conduct. I always knew Tony was a rogue. I'd heard the gossip. But intentionally taking advantage of you in order to spite my father?" She bit her lip. "It's intolerable, Margaret."

Was that what he'd done? Compromised her to embarrass his father? Margaret's stomach pitched at the thought.

Another twitter came from the direction of Miss Turnbull and her friends.

Romy's eyes, so much like her brother's, narrowed into slits.

"I am the daughter of the Duke of Averell. She won't dare disparage you in my father's ballroom." Romy squeezed her hand and made a beeline for Miss Turnbull.

Miss Turnbull looked around the room, eyes wide, searching for any escape from the angry woman in the blue dress who was striding her way.

Margaret appreciated Romy's loyalty but knew it would do little good. The damage was done.

Aunt Agnes, chin pointed and sharp, nodded to Winthrop and made her way to Margaret's side. Curling her spindly fingers around Margaret's elbow, her aunt steered her out of the ballroom without allowing Margaret the chance to say goodbye to either the duchess or Romy. She pushed Margaret into Winthrop's waiting carriage without so much as a word, her boiling rage at Margaret so fierce it threatened to suffocate them both.

Margaret turned to look out the window as the coach rolled back to her aunt's house. Well, she had *wished* to be compromised tonight, though the evening had taken a rather sharp departure from what she'd originally intended. Had it been Carstairs who'd compromised her, he would have asked to speak to her aunt discreetly and promised to arrive the following day with his solicitor bearing a formal proposal of marriage. Instead, Margaret had become merely another young lady whose reputation was irrevocably destroyed by a notorious rake. Welles was known for his sexual exploits and his pleasure palace, *not* for his honorable intentions.

Welles would *never* offer her marriage. It simply wasn't in his character.

If there was one bright spot in this entire fiasco, it was that being compromised by a man with Welles's reputation *did* ensure one thing. Not even Winthrop would have her.

Margaret would have to live the remainder of her days outside society due to her fall from grace. That didn't actually bother her too much, except she would be dependent on her aunt's charity until she could find some sort of employment. Once she turned thirty, a portion of her inheritance would revert to her. Perhaps she could teach piano or become a governess.

Unlikely once your indiscretion becomes public knowledge.

Aunt Agnes may well turn her out. Margaret had no other family to seek refuge with, except for a distant cousin on her father's side whom she'd never met and who lived in Scotland.

Once they arrived at her aunt's home, Aunt Agnes left Winthrop's carriage without a word to Margaret. Thin shoulders stiff, her aunt picked up her skirts and walked up the stairs to her rooms without bothering to see if Margaret followed.

Margaret slept little that night, her thoughts anxious and disjointed. There had to be a way out of the situation she found herself in. She'd worked so *hard* at endearing herself to Carstairs. My God, she'd studied *fly fishing*. Her mistake, Margaret could see, was confiding in Welles. The pain at his betrayal was made worse by her own feelings for him. Why had he ruined everything for her? Because he could?

The question kept her in bed for the remainder of the day.

Margaret, by nature, was a problem solver. Her intelligence set her apart, she told herself, from those poor girls who depended on others to think for them. She accepted her limitations, namely the fact that she was only passably pretty and came from tin miner stock. Instead of lamenting her circumstances, she had always chosen to find ways to circumvent obstacles. When her aunt had thrust her into the season against her wishes, Margaret had adopted a shy, retiring manner to remain beneath the notice of any fortune-hunting lord. When she had rebelled at her aunt's rules, and the piano had been taken from her, Margaret had become docile as a way to get what she wished even though it chafed at her constantly, like an itch begging to be scratched.

A wave of self-pity engulfed her.

All she'd wanted was a pleasant, slightly stupid husband so she could play the bloody piano and help her fellow female musicians.

Two days after the duchess's ball, Margaret decided it was finally time to face the music, so to speak. She could not continue to wallow in self-pity and lie in bed cowering from the world. Margaret was made of sterner stuff, though she'd pretended not to be. She would discuss the situation calmly with her aunt, apologize profusely, and make it clear to her nothing except a kiss had been exchanged. She would express her regret to Winthrop for any discomfort she'd caused him. Then Margaret hoped to convince Aunt Agnes to send her away to the country, preferably back to Yorkshire. At least it was familiar.

Her aunt sat on her favorite chair in the formal drawing room, as if knowing Margaret would seek her out. The painfully thin, sticklike figure became rigid at the sight of her niece, clearly poised for attack at the slightest provocation.

"Good morning, Aunt."

"Margaret." The flinty eyes ran over Margaret, not bothering to hide her dislike. "I did wonder when you would decide to face me after what you've done. An heir to a duchy. My, my, I would not have thought you so ambitious, or so stupid. Are you still a virgin?"

"Yes," Margaret lied feeling the rush of heat up her neck at the memory of Elysium. "It was *only* a kiss."

A horrid cackle left her aunt. "Only a kiss? You've been *compromised*. No one thinks you shared *only* a kiss with the Earl of Welles. I saw your face when you returned to the ballroom. And the mark on your neck. Thankfully the duchess interrupted before he'd seduced you completely. What *were* you thinking?" Her voice raised an octave.

She had been *thinking* she was going to compromise Carstairs.

"All of London is holding its collective breath to see if Welles will do the honorable thing." A shrill laugh escaped her as she shook her head. "We will wait *forever*. Welles hasn't an honorable bone in his body. Did you really think being compromised at the Duchess of Averell's ball would result in marriage?"

I did. Just not to Lord Welles. "Of course not. It was only a kiss," she said again.

"Perhaps you aren't nearly as clever as you think you are, my dear. Marriage to Lord Welles!" Another ugly laugh escaped her. "This entire affair smacks of a jaded rogue who decided to make sport of a plain girl for his own amusement. Had he managed to seduce you, I would have had to send you away."

It was on the tip of Margaret's tongue to confess Welles had seduced her over a week ago; if the end result was expulsion from London, she was ready to pack her bags. Possibly if she mentioned Elysium, Aunt Agnes would send her all the way to the Continent. Gathering her courage, she opened her mouth to confess everything, but the next words from her aunt stopped her cold.

"As it is, you'll still be able to marry Winthrop."

Dread swirled deep and dark in her stomach. "But you just said—"

No. This would never do.

"Lord Winthrop is distraught, of course. But I've explained your...*impassioned* response to music. A flaw inherited from your mother who was similarly afflicted." She waved her hand in the air. "As if you were slightly addled."

"Do not equate my musical talent with a sickness. It is a talent."

Her aunt's lip curled at Margaret's show of defiance. "You were merely playing the piano as you had on *many* occasions when you visited the duchess. Welles came upon you while you were in the throes," her mouth tightened, "of your music. Welles is a seasoned rake, a seducer, who took advantage of an innocent young girl. You were only *stupid*, not despoiled. Winthrop has assured me he won't tolerate such nonsense in the future. I doubt you'll ever be permitted to play again." A smug look crossed her skeletal features while the feather atop today's turban, a pheasant's, quivered with triumph.

"No. I mean, that's not—" Margaret's throat felt as if it would close and leave her begging for air. Once, when she was a child, she'd escaped her nanny to explore a small lake at the edge of her father's property. Slipping in the mud, Margaret had fallen into the dark water, her limbs tangling in her skirts. She'd held her breath for as long as she could even though her lungs screamed for air. One of her father's men had seen her fall in and saved her. That's what this conversation with Aunt Agnes felt like, only *no one* was going to pull her out of the deep waters her aunt had pushed her into.

"A quick marriage to Winthrop and you'll be shipped off to his country estate where, he assures me, there isn't a piano within miles. By next season, Welles will have seduced some other young girl and you will be forgotten."

The truth, as told by her aunt, was painful.

"My dear, did you think you were the *only* young lady Welles has ever compromised?" An ugly, choking sound left her. "Goodness, there's at least one each season. You can nearly set your clock to him."

Margaret said nothing. She was afraid if she opened her mouth she would begin to scream and not be able to stop.

A knock sounded on the study door. The heavy oak swung

open to reveal a slightly ruffled Henderson. The butler bowed low and carried a silver platter over to Aunt Agnes, whispering in her ear.

Her aunt's mouth quivered as Henderson spoke to her. She looked down at the note sitting on the salver and nodded. "You are excused, Margaret," she croaked before waving Margaret upstairs.

"Has something happened?"

Her aunt blinked as if surprised Margaret was still in front of her. "I said you are excused. Go to your room. This instant," she snapped.

Dismissed, Margaret had no choice but to make her way upstairs. After reaching her room, she closed the door behind her and told Eliza she wished to take a nap. As soon as the maid retreated, Margaret locked the door before squeezing under her bed, feeling beneath the mattress for her composition book.

Opening to the sonata she'd been working on, Margaret traced the notes with a fingertip, hearing the corresponding music in her head. A sob escaped despite the fist pressed to her lips. Even after all her careful planning and preparation, Winthrop would still have her.

She shut the notebook with a slap, pushing it back beneath the mattress. For the first time in her life, Margaret had no desire to play the piano, even though she could hear the music of Welles quite clearly. Disgusted with herself for still longing for him when he was the cause of her ills, she fell to the floor, the rug chafing against her cheek. Tears fell from her eyes and for once, Margaret didn't blink them back.

She had no idea what she was going to do.

26

The next morning after crying herself to sleep, Margaret awoke with renewed faith in her ability to find a way out of her situation. She was nothing if not resilient. Today she meant to walk her aunt's garden, avoiding the rosebushes, and contemplate her future. There was a way out of this mess Welles had laid at her feet, she had only to find it. It was exhausting to be so heartbroken.

Leaving her room, she headed for the stairs.

Noises sounded below. Her aunt had visitors. Margaret's foot halted on the step as two men, both dressed in crisp, dark suits exited the drawing room. The low murmur of their voices reached up the stairs, though she couldn't make out their words. Efficiency hovered around both men, their movements quick and businesslike. One held a thick packet under his arm. Without looking in her direction, they strode past Henderson, who threw open the door, and into a carriage sitting outside.

Winthrop's solicitors. Her heart sank.

She would *not* accept the idea of marriage to Winthrop. Margaret had spent the better part of the morning calculating how much pin money she'd squirreled away in her armoire. The book on fly fishing could be sold, though it wouldn't fetch much. How ironic to be a wealthy heiress and have not so much as a farthing on her person.

"Margaret."

She looked toward the drawing room to see her aunt, hands clasped and turban straight, looking at her with heightened anticipation. Aunt Agnes looked...*happy*. Possibly even elated. The last time she'd looked so thrilled had been when Winthrop had proposed. Margaret was immediately on guard.

"Please come in. I've some things we must discuss." Her aunt's chin pointed to the hated drawing room.

Margaret nearly declined her aunt's request, but told herself *nothing* her aunt did to her could be worse than marriage to Winthrop. Cautiously, she made her way to the couch. The remains of the men's visit sat on the table: A cold pot of tea and a pile of papers stacked neatly next to her aunt.

"Henderson," her aunt said to the butler hovering about, "please bring a fresh pot of tea. And those delicious scones my niece enjoys."

Margaret sat down on the couch with a plop, the dread spiraling out of control, making her insides ache. Aunt Agnes looked far too pleased; she'd never cared what Margaret preferred before as evidenced by her forcing Margaret to marry Winthrop.

"It would seem," Aunt Agnes bent her boney form to perch on the end of her favorite chair like a turban-wearing vulture, "that *you* are to be a duchess one day."

27

Margaret glanced back at her reflection in the mirror, admiring the simple, if hardly modest cut of the gown she would be married in. Tightly fitted around her breasts, the bodice pushed the small mounds up against the froth of lace edging the square-cut neckline. A large expanse of her chest and neck was exposed.

"The color suits you, miss," Eliza said.

Margaret had to agree. The deep rose blush of the gown complemented her dark hair and pale complexion. She looked like one of the roses decorating her aunt's bone china.

"I'd like a few moments before I come down," she instructed her traitorous maid. The girl would not be coming when Margaret left this house, despite Margaret not having hired another lady's maid. Eliza hadn't been told the news yet.

The maid bobbed and left her alone.

Another delivery from the same modiste who'd designed her gold gown had arrived this morning, the card inside signed with love from Romy. It appeared her friend was to blame for the stylish but somewhat scandalous neckline and expensive Belgian lace. The duchess had sent her a lovely pair of earrings. Pear-shaped diamonds, which now dangled from Margaret's ears, catching the light every time she moved. Margaret had exclaimed in surprise when she saw the diamonds, sitting in a red box with a silver ribbon.

The earrings had come with an apology that neither the duchess nor her daughters would be present for Margaret's wedding to Anthony Marcus Barrington, 10th Earl of Welles and heir to the Duke of Averell. The duchess and her household had departed unexpectedly the day prior for Cherry Hill, the duke's seat. The duke had taken a turn for the worse and the duchess, ever devoted, wished to be at her husband's side.

Margaret understood. Besides, she wasn't certain she *would* be married today.

Aunt Agnes was beside herself that Margaret had brought Welles up to scratch. Dozens of invitations for her aunt had arrived in less than a day and had begun to stack up on the table in the foyer. As the aunt of a future duchess, Lady Dobson was more in demand than ever. Despite her aunt's almost frightening bliss at the marriage, Margaret was less than happy.

This entire marriage was bound for disaster.

When her aunt had first informed Margaret that Lord Welles had offered for her, she had been certain Aunt Agnes was joking. Or having a hallucination. Welles would *never* marry. He'd told her so on more than one occasion. His aversion to marriage was well known in the *ton*.

Margaret should have been thrilled. She would not be a pariah, but a duchess. There was also the immense relief, of course, of escaping her future as wife to the pear-shaped Winthrop, but it was tempered by the thought that Welles was being forced. Had the duchess held something over his head?

He compromised you intentionally.

If he actually showed up to marry her today, she would have to ask him why.

"Don't dawdle." Aunt Agnes appeared in the doorway of Margaret's room, now devoid of most of her things. Her trunks had already been sent ahead to Welles's town house. Contrary to Margaret's earlier assumption, Welles did *not* live at Elysium, but only kept a room there. He had a lovely home not three blocks from Averell House.

She didn't really know him at all.

Margaret turned and followed her aunt downstairs to the drawing room. Strange, she'd managed to avoid this room, her least favorite in the entire house, for years. She'd never thought it would be the place where she'd be married.

"Come, Niece." Aunt Agnes took her hand.

Margaret looked down at the claw-like fingers encircling her wrist. It was the first time Margaret could ever remember her aunt touching her with anything resembling affection. That she did so now seemed more disingenuous and impossible than marrying Welles.

She shook off her aunt and marched into the drawing room, blinking at the two men standing before the vicar. Welles and his brother, standing side by side, looked so alike it took her a moment to realize it wasn't her anxious mind playing tricks on her. She'd seen Leo Murphy before, the night she'd visited Elysium, but that had been at a distance.

The two men were of like height; both possessed the same dark brown hair, handsome chiseled features, and identical pairs of Barrington blue eyes. Welles was leaner, the lines of his body more elegant. Leo was broader across the chest and stockier. When Leo smiled, as he was doing now in her direction, a dimple appeared in his cheek. But even if she hadn't seen those differences, the splashy waistcoat Leo wore with its swirl of sapphire and gold thread was enough to separate them. Welles, who only wore dark-colored, exquisitely tailored and understated clothing wouldn't be caught dead in such a thing.

I guess I do know him a little.

"Miss Lainscott." The deep baritone melted over Margaret's skin, luring her closer to Welles even though there wasn't anything remotely welcoming in his tone. His chiseled jaw was hard, sculpted from pure ice. She might catch frostbite only by standing near him. "May I present my brother, Mr. Leo Murphy."

Leo took her hand, his fingers tightening over hers. "A pleasure, Miss Lainscott."

"I'm happy to finally meet you," she said. Leo had the same deep resonance to his voice as Welles, though his didn't sink into her bones and cause her skin to hum.

"Now that the pleasantries are over, shall we get on with this?" Welles practically snarled at the vicar, causing the poor man to redden. He was ignoring Margaret completely; she could have been Aunt Agnes for all he'd noticed.

"I would have a word with you, my lord," Margaret interjected and smiled politely to the vicar, "before we continue."

Welles's eyes were glacial, the beautiful blue rings like frost on a pond. "Now?"

"Yes." She turned toward the door without waiting for him to agree.

A nervous, cackling laugh left her aunt before catching Margaret by the sleeve to bestow a brutal pinch to her upper arm.

Margaret winced and jerked away, glaring at her aunt. Aunt Agnes didn't care for the recent changes in her niece's temperament. Which was fine with Margaret since she didn't care for her aunt.

Welles stared down at Aunt Agnes from his much greater height. His voice lowered dangerously. "If you *dare* touch her again in such a way, *I* will *pinch you*, Lady Dobson. And I promise you won't find it pleasurable in the least." He leaned close. "Despite what you may have heard."

Her aunt's smile faltered, jet black eyes flashing with dislike. "I understand *completely*, Lord Welles."

Leo chuckled softly from his place by the vicar.

"Good. I *suspected* we'd get on." He gripped Margaret's arm and began to pull her out of the drawing room. "Please excuse us for a moment." He walked her into the hall. "Where?"

"My aunt's parlor." She shrugged off his hand.

Welles scowled reluctantly, letting go.

Opening the door to her aunt's parlor, she waited for him to enter and then shut the door quietly. Margaret paced across the worn Persian carpet several times before coming to a stop before him. "You don't want to marry me."

A dark brow lifted. "It isn't you in particular, Maggie. I don't wish to marry anyone at all. But I am, *in fact*, getting married today. To *you*. You've ten minutes before I haul you back in front of the vicar."

"You don't have to do this."

"I'm fairly certain I do."

Margaret took in every glorious bit of him. She was in love with Welles and had been for some time. But marriage to a man who would never love her in return, when her own heart was so involved, was daunting, to say the least, especially since she was certain he would only grow to resent her over time. Eventually, her heart would be broken and shattered by his dislike. Welles hating her was in many respects a far worse fate than being married to Winthrop. "It was only a kiss."

"Yes." He gave her a lascivious look. "Between your legs."

A tremor rippled across her skin. Margaret remembered every moment of their night at Elysium. "But not the night of your stepmother's ball. No one need ever know about…

the other," she stuttered. "I never expected marriage of you—"

"And let us not forget Winthrop. Should I disappear, you'd still have that waddling pear-shaped problem. What are you going to do, Maggie, if we don't marry? Form a rope out of bedsheets and rappel down the side of your aunt's home to make your escape?"

"I would leave by the front door."

Welles snorted in derision. "You've no choice and neither do I."

"I *had* a choice," she said, growing irritated at his mocking attitude. "And *you* deliberately ruined my opportunity with Carstairs." She saw not a shred of affection for her in his eyes, only icy resignation and resentment, as if she were to blame for all his ills. Anger simmered and burned beneath the snowy white shirt and indigo coat he wore, spoiling the air around them. And every *bit* of his rage was directed squarely at her.

"You blame me for this."

A tic appeared in his cheek. He looked as if he wanted to strangle her.

Dear God, he did.

The unfairness of the situation, the feeling she was nothing but a burden, a piece of bloody spoiled fruit no one wanted but couldn't dispose of, bubbled to the surface, exploding in a torrent.

"I don't want to marry you, either." Her hands curled into fists as she faced him. "I've no desire to be subjected to your foul mood and resentment for the remainder of my days. Good Lord, I already live with someone who hates me. I didn't *trap* or ensnare you, my lord, so please cast your withering stare elsewhere."

"Ah, there she is." The corner of his mouth ticked up.

"I had *no* expectations. No illusions. I knew what you were."

"And what am I, Maggie?" he said in a deceptively quiet tone.

"A rake. A libertine. Then you had to go and play Chopin."

"I'm not the one who left the conservatory door open, Maggie."

She sucked in a gulp of air, shocked at his inference. "I *wanted* to marry Carstairs. You were playing—"

He flicked a piece of lint off his coat. "*Christ*, I'm so tired of hearing how you prefer that dimwit to me. And on our wedding day."

"*Bloody Chopin*." She finished, taking a gulp of air, her breasts pushing painfully against the tight constraints of her bodice. "Wait—what?"

Welles was staring at her with such savage possessiveness that Margaret took a step back.

"I said, I am *sick to death* of hearing of your preference for Carstairs. Because he's kind. Pleasant. *Stupid*. So you could walk all over him." He moved to stand over her, a large, angry male, who unbelievably, had decided she belonged to him. Under different circumstances, she would have been...a bit *thrilled* with his declaration.

She stared at him, frozen in place by his words.

"Unfortunately for you, Maggie, I am *none* of those things."

His forefinger reached out, lingering over the tops of her breasts, pausing only to dip below the delicate lace to circle one nipple.

Margaret gasped, hating the way her body immediately arched toward him, a low hum starting between her thighs at his touch.

He removed his finger, pausing only to brush the lace at her bodice. "Lest you think to *demand* the vicar *not* perform the marriage, you should know that I've apprised your aunt of how I debauched you well before my stepmother's ball and took your virtue. I've also informed the duchess. I may have let such a thing slip in my conversation to Carstairs just the other day." He shrugged and took her elbow.

Margaret's mouth popped open in shock. "You—" A flush crept up her cheeks, mortified. She would never be able to look the duchess in the eye again. "Bastard." She tried to pull her arm free.

"No, that is the *other* brother, the one you aren't marrying. Pay attention, Maggie." He dragged her back into the drawing room.

Margaret continued to swat at him, startling the vicar. Leo was smiling. Aunt Agnes moved forward to pinch her, and Welles made a low growl.

Her aunt stepped back so swiftly she stumbled over the chair leg.

"Now that we've cleared things up," he said, nodding to all of them before addressing the vicar, "you may begin."

Margaret barely heard a word of the ceremony. A mounting sense of despair filled her along with a great deal of anger. She didn't want to marry Welles under these circumstances. Aunt Agnes seemed the only one in the drawing room to be even remotely pleased, although Leo didn't look put out.

Her soon to be brother-in-law cleared his throat and gave her a nudge.

"I will," she said automatically.

Welles made a sign of irritation at her having to be prompted to respond before settling a large square-cut diamond onto her finger. The weight of the ring was heavy, the band far too large. Her fingers immediately curled into a fist, wishing she were taller so she could punch him right on his perfect nose.

Welles brushed a perfunctory kiss on her lips, prompting a spark down the length of her traitorous body.

Barely fifteen minutes later, Margaret found herself sitting in the same well-appointed carriage Welles had first propositioned her in a lifetime ago. The same one she'd ridden in after their night together at Elysium.

Only now, Welles was her husband.

28

That could have gone better.

Tony's temples ached, mostly from the overabundance of scotch he'd had the night before. Scotch had helped him come to terms with a variety of current issues, namely marrying Miss Margaret Lainscott. Having to endure the company of Lady Dobson, more greedy and conniving than he'd given her credit for, only added to the dull ache in his head. He had been assured by his solicitors that the sum settled upon Maggie's aunt would keep her away. Lady Dobson hadn't spared Winthrop a thought before agreeing to Tony's terms.

Tony rubbed his forehead while taking in the cause of this entire mess. His wife.

She had chosen to ignore him since their heated discussion in the parlor after Tony had explained he'd informed all concerned her virtue was no longer intact. The look on her face had been priceless. He couldn't have her balking as their vows were said, not after the lengths he'd gone to in order to have her. Instead of being grateful—after all, Tony had tossed aside a vow to never marry he'd made when only fifteen, in order to rescue her from the clutches of Winthrop—she'd castigated him for not leaving her to Carstairs.

I was never going to give her to Carstairs.

The flash of jealous anger spread across his chest. It wasn't the first time, and he doubted it would be his last. Another thing he laid at her feet. Tony's fingers drummed on his thigh, wanting to itch at the ugly possessiveness climbing down his limbs. He'd known the moment Maggie had left Elysium spouting the nonsense about no expectations. What kind of a *man* did she think he was to take her maidenhead and then give her to his friend?

A rake. A libertine.

Tony studied the new Lady Welles discreetly. Her opinion of his character today notwithstanding, she looked lovely. *Incredibly angry.* But lovely.

The rose silk nestled against her petite body seductively, emphasizing her tiny waist and pushing her delectable breasts up in an almost wanton manner. And Maggie did have a tendency toward wantonness; he'd experienced such a thing firsthand at Elysium. Reading the memoirs of a courtesan. Never once blushing while he stripped her of her chemise. Touching his cock. Wicked little thing.

Another part of his anatomy besides his head began to ache, and she wasn't even playing the damned piano.

He bit back the curse forming at his lips. While his anger had simmered to a cool, icy burn in his veins over the last few days, thanks to several bottles of Elysium's best scotch, his fury was still there, threatening to crack through the surface of the skin. Marrying Miss Lainscott felt an awful lot like pleasing the Duke of Averell, something he was adamantly opposed to. He'd been so *bloody* angry when he'd left the ball that night. Amanda's comparison of Tony to his father had sickened him so much it had blotted out everything else, including Maggie.

Tony had immediately retreated to his rooms at Elysium.

He drank himself into a stupor the first night. *And* the second.

It was Leo who had stormed into his rooms, furious at him for leaving Miss Lainscott out to dry, so to speak. Amanda and the girls had refused to see him until he did the honorable thing. Romy, in particular, had sent Tony a *scathing* note; he had no idea his sister knew such vile curses. The entire *ton* was awash with ugly rumor and conjecture. His reputation, already not the best, had been battered further, though he didn't actually care what society thought of him.

Tony gave a great sigh while studying the delicate curve of his wife's breast, wanting her comfort for the pain he felt, even though she was the cause of it.

Contrary to what his family believed, having Leo remind Tony of his numerous character deficits and Amanda vowing *never* to speak to him again was not what had induced him to marry Miss Lainscott. Nor did the *ton* have to proclaim him the most wicked of all rakes or laugh at the fact it had been Lady Dobson's much-unloved niece which had forced Tony to relinquish his vow of bachelorhood.

He'd known exactly what would happen when he played Chopin for her the night of the ball. He just didn't *like* it.

Tony kept his focus on his wife's petite form, mentally stripping the rose gown from her. She was still fuming and possibly mourning her thwarted attempt to become Lady Carstairs. Another rush of jealousy washed over him. He'd never thought to ever be envious of Carstairs or have a woman prefer him to Tony. The thought chafed at his ego.

As the carriage rolled to a stop before his town house, the expression of Lady Welles didn't change except for a slight tightening of her delicious plump lips. Tony allowed himself a moment to study her mouth, remembering the taste of her. There were many uses for a mouth.

His trousers tightened alarmingly at even the wisp of such a thought.

The carriage rolled to a stop in front of his rather modest town house.

Thank God. If he didn't get out of this carriage and work off some of the havoc of today's events, Lady Welles would likely pay the price. He needed a short stroll and a glass of scotch to clear his mind before dealing with his wife. Maybe he'd spend his entire marriage foxed.

His brother jumped out first, shooting Tony a look that warned of an upcoming lecture.

Leo was *very* good at instructing others on how to conduct their lives. Less so when doing the right thing himself. If Leo so much as uttered a word about Tony's conduct, Tony meant to fling Lady Masterson at his brother's head. That would shut him up.

Leo held out his hand to help his new sister-in-law out of the carriage.

Maggie smiled up at his brother, plump lips wide as if she meant to bestow a kiss.

Possessiveness stung Tony again. He was beginning to detest the sensation. He should *never* have encouraged her ridiculous scheme to wed Carstairs, nor requested she play the piano half-naked. It had only delayed the inevitable. Tony had known the moment he'd seen her at Gray Covington last year, arched over that fucking piano, that he was going to have her. He should have taken action then and convinced her to become his mistress.

He glanced at his wife.

Damn her.

Perhaps after he'd had Maggie a time or two, the desire for her would wane and he could go back to his life. He'd give her this house and she could invite every female musician in London to tea if she wished. Play the piano until her fingers bled. Tony would live at Elysium and have as many mistresses as he liked. Opera singers. Maybe an actress or two for variety. He'd insist none of them have the least musical inclination.

The idea had sounded more appealing last night after half a bottle of scotch.

"Welcome home, my lord." Fenwick, Tony's butler, swung open the door.

"Fenwick." Leo clapped the butler on the shoulder. The first time his brother had done such, the very proper Fenwick had nearly expired on the spot.

"Mr. Murphy." The butler gave him a weak smile.

"Fenwick," Tony said not moving further up the stairs, "this is Lady Welles."

The butler bowed politely. "Lady Welles, your trunks have already been brought upstairs. Daisy arrived a short time ago and has unpacked your things and prepared your rooms."

"Thank you," Maggie said in a quiet voice. "Daisy is...?"

"Romy's maid," Tony interjected. "I thought you might use her until you find a replacement for your own. My sister was more than happy to lend her to you. Fenwick will show you up. I need to stretch my legs a bit." He kept his expression bland.

Annoyance flared in Maggie's dark eyes. Her lips pursed, not caring for his abrupt dismissal.

Tony glanced down to see her hand on Leo's forearm. Was she intentionally trying to annoy him?

"Tony—" Leo said under his breath.

"Have a drink. I'll join you shortly," he shot back. It was rude and completely inappropriate to leave his new bride with his brother without even walking her inside, but Tony thought he'd explode if he didn't at the very least walk around the block. Or perhaps take a ride through the park. He was a storm of emotions at the present, and none of them were good.

"Of course, *my lord*." The new Lady Welles barely glanced back. "Mr. Murphy, I'm sure you know the way. I could do with a drink myself."

Ah. There she is.

Tony detested the meek demeanor Maggie had adopted as a way to survive both her aunt and society. He much preferred her obstinance.

Maggie turned away from him, stiffened her shoulders and walked purposefully into the foyer.

Leo waited until she'd disappeared inside before he said, "You're behaving like an ass. None of this is her fault."

"It's *all* her fault," Tony spat back at Leo. "But at least you've made a pretty penny on whether I'd marry her or not. Did you think I wouldn't find out about the open betting at Elysium?"

"I did," Leo said unapologetically. "I was fairly certain of the outcome."

"You don't know anything, Leo."

"Why? Because I'm not the bloody heir?" Leo shook his head. "Regardless, take your walk. Ride your horse until you collapse. Just don't come back here until you've burned away some of your anger toward your bride. She doesn't deserve it."

If Leo didn't stop talking, Tony might well punch his brother. "She deserves every bit."

Leo leaned close to him. "Imagine, you've seduced literally *dozens* of women. And not one of them as carelessly as my new sister-in-law. You *meant* to do it." Leo jumped up the steps away from him and into the house. "You wanted her and decided to give yourself no choice in the matter. Or leave her a choice, either."

Leo was remarkably astute. Tony hated him for that.

29

How dare he?

Margaret deserved, at the very least, to be treated with some respect. Not discarded like an old coat on the doorstep of her husband's home in front of his staff *and* her new brother-in-law...barely an hour after marrying.

"A scotch?" Leo walked into the drawing room and shut the doors.

She nodded.

"I knew there was something about you I adored, Lady Welles."

"My drinking habits?" She gave him a weak smile. Leo was as flirtatious and charming as his brother, with the same graceful way of moving. "I've only ever had scotch two other times, but it seems the right sort of thing to drink under the...circumstances." She made her way to the comfortable-looking settee covered in damask nearly the same color as her gown and looked up at her brother-in-law.

The inflection in Leo's voice was different than her husband's. Welles had a much more cultured accent while

Leo's voice didn't have such snobbery tinting his words. The arrogance in their manner was the same, though, the air of entitlement marking them both as sons of a duke, bastard or not. Leo Murphy, much like his brother, was also intimately aware of the effect of his looks on the fairer sex.

"May I call you Maggie?"

Margaret looked up into the face so like her husband's. "Your likeness to Welles is rather uncanny." It was on the tip of her tongue to tell Leo she'd seen him at Elysium and thought him Welles, but she didn't wish to announce her visit there, though he likely already knew.

"Is that a yes?" Leo handed her a scotch and waved for her to sit down. "We do look very much alike, but we aren't twins, I assure you. Welles is actually a year older than I am." He sipped his drink. "The same father, different mothers." He gave her an assessing glance. "Would you like to hear the story? We've some time, I suspect, before Tony returns."

Margaret nodded, palming her glass.

"Tony's mother was the daughter of an earl. My mother, her lady's maid at Cherry Hill. There's not one cherry tree there, by the way. Have no idea where the name came from." He shrugged. "I grew up at Cherry Hill. Thought my father was a groom my mother had dallied with. Tony and I were childhood playmates, neither of us knowing we were brothers."

"But you look so much alike." Margaret's brow wrinkled. "Surely the resemblance was remarked upon."

"Tony was tall and lanky as a child, while I was pudgy and small for my age. We didn't look much alike then, except for our eyes. I was only the son of a maid, so no one looked too closely at me, not even Katherine, Tony's mother. At least, not then."

Her grasp on the fine cut crystal tightened. The two women would have had a close-knit relationship. How horrified Welles's mother must have been to realize her maid was also sleeping with her husband. And had borne him a son as well.

"My mother had been brought to Cherry Hill as a child. She'd known Averell, Marcus she called him, her entire life and was in love with him for most of it. Molly, that's my mother, broke off her relationship with the duke when he married, but their estrangement didn't last." He gave a small laugh. "I'm living proof of that. At any rate, some years later, Katherine found out about my mother and the duke. They'd grown careless, and she saw them together. She was heavy with child when she tripped going down the steps on her way to confront him. I'm sure you can see where this story ends," Leo said quietly. "Welles found her, bleeding to death at the base of the stairs. I think he was fourteen at the time and home from school on holiday. He held her as she bled all over the rug at the base of the stairs. Tony was covered in her blood, screaming for help."

Margaret was physically ill as she imagined the scene in her mind. A young Welles, finding his beloved mother bleeding to death on the floor. "She taught him to play the piano."

Leo's eyes widened in surprise. "She did. And to appreciate and love music. Tony rarely speaks of her. They were very close. He blames our father for her death, as you may have surmised."

She had, only Margaret hadn't thought the truth to be so awful.

"My mother was horrified at what happened and the part she played. She collected me and fled to London. The duke found Molly eventually, of course, and begged her to come home. I think he bore her a great deal of affection. He may have even loved her in his way. My mother refused and never spoke to him again. She allowed him to see me when he came to London, though I always thought of him as the prick who made my mother weep. My stepfather put a stop to the duke's visits but continued to take the money he sent for my care. I grew up quite comfortably as a bastard. Much more well off than most."

"You don't seem to hate him nearly as much as Welles," Margaret said quietly.

"Tony has enough hatred for both of us, and I was glad to have a brother. But I don't care for the man, if that's what you're asking. I suspect the young, overindulged duke who kept two women under the same roof is not the man whom Amanda and my sisters speak of with such love. He is a different father to them than he was to Welles. And he *did* claim me, bastard or not."

Margaret nodded, lifting her eyes to his. It was a horrible tragedy, altering the course of Welles's and Leo's lives forever. And the life of the Duke of Averell. "He sounds as if he had an epiphany, your father. Perhaps the death of Katherine and losing you and your mother changed him for the better."

She took in Leo's stance, the same careless one Welles often adopted, which gave away none of his true feelings. There was no mercy in his eyes as he spoke of the Duke of Averell. "Our relationship cannot be repaired no matter any change wrought in him. Tony has been punishing the duke for years by not marrying. You see that, don't you? By depriving the duke of an heir and allowing his line to die?"

Margaret did see, with startling clarity. "How Welles must detest me for forcing him to break such a vow." She drained her glass as desolation swept over her.

"Averell has threatened Tony with everything over the years in order to get him to marry. Cut him off without a cent. Vowed to never allow him near the girls. Swore he'd dismantle Elysium brick by brick."

"Gifted him a Broadwood," Margaret said softly.

A genuine smile crossed his lips. "Tony doesn't hate you. He's pissed. Angry. And he does blame you." Leo drained his own glass. "But he's never played the damned Broadwood in Amanda's conservatory, not once. Not even when Phaedra begged him to accompany her. Not until he played it for you."

He bowed to her and walked toward the door, pausing to squeeze her shoulder.

"Rest assured, Lady Welles, while I don't expect the path to be smooth, nothing on earth would have forced Tony to marry you if he didn't *truly* want to."

30

Margaret paced across the rug, glancing every so often to the closed door leading to her husband's rooms. After Leo had taken his leave, Margaret had allowed Fenwick to show her upstairs. While Margaret had flounced down on the bed, admiring the pale green décor and elegant furnishings, Daisy had introduced herself and bustled about the room. Tea was sent up. The sun began to set. Margaret thought of changing but didn't. And there was *still* no sign of her husband. When Daisy asked if she'd dine downstairs or take a tray, Margaret asked for the latter. She was simply too embarrassed to dine by herself on her wedding night.

Despite Leo's reassurance, Margaret wondered if Welles meant to return.

Her new brother-in-law's tale of the series of events that had shaped Lord Welles had given Margaret some insight, at least in dealing with her husband's mood and the enormous obstacle she faced in her marriage. She understood now, truly knew, what was behind his vehement dislike of the Duke of Averell, as well as the punishment Welles had devised for his father. She wondered how it was that Welles didn't resent Leo for being the son of his father's mistress, but as far as Margaret could tell, the two were close and had no bitterness toward each other. Welles seemed only to blame the duke for Katherine's death.

After picking at the chicken and roasted vegetables on her dinner tray, Margaret placed her fork down, looking out the window of her rooms at the small garden behind the house. She could stay upstairs and allow this mood to fester which would lengthen the void between them, or Margaret could take action. Welles could avoid her for significant stretches of time if he chose, and regardless of the reasons for their marriage, she didn't want to become yet another politely distant marriage of the *ton*. Margaret had taken Leo's words to heart as well as the small bit of honesty Welles had afforded her before the ceremony uniting them. He *had* compromised her intentionally. And as absurd as the idea was, Welles was *jealous* of Carstairs. Over her.

If what Leo had told her was true, Welles desired her and might even care for her. But Margaret would need to be careful with him. First, she had to find him.

She assumed Welles had retreated to his rooms at Elysium to brood, and that was where she was most likely to find him. Opening the armoire, Margaret brushed aside the row of dresses Daisy had neatly organized and gave a sigh of relief at the sight of her old cloak. She took it out, inhaling the moth-eaten smell, and wrapped it tightly around her shoulders. Margaret would march down the stairs and ask Fenwick to have the carriage brought around. There would be no hailing a hack or sneaking out the servants' entrance.

She was Lady Welles now.

31

Half an hour later, Margaret stood before Fenwick, who only gave a cursory glance at the ratty cloak the lady of the house was wearing. He was far too well-trained and had likely seen much worse as Welles's butler.

"May I be of service, my lady?" He bowed to her.

"Can you have the carriage brought around? I'm meeting Lord Welles." She lifted her chin in case the butler should deny her.

Fenwick's brows knit in confusion. "Of course, my lady. I shall call for the carriage immediately, but his lordship is in the study."

Margaret's hands stilled against her skirts at the information. "I see. He must have decided to return home after all. I'll join him." How absolutely mortifying, especially since she assumed Fenwick knew she'd dined upstairs alone. Nonetheless, she gave him a bright smile. "Where would I find the study?"

"Two doors down, my lady." Fenwick inclined his head. "Please ring, should you need anything."

"I will. Thank you, Fenwick."

How long has he been here? Margaret fumed. She'd been sitting upstairs, by herself, for hours. Pacing the floor. Wondering at his whereabouts.

Nothing on earth would have forced Tony to marry you if he didn't truly want to.

Margaret drew the words close to her heart. She needed every bit of hope she could muster as she confronted her husband. Lifting her chin, she swung open the study door.

Only the fire was lit. No lamps. At first glance, Margaret wasn't certain Welles was even in the study. Perhaps Fenwick had been mistaken.

"Hello, wife." The coldly mocking baritone greeted her. "Looking for something?"

"Yes, my lord. I am in search of my husband. It appears after forcing me before the vicar he has chosen to abandon me, on our wedding night, no less. I'm sure Carstairs wouldn't have done so."

A growl came from the direction of a large chair before the fire. "I find your increasing show of stubbornness and your need to be argumentative out of character for Miss Margaret Lainscott. I feel certain you should go back to being timid."

"I'm just as certain I should not. I am Lady Welles now."

Another low sound of irritation. "And do not dare mention your longing for Carstairs again to me. You would have ruined him in a matter of weeks. The poor man would have had no idea the type of woman he'd married. Were you going to allow him to make any decisions at all? Or would you have just thrown open his house to invite a horde of destitute musicians to take up residence?"

"I'd allow him to hunt in peace."

"Though not join him yourself? No hunting for grouse as a married couple?"

"After my lack of aptitude for fishing, despite the help of the book you gifted me, I would probably have taken up firearms. In fact, I'm considering doing so now." Despite the familiar verbal sparring, Margaret detected the cold bits of sarcasm and anger lingering in his words. And the pain. Steeling herself, Margaret strode confidently into the room, nearly tripping on the carpet as she caught sight of the Broadwood against the wall, the firelight dancing off the polished wood.

Her heart beat in a hopeful rhythm. Welles had brought it here for her.

"I thought you would like to have the *instrument*," he emphasized the word, "of your ruination close at hand. Besides myself. I moved my desk into a smaller parlor to make room for this monstrosity. I am not so fortunate to have a conservatory in this house."

Margaret was deeply touched he'd done such a thing for her, especially given his mood. "Thank you." Her fingers ran over the ivory keys of the Broadwood, fingers tingling with anticipation at the thought of being able to play whenever she wished. It was a rather grand, romantic gesture for him to make and so very unexpected.

"You may play until your heart's content."

He was her heart's content, only Welles didn't realize it. Moisture gathered behind her eyes. *Bloody idiot.* Did he really think she'd preferred Carstairs? She'd *given herself* to him. Margaret told herself to tread lightly. If everything Leo had told her was the truth, and she'd no reason to doubt him, it would take time and patience on her part to make Welles come around to the idea of being married.

And what of children?

Margaret brushed the idea aside. She needed to focus on one thing at a time. Approaching her husband as if he were a wounded lion or other wild creature, Margaret made her way to stand in front of him. Confrontation was not her strong suit, as evidenced by the way she'd handled the last several years living under her aunt's thumb.

"You're blocking the fire."

Margaret gave a snort. "My lord, we both know I'm far too small to accomplish such a thing. Now who is being argumentative?"

Welles had discarded his coat and it now lay in a heap on the floor. His shirt had been unbuttoned, exposing a beautiful triangle of skin and dark hair to her view.

Margaret shivered, remembering the feel of those crisp hairs against her naked breasts even as her body hummed madly at his nearness.

He smelled of scotch and the outdoors. Wind and leather. She suspected he'd gone riding, something Margaret realized he did when he needed to think. Or was angry, as he'd been today and still was, apparently. The light of the fire caressed his striking features as he stared back at her, a frown tugging at the corners of his wide, sensual mouth. A letter sat open on his lap, the corners torn. Welles's name, his Christian name, was scrawled across the top in a spidery, shaking hand.

The writing of someone who is gravely ill.

The fumes of scotch grew stronger as she took a step closer to him. "You're foxed." She reached out to take his hand, as she'd done the day of Lady Masterson's garden party.

His fingers curled away from her.

The rejection stung, but Margaret was determined. The Broadwood glistened behind her as a reminder he must bear her some affection. "Did something happen?" She nodded toward the letter laying discarded in his lap.

"I chose the color especially for you." One finger waved elegantly in her direction. "Rose blush. I saw it at the modiste's when I ordered the gown made from gold. It reminded me of you. Blushing for me, the cream of your skin turning pink when I say such inappropriate things."

"You sent me the gowns?" In retrospect, she should have guessed, given the immodest necklines. Another romantic gesture. Despite his manner, Margaret's skin buzzed in a delicious fashion, begging her to draw closer. She raised her hand, intent on touching him.

"I couldn't imagine how a girl of gentle breeding would have picked up on every innuendo I made. It was a shock to discover you were a virgin." He lifted his glass and took a sip. "And a great *many* things have happened." An ugly thick sound came from him.

Margaret stepped back from her husband, hand dropping back to her side. The comment stung as he'd meant it to. "That was unkind."

"Do you know what this is, wife?" Welles held up the letter.

Margaret was fairly certain she did. Her stomach pitched in apprehension as she stared at the vellum, recognizing the broken ducal seal. "Welles—"

"This, *dearest* wife, is a congratulatory letter from His Grace the Duke of Averell on our marriage. Doubtless, his joy at our nuptials has extended his miserable life."

"And you blame *me*," she said, her words as mocking as his. "This is *my* fault. Because I *forced* you to compromise me."

Another ugly laugh came from him. "Wasn't that your plan all along when you came to Elysium?" The words flung at her like a dozen daggers, slicing and digging into her heart. "For all I know, you are in league with that old prick and my stepmother. You're quite Machiavellian, Lady Welles."

If she had dared to come any closer, Margaret would have slapped Welles across his beautiful, smirking face. "I didn't do this. *You* did." He'd whittled down the most beautiful night of her life to nothing more than sexual manipulation. The dread settled firmly in the center of her chest.

"He's not going to win. I'll have no children. No heir for him to coo over." His eyes ran down her form. "Go to bed, Lady Welles. You will wait in vain for the consummation of this marriage."

The words struck her hard, the hatred of his father thickening the air between them.

Gathering her courage, Margaret leaned in, sorely sick to death of his bitterness and anger, particularly the parts directed at her. "I am exhausted with your moods."

"Ah, there she is. It's unfortunate I don't want her here."

"I grow weary of your temper tantrums. Your wild accusations. Your inability to be happy because it is so much more important to hang on to your bitterness. Your father will die, surrounded by his loving wife and daughters, and you will *still* be *miserable*. Your mother will *still* be dead."

"Get. *Out*."

"Since I am now free to take lovers, perhaps I shall."

His fingers tightened on the glass and Margaret waited for him to hurl it at her.

"Just remember," she said in a low tone, daring to whisper close to his ear. "It was *Carstairs* I wanted." She refused to play meek and mild another moment, especially not for this man who'd demanded otherwise from her the entire time she'd known him.

He sat in the chair unmoving, refusing to look at her. After a few moments, Margaret wrapped her dignity about her and strode to the door, flinching only when the sound of glass breaking in the fireplace met her ears.

Once upstairs, Margaret tossed the cloak aside and looked into the fire. She would not sit back and put her own desires on hold until Welles came to terms with their marriage. And she refused to walk daintily around him while he wallowed in resentment, pretending it didn't bother her.

The sound of the front door slamming echoed up the stairs.

He would probably live at Elysium for a time. Maybe forever.

Daisy arrived later with a quiet knock and began to help Margaret get ready for bed. When she pulled out a silky nightgown meant for her wedding night, Margaret waved her away. Her husband's accusations had devastated her. Welles had meant to push her away and he'd succeeded. Brilliantly.

The maid left her with a murmured good night, and Margaret climbed into her bed. She was used to being unwanted. Unloved. Margaret had existed in such a state since her father's death. Welles doing much the same was a disappointment, but not unexpected.

Tomorrow, she would visit her father's solicitor. The sum to come to her upon her marriage would now be hers entirely to do with as she wished. If nothing else, Margaret meant to have a rich, fulfilling life. Welles could go hang.

For the moment.

32

"Do you plan to live here indefinitely?"

Tony looked up from the desk in his rooms at Elysium—he'd been reviewing some of the accounts—to see his brother enter.

"Do you ever knock?"

"If you are moving in, you should have a bed brought up. You've room for it now since the piano is gone and it must be bloody uncomfortable to sleep on the chaise every night."

"The chaise is fine."

Leo took hold of one of the chairs by the fire and dragged it over to Tony's desk. "I can't imagine what is keeping you at Elysium. Do you not trust me to handle the accounts? Or are you hesitant to return to your bride after behaving like an ass?"

"We may have had an argument."

Leo shook his head. "I assumed as much."

After his wedding night during which he and Maggie had snarled at each other, Tony had retreated to his rooms at Elysium. He needed time to think, something he couldn't do with Maggie in such close proximity.

"Averell sent me a congratulatory note. Did I tell you, Leo?"

"I thought he might."

The note, written in his father's shaky hand, had set a match to Tony's already combustible emotions. He'd exploded, sending bits of verbal shrapnel all over the one person who least deserved it. Rage at his father and guilt over betraying his mother led him to accuse Maggie of conspiring to trap him in marriage. She'd stood fearlessly in the face of his hostility and with a smile on her face told him she *preferred* Carstairs.

Brave little thing. A bolt of longing for her shook him.

"I wondered what had set you off." Leo shot him a look of empathy. "So he sent you a letter. What of it? You went to great lengths to marry her, but now you don't wish to be under the same roof as she? Seems a waste."

"We can have a politely distanced marriage. Many do."

"True. But why marry her at all if you weren't going to have her?" Leo shook his head. "You realize, Tony, that every impoverished, anguished artist with mediocre talent is sniffing about her ankles under the auspices of wanting her patronage."

Tony knew his wife was carrying on splendidly without him, hosting small gatherings to discuss art and music, garnering a host of admirers. He received regular reports from Fenwick. Maggie had finally blossomed without him, earning a reputation as a charming and witty hostess in the weeks they'd been parted. Her true self had finally been revealed, and she was touted for it.

I always saw who she was. Always.

"Yes, she's busy turning my home into a refuge for parasitic musicians," he snapped at Leo. "What of it?"

"Especially one *impoverished* parasite by the name of

Henri Bouvard." Leo watched him closely. "I'm told he plays Chopin with much passion."

Jealousy sparked and flared inside him. "She's free to do as she wishes," Tony heard himself say, knowing his brother was deliberately goading him. "As am I." He'd tried to return to his former state of rakishness after their marriage, but Tony was having little luck doing so. Not one woman who propositioned him could play the piano, and only two possessed more intelligence than a potted fern.

"The duke is dying, Tony. Your wife is very much alive." His brother shook his head. "For the love of God, go home. Christ, you're miserable." Leo stood and walked toward the door. "But if you are so stubborn as to stay, take my advice, and at least bring yourself a proper bed."

Tony waved his brother out. "I've work to do. Your concern for me is duly noted." He didn't need or want his brother's advice. What did Leo know anyway? Tony would be perfectly content living at Elysium, bed or not. He could avoid his wife forever. Pushing the conversation with Leo aside, Tony bent again to his task.

Another sharp pain of longing struck him.

He stared at the ledger before him for a good thirty minutes after Leo left him, not seeing the lines of numbers or lists of transactions.

All he saw was Maggie.

33

Her husband had returned home.

After weeks of living apart with no communication from Welles, Margaret had gotten used to her more solitary existence and her independence. She was content. Not happy, but happiness was overrated. Purpose and passion were what mattered.

In control of her inheritance, *finally*, Margaret had recently made a large contribution to the Royal Society of Female Musicians and had even hosted a very small, charitable event in support of the organization. She'd played the Broadwood, much to the admiration of the guests in attendance, although her performance lacked some of the passion with which she usually played. The colors of her music had become less vivid. Muted. *Dimmed*.

She blamed Welles.

Today after paying an overdue call to Mrs. Anderson, Margaret was greeted by Fenwick with the startling news that Welles was back in residence.

About bloody time.

She looked at the doors separating their rooms,

wondering if Fenwick had been mistaken. No sounds emanated from behind the door nor did she hear Welles in the house.

Perhaps he'd only come back to collect his things.

The thought was as painful now as it had been on their wedding night, but Margaret refused to go to Elysium and retrieve her husband. If Welles was determined to be stubborn, so could she. After instructing Fenwick to have a dinner tray brought to the study and intentionally not asking after her husband, Margaret made her way downstairs. She often had dinner with the Broadwood before a warm fire, finding that doing so made her feel closer to Welles and helped heal the pain of the separation he'd forced upon them both.

She swung open the door, glad to see the fire was already crackling merrily in the hearth, and the candles lit. But there was no dinner tray in the usual place. Wondering if she'd beaten Fenwick to the study, Margaret turned, meaning to go in search of the butler.

"Hello, Lady Welles."

Margaret halted at the sound of his voice. She hadn't heard the low, rumbling baritone in so long, she thought, for a moment, that she'd imagined it. Ignoring the sudden fluttering of her heart, she turned and made her way to the piano bench, meaning to sit down.

"Were you expecting Henri, perhaps? Or another one of your destitute artists?"

"What are you doing here, Welles?" He'd been lying in wait for her, that much was obvious, but Margaret assumed he would choose the drawing room or even her chambers should he wish to speak to her. But *not* this room.

"I live here. Christ, what have you done to my study, Maggie?"

This was now *her* conservatory and to that end, she'd

replaced some of the starkly masculine furnishings with lighter pieces of furniture and redecorated. The room was now all pale blues with only a touch of brown and she'd replaced the heavy velvet curtains with a wispier fabric.

She came toward her husband. Welles was glorious, as usual. He sprawled across one of the dainty chairs she'd recently purchased, his big frame far too large for the delicate piece of furniture. One long leg was hooked over the arm. There was no coat of indigo tonight, only a stark white shirt unbuttoned at the throat, half-tucked into a pair of leather riding breeches. Her heart twisted pleasurably at the sight.

"This is now my conservatory, my lord. I entertain guests here."

"Oh, yes, your hordes of penniless musicians. Like Henri."

There wasn't anyone of Margaret's acquaintance named Henri, but she didn't bother to mention that to him. An open bottle of wine sat on a side table to his right; a Bordeaux. Welles held a glass of the jewel-toned liquid, while another sat waiting for her. Margaret picked up her glass and took a seat in the chair beside him. Her heart was beating madly, unsure what his presence here meant.

"I am a supporter of the arts." She took a sip of the wine.

"I'm glad." He gazed at her intently, as if considering what else to say. Welles was rarely at a loss to be charming or conversational. It was unlike him to be so hesitant with her.

Margaret stared into the fire. She was still hurt from their last encounter, bruised and bleeding from the accusations he'd thrown at her, even though she knew the source of his anger. The remnants of the letter from the duke, which had sent him from her, had been sitting charred in the fire grate for her to find after Welles left the house that night.

Welles reached out and took her hand in his, surprising her. He laced their fingers together. "I miss you." The words were low and thick. "I don't want to, but I do."

The room grew silent except for the sound of the fire.

"Now would be the appropriate time for you to say you've missed me as well." He turned to her.

"Why did you marry me, Welles?"

A log popped in the fire. "Because I wanted you," he said, confused. "You *know* that." The dark waves of his hair fell to touch his cheek. "*All* of you. Not only the naughty bits, although they are very lovely indeed." A deep sigh. "I'm making a mess of this."

"I don't want you to be here in spite of yourself, Welles. I don't wish to be the source of your resentment especially since I would have been perfectly happy with Carstairs."

"Would you? Been perfectly happy? I think not."

"If you have come to lay blame at my feet again, please rethink your position. We can continue to have a distant marriage. I'd prepared myself for such a thing before I met you. I find I enjoy my independence with no husband underfoot."

He put down his wine glass and stood. For a moment, she thought he meant to leave her again, with the Broadwood and her hopes, but instead, he came to her, kneeling at her feet. His hands went to her thighs as he placed his head in her lap, nuzzling at her stomach.

"I was gone overlong," he whispered, the words vibrating down between her thighs. "Forgive me."

Margaret shook her head, all her pain over their separation coming to the forefront. A tear ran down one cheek. "You were," she choked out before sinking her fingers into the dark waves of his hair. "We should talk, Welles. There are a great many—"

"No. Later. No talking."

Hands dipped beneath the hem of her dress. The warm caress of his fingers traveled up her silken-clad legs to her thighs where he toyed with the tops of her garters.

The slow rush of Welles crawled up her skin, his very nearness more potent than any drug. Nothing between them had been settled, although apparently his promise never to consummate their marriage was about to be broken.

The warmth of his hand moved against the inside of her thigh. His fingers trailed through the soft hair of her mound, teasing the very top of her crease and the small bit of flesh hidden there, already swollen and aching.

"Lady Welles, it appears you are much happier to see me than you originally let on." His finger dipped through the moisture coating her flesh. Gently he pressed two fingers inside her as Margaret shivered in response.

Her forehead fell against his shoulder. Brazenly she tipped her hips in the direction of his questing hand and heard a low chuckle in his chest. "I'm still angry," she breathed.

"Good. So am I." He lifted his chin, mouth seeking hers for an urgent kiss that spoke of his ultimate possession of her. Coaxing her lips to part, his tongue sought out hers, deepening the kiss until Margaret went limp. His mouth moved from hers. "But I won't leave you again."

Pressing a kiss to the corner of her mouth, Welles stood, despite her protests, taking her with him. His mouth trailed over the skin of her neck as he turned her to face the chair. "Get on your knees," he whispered.

Shaking, Margaret did as he asked. Her breasts pushed against her bodice painfully, her nipples hard and aching. His hand ran up and down the length of her spine. "Stay, Maggie." Fingers toyed with the delicate hairs at the base of her neck. "Don't make me tie you," he murmured. His lips brushed against her ear. "Though I admit, I wouldn't mind doing so. Especially if I find out Henri is your lover."

"Welles—" Why did he think she had a French lover?

"Is that why you came home?" She gasped as he started lifting her skirts. "Because you thought I had a lover?"

"No, Maggie. I came home because I can't stay away from you." Another kiss. "So many petticoats." She heard a rip as material fell away from her backside. "A waste of good cotton, in my opinion. But not to worry. I'll buy you a whole slew of new underthings if you like."

The air of the room touched the bare skin of her buttocks as he traced the base of her spine to cup one cheek.

"Christ, you've a lovely, beautiful ass, Lady Welles."

His declaration was followed by the press of his lips against her skin, then the graze of his teeth. Fingers ran the length of her slit as Margaret struggled to breathe. Waiting. He had aroused her so thoroughly with the barest touch, her entire body was throbbing. Perhaps she'd been wanton her whole life and never realized it until Welles.

Margaret reached out, her fingers digging into the cushions of the chair.

"Good girl, Maggie." He kissed the exposed skin of her lower back. "You've ascertained I'll be breaking my earlier promise never to consummate our marriage?"

"Yes," she breathed as the heat coiled within her.

"I find it an unacceptable way to live, not being inside you."

He moved his fingers along the slick folds of her crease, his movements measured. Controlled. Intentionally avoiding the one spot which would give her the most pleasure. She bit her lip to keep from begging. "You still blame me."

"I am working through that. Your current efforts to meet me halfway are helping immensely." He nipped at her skin.

She whimpered, pushing back with her hips against the pressure of his fingers.

"I know, sweetheart." The rustling sound of his clothing met her ears.

Her cry echoed loudly in the study as Welles drove inside her with one, hard thrust, pushing her face against the seat of the chair. One arm gripped her around the waist, holding her so she couldn't move. The other hand moved between her thighs, fingers brushing with the lightest of touches until Margaret was begging, shamefully, for release.

Welles took her roughly, his pace steady and hard. If this was her punishment for making him want her, it was a price she would gladly pay. Her entire body sharpened, honed to a fine point as her muscles clenched in anticipation of her release. Margaret hung on the edge of the precipice waiting for the fall.

Welles stopped moving. Stopped the gentle caress against her.

"Please." She pushed back futilely against him. She tried to press herself against the chair to relieve the ache, but he wouldn't allow it.

"Oh, Maggie." Gently he kissed the back of her neck and the curve of her shoulder before pressing his forehead against her back. He was saying something, repeating a string of words into the silk. The same cadence as what he'd whispered to her at Elysium.

He withdrew and pressed forward until she moaned.

"Whatever our souls are made of," she heard him say softly against her back as his fingers moved against her flesh again, "hers and mine are the same." He kissed the skin of her back and then gently pinched the tiny bud where her pleasure pooled between his fingers.

Margaret screamed out his name as the release roared through her. Her hips bucked wildly against him, the ridge of her teeth biting into the chair cushion. Welles held her tightly, groaning at the clench of her muscles pulling him deeper inside. The pleasure was so exquisite she couldn't think how she'd survived these last weeks without him.

Welles thrust hard into her again. Each stroke deeper

than the last until, with a muttered oath, he withdrew, and warmth splashed across her buttocks.

JESUS.

Maggie still trembled, her body shaking with the intensity of her release. He'd wanted nothing more than to stay inside her as his own climax ripped through him, but he couldn't. Tony may have come to terms with his marriage and his need for the small woman beneath him, but his mind refused to contemplate a child.

Taking a ragged breath, he laid his head against her back, struggling to regain control of himself. He told his racing heart, in no uncertain terms, to stop stretching in her direction. The sensation was bloody painful.

This was why he'd never sought her out after the house party at Gray Covington. Maggie had an inconceivable amount of power over Tony which was, frankly, *terrifying*. He'd come to the realization after staring at the account books and having no idea what was written. He was in love with her. It would take some time to get used to the idea.

Whatever our souls are made of, his and mine are the same.

It was a quote from a torrid love story his stepmother had been reading years ago that he'd happened upon in the library. She'd underlined the passage, probably thinking of Tony's father. Tony had shaken his head at Amanda's romantic nature even as the quote stayed with him. The words had spilled from his mouth tonight and when he'd made love to Maggie at Elysium, speaking his heart's truth.

Gently, he turned her over and cupped her face, pressing their foreheads together. "Did I hurt you?"

Her eyes were heavy-lidded and dazed. The plump lips of

her mouth turned in a seductive smile. "Not in the least. I am much sturdier than I look."

Tony's chest contracted. "I know." He pressed a tender kiss to her mouth. It was one of the reasons he felt so strongly about her. Maggie was a tiny ship, who though pitched about with sails shredded, nonetheless weathered all storms. She was far stronger than he would ever be.

"I think," he tucked a strand of hair behind her ear, "we should have something to eat and continue this conversation upstairs." Taking her torn petticoats, Tony wiped gently at her buttocks and thighs. He picked her up, gratified when she didn't object and instead hid her head in the curve of his shoulder, clinging to him like a small monkey.

"Would you like a bath?"

She nodded.

"With me?" He nibbled at her earlobe. She would want to talk about their separation and his feelings for the Duke of Averell. But Tony had decided one had little to do with the other.

"Definitely." She kissed his neck.

Holding on to her, he grabbed her ruined petticoats with one hand and tossed them into the fire. He walked to the door, smiling as she glanced over his shoulder at the Broadwood.

"You can play the piano tomorrow." He pressed a kiss to her temple. "There's another instrument I wish you to play tonight."

"I can't believe I'm saying this, but I've missed your improper comments."

"Henri doesn't ply you with flirtatious innuendo?"

Maggie cupped his face between her slender hands. "There is no one but you, Welles."

He knew that. There was no one else for him either.

Carrying her upstairs, Tony saw her surprise as he

bypassed her room in favor of his. Tossing her on the bed, he stood over her, skirts spread out with her torn petticoats sticking out from beneath the hem, admiring the shape of her calves and ankles. "I'm going to find Fenwick and have the bath and food sent up." He leaned over her and pressed a kiss to her lips. "Stay where you are."

"Or you'll tie me?" She sat up on her elbows and regarded him with her lips twitching.

Naughty thing.

"I was correct, Lady Welles. You aren't nearly as nice as you appear."

34

Margaret awoke the next morning to a slow crawl of butterfly kisses against her eyes, her lips, her cheek, the curve of her ear and her neck. The kisses moved lower, circling her naked breasts and her stomach. Somehow without waking her, he'd managed to pull the sheets off. Margaret was sprawled naked on the bed, her hair spread over the pillows. She'd fallen asleep last night as soon as Welles had carried her from the tub, fed her, and made love to her again.

Welles looked down on her, impossibly handsome, the sapphire circles making up his eyes clearly discernible in the early morning light. One leg was thrown over her so she couldn't move. A tactic of his, she was learning, so Welles could position her any way he wished.

"Welles."

"Tony." He pressed a kiss to the corner of her mouth.

"Tony," she said, her head falling back as her husband's mouth latched around one taut nipple. "Should we not speak—"

"No. I've other things on my mind."

Margaret immediately softened at the caress of his fingers through the soft down at the apex of her thighs. Welles would *have* to talk to her at some point. He couldn't pretend the Duke of Averell didn't exist except as an object of hatred. Her husband must come to terms with a great many things if they were to be happy. But Welles was stubborn. It would take time.

I won't give up.

He made love to her slowly, taking his time, every touch and caress drawing Margaret's blood to the surface of her skin. He brought her to the edge of her senses repeatedly, until she was writhing on the bed, her wrists captured above her head in one of his hands, begging him.

When he at last thrust inside her, agonizingly slow, and released her hands, Margaret wrapped them around his neck, meeting each stroke with the tilt of her hips.

"I love you, Tony," she whispered. "I love you." It didn't matter that he wouldn't say it back; she could no longer contain the feeling of her heart. He needed to know, even if he didn't feel the same. But Margaret hoped he *would* come to love her one day.

Much later, Margaret dozed off, her head on Welles's chest. Music played in her mind, the beating of his heart keeping time while the notes and colors floated about them, becoming bright once again now that he was with her.

A lingering fear tempered her happiness, hovering just behind Margaret like a dark shadow. No matter how much Welles cared for her or promised never to leave her, he had still not completely let go of his anger toward his father.

Or her.

35

"There you are. Up to mischief, I expect."

Margaret looked from her stack of chips to the sapphire of her husband's eyes. Welles leaned against the card table, a glass dangling from one hand. His gaze dipped to the bodice of her dress which was rather modest in comparison to Lady Masterson's.

"I'm teaching her faro," Georgina said. "She's quite good, Welles."

Her husband leaned over and pressed a kiss to Margaret's temple. "I expected she would be. Lady Welles is quite intelligent and very accomplished. She also takes instruction with enthusiasm."

Margaret's cheeks warmed. "It depends on the talent of the instructor, my lord."

Welles gazed back at her, fire sparking in his eyes. He trailed a finger along her collarbone, chuckling softly.

If the onlookers at Elysium were surprised to see the infamous Lord Welles, consummate rake and libertine, doting over his bride, a woman most had dismissed earlier as too plain and unassuming to garner much attention, they didn't show it. No one at Elysium dared ask why Welles didn't stay out until dawn drinking as he used to, nor why he'd declined to take another mistress.

"I've won handily." Margaret's hand reached up to tug at the lapel of his coat. Indigo, of course, though her suggestions to wear another color resulted in only black and a brown so deep it was *nearly* black. She supposed it didn't matter. Dark colors, with little decoration, left his masculine beauty to shine like a jewel. There were times Margaret felt like a drab little mouse next to her stunning husband.

"Indeed, you have, Maggie." His eyes dropped to her mouth. "I've got to speak to Leo, but then we should head home."

"Welles, it's early. You'll spoil all her fun." Georgina laughed.

"Oh, Maggie will have fun tonight, won't you?"

"I expect I will, my lord." She shot her husband a saucy look.

"She's promised to play another duet with me." A low, amused rumble came from Welles. "I quite enjoyed the last one."

The previous 'duet' had resulted in Margaret on top of the Broadwood with Welles's dark head between her legs. A maid had nearly walked in on them. She blushed furiously and looked away.

"Good Lord, Welles," Georgina said. "What on earth are you *doing* to Maggie? I wasn't sure a person could turn such a shade of red."

Her husband ignored the question, his heated eyes still fixed on Margaret. "I'm entrusting her to your care, Georgina."

"Do you think that a good idea, my lord?" Margaret said. "There's no telling how I will corrupt Lady Masterson."

He laughed at her reply, a glorious bubbling sound that

never failed to awaken butterflies in Margaret's stomach. He tucked a strand of hair behind her ear before striding off, headed in the direction of the stairs, and up to Leo's office. When Welles reached the steps, he turned and paused, his eyes lingering on her before he continued up the stairs.

"Dear God, he's in love with you," Georgina said under her breath. "You've ruined him." Draining her wineglass, she motioned to a nearby servant for another. "I never thought I'd live to see such a thing."

"He cares for me, but it isn't love." Since their reconciliation, Margaret had whispered her love for him many times, but he'd never said the words back. It bothered her, but she remained hopeful.

"Any idiot can see it. That pea-wit certainly does." She nodded toward a stunning redhead who was looking at Margaret as if she were something distasteful. "Lady Isley." Georgina waved in the woman's direction with a false smile. "Bitch," she said, smiling.

Lady Isley's lip curled.

"I've no complaints," Margaret said.

Georgina raised a brow. "I know you don't believe me." She rolled her shoulders and Margaret watched in horror as one of Georgina's breasts appeared to break free. "I will admit you've some work to do in regard to his father, the duke, though Welles seems to have reconciled himself to marriage, at least."

Welles still refused to discuss his father. When a letter arrived from Cherry Hill, whether from Amanda or one of his sisters, her husband's mood would shift ever so slightly. Sometimes she would hear him in the study, in the middle of the night, playing the piano as he tried to make peace with himself.

"Reformed rakes do make the best husbands." Georgina wiggled her brows.

"So I understand." Yet another topic Margaret hadn't broached with her husband. The vast majority of men took a mistress at some point in their marriage. She wasn't sure he hadn't done so. She looked down at her cards. Though she couldn't imagine where he'd find the time. And his attentions toward her had only intensified.

"He's terribly complicated. But if anyone can...*mend* him, it will be you, Maggie." Georgina lifted her glass. "I've known Welles a long time and this is the first I recall him actually being...*happy*."

"I appreciate your faith." Margaret thought she would be in need of it. Shortly after they had reconciled, Welles had produced a card with the address of an apothecary, instructing Margaret to visit the establishment and ask for items to prevent a child. At first, she thought he was joking.

The look on his face told her he was not.

"You are a good friend, Georgina," she said.

Georgina took her hand. "I adore you and Welles." She tapped her finger for the dealer to give her another card. "But what brought on such sentiment? Because I went with you," she lowered her voice, "to find those little sponges? I'll admit I never knew Mr. Coventry's establishment existed let alone what sorts of interesting items could be found there."

"Among other things." Georgina *had* gone with Margaret to the apothecary. For a woman who all of London thought little more than a harlot, Georgina was surprisingly prudish. Margaret had purchased several small sponges, trying not to fall to the floor in mortification when the wizened elderly man instructed her on their use. She never told Georgina Welles had sent her there, though Georgina had surely guessed. He was determined to remain childless, despite his appetites in the bedroom.

"You're turning bright red, Margaret." Georgina nudged

her shoulder. "Good Lord, what *does* Welles do to you that has you constantly blushing?"

Everything. Anything. Apparently, she *was* wanton.

A scuffle sounded from the front of Elysium along with a string of curses. The giant who stood guard at the door, Margaret had learned was named Smith, had a hold of a rotating blob of velvet-covered, pear-shaped flesh by the arm.

"I'm a member and I *demand* to be let in. You will release my arm. Don't you know who I am?"

Margaret looked up from her cards and froze. "Bollocks."

Georgina never even raised her chin. There was always at least one altercation in the evenings at Elysium. "What is it?" She tossed a card toward the dealer.

"You tell Murphy I'm here." Lord Winthrop wailed and thrashed at Smith like a worm on a hook. "I am once again a member in good standing."

"You aren't on the list. Send a runner," Smith grunted to another one of Leo's employees standing near, his arm muscles bulging as he held the struggling Winthrop.

Georgina's admiring gaze settled on Smith. "I don't think I've ever seen an arm muscle so large."

Margaret barely heard her friend's admiration for the giant doorman. She was too unsettled by the appearance of Winthrop. Hopefully, he wouldn't spot her and try to renew their acquaintance.

"May I have a scotch, please?" she asked, stopping a passing servant. Something stronger would be required if Winthrop's presence was to be tolerated. She hadn't seen or spoken to him since the night of the duchess's ball when Welles had compromised her.

"I tell you, my debts are cleared." Winthrop's eyes roamed over the room, passing by Margaret before he uttered an oath and his gaze moved back to her. His florid face scrunched into dislike. "Taken care of by Lord Welles." He shook off Smith's arm.

※

"I WONDERED WHERE YOU'D GONE, LORD WELLES. I'VE been looking for you."

Tony paused at hearing the voice of Lady Isley on his way up the stairs to his brother's office. He meant to speak to Leo about the merchant who supplied the wine for Elysium before taking his wife home. Tony had found an irregularity in the accounts and suspected the man was skimming off the top. The last thing he wished to do was be accosted by a former lover, especially when Maggie sat downstairs.

"Good evening, Lady Isley. You shouldn't be up here wandering about unsupervised." He took her elbow to escort her back down to the first floor. This part of the second floor was off-limits to patrons, as Lady Isley was well aware.

"I thought," Lady Isley purred, "we could make use of one of Elysium's private rooms as we have in the past." Her skirts twisted around his legs as she pushed against him, the floral scent of her perfume flooding his nostrils.

"I don't think so." Lady Isley had been an occasional lover of his, but nothing more. "I thought you'd retired to the country, Lenora." He tried to steer her in the direction of the stairs.

"I found I missed the delights of London." Her fingertips trailed down his chest. "When I heard the rumor you'd married," she said, "I didn't believe it at first. You've always had an abhorrence for the institution. I was shocked to find out your little bride was Lady Dobson's niece. The tin miner's daughter."

Tony disengaged her fingers. How had he ever found Lenora remotely interesting? He couldn't recall one conversation they'd ever shared or anything remotely intelligent coming from her mouth. Lenora was painted and primped, like an overdone cake. Or a tart. He no longer found her appealing.

"I must decline, Lady Isley." A number of beautiful women had tossed themselves in his direction since his marriage, with similar results. Tony had no interest in any of them. He only saw Maggie.

His marriage didn't terrify him nearly as much as it had a few weeks ago. Instead, wedding his little pianist now gave Tony a deep sense of peace.

Lady Isley's eyes widened slightly, surprised her charms were having no effect. "You don't need to pretend to be the dutiful husband. We all know you *had* to marry her, Welles. You, of all people, getting caught in an indiscretion and then having a burst of honor." She leaned closer. "Which we all know you don't have."

Tony's jaw tightened. "If you'll excuse me, Lady Isley, I need to return to my wife."

He dropped her arm, not caring if she found it impolite. One of the runners could be sent upstairs to escort Lady Isley back to the public area. Before he could turn, she grabbed the lapels of his coat, stood on tiptoe and pressed her lips to his.

36

Margaret glanced down at the table, making herself as small as possible lest Winthrop decide to come her way, and attempted to hide herself behind Georgina.

"What in God's name are you doing?" Georgina glanced toward the door, noticing for the first time, not Smith, but the man the giant actually held in his grip. "Oh, dear. Winthrop. I was certain he'd been banned."

Margaret snuck a peek around her friend's shoulder. Her former suitor was mopping at his forehead with a handkerchief and scowling. Garbed in a brown velvet jacket trimmed in gold braid, he looked like an oversized chocolate truffle wrapped in foil and spoiling in the sun.

"Good Lord, he's *terrible*," Georgina said with a glance down at her cards. "Your aunt meant to give you to that sweating mass of velvet?"

"Yes," Margaret said, scanning the room behind her, looking for Welles. Movement caught her eye on one of the second-floor balconies. A woman pressed herself rather seductively into a gentleman who didn't seem to be resisting her. Lady Isley and—

Bile turned her mouth bitter. *Surely not.*

Lady Isley, the redhead who'd so *scornfully* examined Margaret a short time ago and found her wanting was now on the balcony directly above the gaming floor, locked in a passionate embrace with...*Welles*. Margaret's head whipped back down sharply, Winthrop and the faro game forgotten.

"Maggie? What's wrong? Are you ill?"

She looked down at her hand of faro, disinterested in the remainder of the game. And she was even wearing one of the new gowns her husband had chosen for her. A deep, jeweled sapphire that matched his eyes. Jerking her head in the direction of the landing, she lifted her glass, draining the contents.

Georgina followed the motion, her eyes widening as she caught sight of what was transpiring on the landing above them. "Maggie, I'm sure it isn't—"

"I need some air. Please excuse me." She closed her eyes for only a moment but even when she did, Margaret could still see Lady Isley and Welles. Pushing away from the table, she brushed off a startled Georgina and started through the gaming floor. Weaving her way between various card tables, roulette, and dice, Margaret's only thought was to get as far away from Welles and Elysium as she could.

At least I won't wonder any longer about Welles taking a mistress.

Wounded and angry, Margaret was at the far end of the floor when the horrible smell of talc and sweat filled her nostrils. A giant, pear-shaped form blocked her way, looming over her in brown velvet.

"You."

THE THEORY OF EARLS

TONY TURNED HIS HEAD AND LADY ISLEY'S MOUTH LANDED on his chin. He pushed her away in annoyance, nose wrinkling at the overabundance of perfume she wore.

She made a poof of surprise at his rejection, the look on her finely sculpted features almost comical.

Had the circumstances been different, Welles might have laughed out loud at Lady Isley's shock. But Winthrop's whine of indignation reached his ears, so loud it could be heard above the din of the gaming tables. The man sounded like a screeching rooster.

Lady Isley pouted. "What is it? Her? Oh, come now Welles, we can be discreet. My understanding is she's a timid thing at best."

Timid was the last thing Welles would have called his wife. Quietly determined would be a better description.

"I have a room set aside for us," Lady Isley continued. "And a friend downstairs who can join us, if you like. You've enjoyed such things in the past. Surely you need a change from the little...*sapling* you've been—"

"Lady Isley," he said in a chilly voice, "I bid you good evening." He had caught a glimpse of his wife's petite form as she sidestepped Winthrop and continued toward the far end of the gaming floor, apparently unaware Winthrop continued to stalk her from behind.

"Welles—" Lady Isley tried to stop him, and he shook her off.

Tony strode quickly down the hallway to the back staircase, intent on intercepting Winthrop before the man could catch up with Maggie again. His wife wasn't in any real danger from her past suitor; Leo had runners all over the floor who all knew Lady Welles. Even now, he saw Peckam cross the floor, his head turned in the direction of Maggie. Nodding to two other runners, the three men spread out to flank Winthrop.

Maggie didn't so much as look behind her. Her shoulders were rigid, and she was stomping toward the back door, clearly upset; he doubted it was because of a losing hand in faro.

Bloody hell.

Either his wife hadn't heard Winthrop's continued squawks of indignation, or she didn't care. She changed course abruptly, heading toward the same staircase Tony was moving down. He'd intercept her in a moment.

37

"You."

The words thundered behind her again. It was Winthrop. She hoped if she ignored his presence he would go away and plague someone else. After his persistent courtship, Margaret should have learned her lesson. What he hoped to accomplish by confronting her in her husband's club, she'd no idea. Nor did she care. Margaret didn't have the energy or time to be concerned with her previous suitor; she was too busy trying to hold her broken heart together. And decide whether she would kick or *toss* Lady Isley's voluptuous form down the stairs. Winthrop and his sweating mass could go hang.

"I'm speaking to you," he threatened behind her.

Margaret turned, the rustle of her skirts hissing dangerously around her ankles. Marching directly over to Winthrop, she didn't bother to conceal her abhorrence for him. She ignored the stares and whispers of Elysium's members, some of whom had paused, cards or dice in hand, to watch the scene unfolding.

No doubt it will be all over the gossip columns tomorrow.

The only question was whether it would take precedence over her husband's amorous attentions to Lady Isley.

"What is it you want, Lord Winthrop?" she demanded. "Speak. Unless you wish to continue our merry chase through the gaming tables."

The rubbery lips pursed before he wiped them with his sweat-stained handkerchief. He frowned, brow wrinkling to scowl at her. When Margaret didn't so much as flinch he stammered, "You"—his sweaty face crumpled—"were supposed to marry *me*."

"Was I?" Her hands went to her hips. "I don't *ever* recall agreeing to a match with you. In fact, I believe I *tossed up my breakfast* at the very thought when you proposed, right into my aunt's rose bushes. Did you take that as my agreement?"

Snickers came from the roulette table to her side.

"We were to be *married*," he stated again, puffing out his chest, which made his much fuller bottom stick out. "Your aunt promised you to me."

"Then perhaps you should take up your complaint with Lady Dobson."

His large hands clutched at his sides, the malice in his gaze thickening to hatred.

Maggie marched closer to him and watched with delight when he took a small step back.

"I'm so sorry you won't receive my substantial dowry, Winthrop. You behave as if you were entitled to it for some reason. Oddly enough, it seems my wealth has ended up in exactly the same spot it would have if I'd accepted your proposal. *Here*. Elysium." She glowered at Winthrop, daring him to contradict her. "Probably at the very faro table I've just vacated. I understand you play abysmally."

A series of shocked gasps echoed around her. Margaret ignored them all.

Winthrop's mouth popped open at her diatribe, no doubt

expecting *timid* Miss Lainscott, a girl who couldn't even meet his eyes during his pathetic courtship. Margaret was no longer playing at being a mouse to navigate a society and an aunt she detested.

I have never been that girl.

I see you, Maggie. Welles had always known. Her heart gave a painful lurch.

"Now if you will *excuse* me, Lord Winthrop," her eyes took in his sweating mass, the derision clear in her tone. "I am needed upstairs. I plan on engaging in fisticuffs with Lady Isley for having the *audacity* to kiss my husband while I was occupied playing cards."

The whispers around her grew louder at her declaration. As if she gave a *fig*.

"I bid you good evening." Margaret tilted her chin, challenging Winthrop to say more. She'd thought about fleeing Elysium, but halfway across the gambling floor, she changed her mind. Her husband *may not* love her despite Georgina's remarks. But he cared for her. *She* was Lady Welles. He had come back to *her*. Margaret would not *tolerate* Lady Isley's disrespect and would make her feelings *abundantly* clear to the red-haired harlot.

Her fingers curled into fists. She was relatively sure she could throw a decent punch.

Turning on her heel, intent on her mission, Margaret was halted by a familiar wall of muscle, clad in indigo and smelling of the outdoors and leather.

She winced as another odor invaded her nostrils.

There was also a trace of what had to be Lady Isley's perfume. *What a cloying scent.*

"Brava, Lady Welles," the wall of muscle rumbled. "Fisticuffs with Lady Isley? Over my honor? I'd no idea you were so bloodthirsty."

Margaret ignored his teasing remark. She was angry and

might burst into tears. "My lord."

Welles looked down on her, one dark brow raised at her clipped greeting, but the corner of his mouth ticked up.

"Do not," she said in a serious tone, "mock me."

His eyes glittered in the light of the chandeliers. "I would not dare to do so, Lady Welles. At the moment, you're rather frightening. Do you require my assistance?" He looked over her head at Winthrop, who was wheezing behind her.

"No. I'm doing quite well on my own, thank you. But I *am* ready to return home, my lord. Will you be staying to escort Lady Isley?"

Welles frowned. "I will be leaving with *you*." Taking her gently by the shoulders, he positioned Margaret behind him. "Stay put," he said for her ears alone. "Good evening, Winthrop. Is there something you'd like to say to *my* wife? If there is, pray continue."

Winthrop shifted back and forth, drawing attention to his choice of footwear this evening. Brown satin with gold buckles and a tiny bit of a heel.

Margaret cringed just looking at him. Now that Welles was here, her anger was rapidly being replaced by mortification at the scene she'd caused. The entire gambling floor had heard her threaten Lady Isley.

"I was not compensated nearly enough," Winthrop sputtered.

Margaret's hand tightened on the back of Welles's coat. *Compensated?*

"Indeed? My solicitors made an error? Or are you inferring I've been dishonest with you?

"Of course not." Winthrop paled, craning his neck around, suddenly aware he had become the center of attention in a most unpleasant way. "But—"

"I understand. You had a verbal agreement with Lady Dobson to marry her niece. You've missed out on her very substantial dowry." The low rumble of his voice became dangerously polite with a distinct chill.

"There was a *contract*." Winthrop looked down at his ridiculous shoes, then back to Welles, his face ugly.

"Which you neglected to sign because you took issue with some of the wording, I believe." Welles gave a graceful flick of his wrist.

"I had agreed." He pointed a finger at Margaret. "She agreed."

"Yes, I believe Lady Welles puked out her response to your proposal."

Laughter burst from the surrounding crowd.

Winthrop's jaw tightened. "I want what is due to me for her loss."

"What *you* are due?" Margaret hissed from behind Welles before his arm snaked around to squeeze her hip, asking her to be silent.

"*I* wiped your debt clean at Elysium, Lord Winthrop, and settled a sum on you for any misunderstanding that you were to wed," he paused, "*my wife*." His deep baritone went frosty, his body beneath Margaret's fingertips taut.

Welles took a step in Winthrop's direction. "If I didn't know better, Winthrop, I would think you were accusing me of *cheating* you."

The tables around them had quieted. *All* of Elysium had quieted. Peckam and several of Leo's runners circled them.

Winthrop turned a horrific shade of purple. "No, my lord."

For the first time, Margaret caught a glimpse of the power Welles wielded within the *ton*. He was already every inch the duke he would one day be.

"I thought not. You've misunderstood. Let me make things clear to you. I'd hate for you to go running about making such outlandish claims again." Welles crooked a finger in Winthrop's direction, a cold smile on his lips.

Winthrop swallowed and leaned in.

"I know *exactly* what Walter Lainscott bequeathed to his only child. *Every* penny you and that conniving harpy thought to take from her. You'd already contacted several businessmen to sell her shares of the mines, a bit prematurely, I might add."

Margaret pressed her forehead into Welles's back, inhaling sharply. My God, was there no end to her aunt's deviousness?

Winthrop's cheeks puffed out alarmingly. "It was perfectly acceptable, my lord. A wife's assets belong to her husband."

"Walter Lainscott didn't think so." Welles took a step back and pulled Margaret beneath the security of his arm. "Do not *ever* approach my wife again or I will take it as a sign you wish to settle the dispute in another way. One which you will like less. Do you understand?"

Winthrop was pale and sweaty, the strands of his hair sticking to his forehead. "I do."

Welles smiled brilliantly. "I bid you a good night, Lord Winthrop." His voice boomed across the gambling floor, as he gave an almost imperceptible nod to Peckam.

"I'll have Mr. Peckam show you to your carriage, Winthrop. Consider your membership at Elysium to be *permanently* revoked."

38

"Maggie."

Her gaze was fixed on the street outside the carriage window after having wedged herself into the corner to avoid touching him. Once he'd ushered her through the remainder of the gaming tables and out to the private garden, Maggie had shaken off his hand before climbing inside and settling herself against the leather with a puff of distress.

"Maggie," he said softly. "Please talk to me." Her declaration over engaging Lady Isley in fisticuffs explained why she'd left Georgina at the faro table. His wife had seen Lady Isley's attempts at seduction and immediately jumped to the wrong conclusion.

Annoyance flared. Why would she assume such a thing?

Why would she not?

"You will eventually need to speak to me, if only so that you can instruct me to position my tongue correctly or—"

One small, slender hand slapped sharply against the seat. "I am *not* in the mood for your blatant sexual innuendo. It ceases to amuse me. I have several things to ask you about Winthrop but first, let us discuss Lady Isley."

"Of course." He tried to take her hand and she twisted her fingers away.

"I saw you on the landing."

"What do you imagine you saw?" Maggie didn't trust him. Expected, but still painful.

"You were *kissing* Lady Isley." A muffled sound came from her.

"I was *not*. The lady in question kissed me." It wounded him that Maggie thought him unfaithful.

"Were you flirting as you...tend to do?"

"Flirting with her *as I do*? What the bloody hell does that mean?" He took off his hat and tossed it across the carriage. "No, I did not flirt with Lady Isley, nor encourage her."

Maggie's entire body shrank back a bit more. "Your reputation precedes you, my lord. Is she your mistress? I would know now, Welles."

Tony fell back against the squabs, for the first time truly *ashamed* of the sexual exploits he was well known for within the *ton*. Maggie knew of his reputation. Christ, everyone did. There was no hiding all the immoral, improper things he'd done; for God's sake, he owned Elysium. But he'd never considered how his past might hurt his wife someday, mainly because he'd never planned on having one.

"Lady Isley is not my mistress." He took a deep breath, knowing Maggie would sense immediately whether he left something out. "She and I shared an encounter or two at Elysium long ago. Well before our marriage." Truthfully, he'd not touched another woman since asking Maggie to play the piano for him in her chemise.

"In the private rooms on the second floor?"

"Yes." His wife made a small sound of pain. "But *nothing* more. She wished to...rekindle our previous association, which I declined. Maggie," he said, trying to draw her against him, "it will be hard to attend virtually any event in London without running into one of my previous lovers. You know of my reputation. My past. I can't change it."

Margaret turned her head to the window again.

"The street outside is more interesting than I am?" He slid across the squabs until she was trapped between the wall and his body.

"I have not been unfaithful to you," he said. He pressed a kiss to the delicate skin beneath her ear. "Not in mind or body." Nor did he intend to, which was surprising. "It's rather shameful, I admit, to be brought to my knees by a woman half my size who is terrible with names no matter the number of times you are introduced to a person."

"Untrue." She slid a little closer to him.

"You can't remember any of the names of our staff. You referred to Peckam earlier tonight as Peachum."

"I know Fenwick's name." She sniffed.

"I hope so. He's our butler and runs our household." Welles wrapped an arm around her. "And you eat all the currant scones, no matter how many Cook makes *even though* you are aware currant is also *my* favorite. I'm left with crumbs and nothing but insubstantial tea sandwiches."

"I wasn't aware you liked them so much. I'll try to leave you one or two in the future."

"My forgetful, scone-eating wife who," he kissed the corner of his mouth, "begged me only last night to turn her in such a way that—"

"Enough, my lord." She finally turned in his direction and grabbed the edge of his coat before one slender hand rubbed absently up and down his thigh.

"You're quite wanton, Lady Welles."

"I've been corrupted," she murmured into the folds of his coat. "I was merely a young lady avoiding marriage to a waddling pear when you came upon me." Her head fell to his chest. "You paid Winthrop to go away, didn't you?"

Tony took her hands and pressed a kiss to her fingers. "I did. He kept flinging about having a verbal agreement with your aunt and alluded to a contract, though I could find no evidence they'd actually agreed on one. Winthrop is greedy. But I understand now why you were so determined to have Carstairs. He would never have delved into your finances or taken control from you. No wonder you wanted an unintelligent husband."

"I failed miserably at that. You meet none of my parameters."

"I don't suppose I do." He held her tightly. "I'm sorry I didn't tell you about Winthrop, but my mind was elsewhere. Quite frankly, I'd forgotten all about him and his stupid shoes until tonight."

Tony had been trying to come to terms with the emotional turmoil caused by his marriage. But he'd made sure, against his solicitor's recommendations, that no matter what happened, Maggie was to be given what was hers.

"There is a bit more, I'm afraid. Your aunt, in return for throwing her support behind Winthrop to overturn that portion of your father's will, was to receive a large chunk of your dowry. Did you know your father supported your aunt for years? Probably out of guilt for the scandal he created when he married your mother. And Lord Dobson left her in dire straits when he died. I suppose she felt she had no choice."

Maggie grew very still. "Everyone has a choice. No wonder she wanted me to marry him."

"I took care of Winthrop. And I settled a sum on your aunt, with the condition that she never contact you again. You may change the terms if you wish."

"No. I don't wish." She snuggled closer. "Thank you, Welles."

"I will never touch what is yours, Maggie. If you wish to start your own bloody orchestra and pension off every ancient accordion player at Covent Garden, I will not object, but please, I prefer they not all practice in my study."

"My conservatory," she corrected him with a smile.

"You could buy dozens of pianos and put one in every room of the house. Or you could donate the entire sum to Mrs. Anderson. The money is yours and will stay yours."

"I feel much better now, my lord." Maggie took his hand and pressed a kiss to the palm before placing it to cup her cheek.

Welles's heart contracted painfully in his chest.

"You are a good husband, Welles."

He blinked, surprised at the compliment. How the *ton* would roll with laughter to know the jaded rake Lord Welles would do anything to hear such praise from his wife. "I hope to be." Voice thick with emotion, Tony brushed his lips against hers, gratified when she attempted to climb into his lap.

"I'm sorry I don't meet all of your requirements for a husband," he said into the curve of her neck. "But I can take up horse breeding or something and attempt to ignore you."

"I suppose that's something." She tilted up her chin for another kiss.

As the carriage pulled up in front of his house, Tony helped her out, tucking her into his side before leading Maggie upstairs directly to his room. Since his return, Tony had insisted she sleep next to him at night, claiming he often grew cold without her. It was the most ridiculous of excuses. The truth was he liked waking up with her next to him.

"Daisy," he called through the door to the maid who was waiting in Maggie's room. "You're dismissed for the evening.

"I'll assist my wife tonight." He shut the connecting door, after assuring his valet he could see to his own needs as well.

"Daisy must wonder why she never has to make my bed." Maggie's eyes were luminous in the candlelight, like brushed velvet.

"She will continue to wonder. I grow cold at night without you." He cupped her face in his hands and pressed a tender kiss to her lips. "I'm sorry about Lady Isley and every other woman in the future who may challenge your patience."

"I know." Her head tilted as she ran a finger down his jaw.

He spun her around and began to slowly undo the row of tiny pearl-shaped buttons at her back. After the first three, Tony pressed an open-mouthed kiss to her spine, breathing in her scent.

"I wanted you from the first moment I saw you," he whispered.

Maggie arched her back against his mouth. "When I played the piano at Gray Covington and made a complete ass of myself?"

Three more buttons, and the dress spread out across her naked shoulders. "No. Before. At dinner the first night." He kissed along her collarbone, feeling her ripple of surprise.

She drew in a sharp breath as his teeth grazed across her shoulder. "At dinner? I barely said a word to anyone. Aunt Agnes had admonished me to be silent."

"Yes, but I *saw* you, Maggie. And when you arched over the piano," he began to untie her stays, "I decided I *would* have you. I thought of nothing but tasting you. Burying myself in you. Savoring you as one does a fine wine."

A quiver shot through her as the stays fell free. "I think myself much more common. Like scotch."

Tony chuckled, sinking his fingers into her hair, pulling at the pins until the dark brown strands fell streaming over her shoulders. His hands reached around and cupped her breasts, carefully rolling her nipples between his fingers until she moaned. His cock hardened at the sound, throbbing painfully in response.

One hand slid down between her legs, feeling how soft and ready she was, though he'd barely touched her. "When I saw you again, hiding in the wisteria, determined to escape the attentions of Lord Winthrop, I had already decided to make you a most indecent request."

"You *never* meant to allow Carstairs to have me," she said.

"Nor anyone else." His fingers moved against her, listening to the delightful sounds she made. He pressed the length of his cock against her buttocks.

"Why?"

"Because you're *mine*," he whispered, turning her face to him.

39

Margaret woke and immediately stretched out her arm, surprised to find the other half of the bed wasn't full of gorgeous, muscular male. She sat up and looked toward the open door of her rooms.

Only Daisy's plump form could be seen busily laying out Margaret's clothing and bath towels. Steam floated around the maid in a thick mist.

Wherever Welles had gone, he'd ordered her a bath before leaving.

Margaret flopped back on the bed. She was ridiculously happy. While Welles hadn't said he loved her, after taking all of his actions into consideration as well as his adamant assertion he had not been unfaithful to her, it was very possible Georgina's assumption about his feelings had been correct.

I need to hear him say it.

Welles was a work in progress. When he was ready, he would tell her he loved her.

She stood and grabbed her robe at the foot of the bed, wrapping the silk around her naked body, and walked into her bedroom, sniffing the aroma of rose oil Daisy had put into her bath. The maid helped her out of her robe and into the steaming water.

Margaret closed her eyes and sank into the heated water with a groan. "Daisy, do you think you could check downstairs to see if there are any fresh currant scones?" She giggled. "Spare one or two for my husband." When the maid didn't answer, Margaret's eyes fluttered open.

Daisy frowned. She'd been doing that quite a bit of late.

"Is there something amiss, Daisy?" Margaret trailed her hand in the water. The maid insisted she was content to stay in London. Romy had been saddened but glad Daisy would stay in the family, so to speak. But perhaps she was homesick.

"No, my lady." But the maid was still looking at Margaret before a smile broke across her face. "I'll go pull out one of your new day dresses. The green sprigged muslin? It's very fetching."

"Perfect."

As she sank back into the water, Margaret's glance fell on the latest letter from Cherry Hill, this one from Phaedra. There was a new barn cat who was quite a mouser, a stray the duchess had taken in. The cat had been christened Theseus for his bravery in clearing the barn of rodents. He was most appreciative of his new mistress and showed his affection by leaving the duchess dead mice and the occasional bird in her rooms. The letter detailed Phaedra's attempts to find out how the feline was entering the house and depositing gifts for her mother.

The duchess had written a small note at the bottom of Phaedra's letter. The duke continued to decline; the brief improvement at the news of Margaret's marriage to Welles had only been temporary. Even the laudanum the doctor prescribed was no longer enough to ease his pain. She begged Margaret to convince Welles to at least return to Cherry Hill to bid his father goodbye.

Margaret pulled her eyes away from the note. Welles *should* go to Cherry Hill. Forgiving his father would not mean forgetting the duke's treatment of Welles's mother, but possibly it would ease the bitterness her husband continued to live with.

Welles had also received a letter from Cherry Hill not two days ago, another note addressed directly to him in the familiar shaking hand of his dying father and bearing the ducal seal. Mindful of what had occurred the last time Welles had received a letter from his father, Margaret had left him alone to read the contents. He'd disappeared shortly thereafter without a word. Margaret had awoken later that evening at being carried from her room to his, where she'd been dumped unceremoniously on the bed, before Welles had collapsed next to her fully clothed, reeking of scotch.

She had wisely chosen not to question him.

As Daisy dried her off, Margaret mulled over the situation, determined to find some sort of an answer to her husband's refusal to address the issues he had with the Duke of Averell. She was hesitant to push him on the subject, not wishing to shake their still fragile but strengthening reconciliation. But still, each day she grew more and more sure of Welles and their marriage. Maybe it was time to sit him down and force him to face the duke before it was too late.

Daisy pulled her stays tight before pulling the green sprigged muslin over Margaret. The maid's hands went to work on the buttons at the back, tugging on the material before pausing.

"Daisy?"

"I'm sorry, my lady. Perhaps the seamstress got your measurements wrong on this dress. It's far too tight."

The bodice hugged Margaret like a glove. If she breathed too deeply her breasts might pop out. "I think I've gained some weight," she said to Daisy. "I eat far more now than I ever did at my aunt's home, where the cook wasn't nearly as good. I'll have to watch myself. I shouldn't eat so many scones. I won't have any today." She smiled. "I don't wish to grow stout."

Daisy didn't return her smile. "My lady, if I may."

"Daisy, what is it?" She touched the maid's hand. "Do you wish to return to Cherry Hill? Please don't be worried I'll be upset. I'll be sad to lose you, but Cherry Hill is your home. I would understand."

"No, what I mean to say is, I don't wish to return to Cherry Hill. I like London and my place here. But there's something—" Daisy looked away before turning back to Margaret. "My lady, forgive me if I'm impertinent, but I've ten brothers and sisters. All younger than me." She paused. "I know what a woman looks like who—"

"That's not possible." Margaret stopped Daisy before she could hear the words she feared most. "No. I am not," she said with conviction. Her husband may have reconciled himself to having a wife, but not children, as evidenced by the more strident measures he took. Welles had been using a device he called a French letter to prevent contraception. She used the small sponges soaked in vinegar. If anything, Welles's determination to not have a child had intensified, as if ensuring he would grant his father no solace at all before he died. She hoped, one day, Welles would relent and accept a child.

But not like this.

Margaret fell back against the bed, struggling to remember the last time she'd had her courses. Not since before she'd played the piano for him at Elysium in her chemise. She calculated in her head as dread filled her.

How could I have not noticed?

She'd been so intoxicated by having Welles, the Broadwood, her music, Margaret had paid little attention to anything else.

"Say nothing, Daisy. I'm certain you are mistaken," Margaret said abruptly, as panic seeped into her veins. She pressed a hand to her stomach. *No. Please. Not yet.*

"Yes, my lady." The maid shot her a look of concern before leaving the room.

Margaret went to the seat by the window, staring out at the garden for the better part of an hour, mulling over every detail of her life, wondering how she could have ignored the signs. She'd become ill in the carriage several times in the last month, blaming it on the rough roads, and told Welles the vehicle needed new springs. Every day at tea she became nauseated, but she blamed it on the milk being spoiled. Or the fact that she hadn't cared for the sugared biscuits Cook put out. She *was* more tired than usual, but she'd been joining Welles at Elysium several times a week in addition to organizing her charitable events. Margaret had just assumed the exhaustion was due to her busy life.

He'll grow to resent me again.

Margaret slowly caressed her stomach, wondering at the life she was now certain grew within. Her husband would not be happy at the news he was to be a father.

Nothing ever works out as I plan.

Welles would be furious. He would blame her, unfairly, as he had before. She could only hope, given the state of their marriage, he would come to terms with the child. Margaret would even agree to withhold the news from Cherry Hill if that was what he wished.

"No. I can't be," she whispered, a lump forming in her throat.

"You can't be what?" Welles appeared in the doorway, smiling and looking ridiculously splendid in his riding clothes. He'd been up early, racing around the park as he liked to do, unaware his wife had just betrayed him in the worst way possible.

Well it's his bloody fault as well. She thought of the things he'd done to her last night.

"Your cheeks are pinking, Lady Welles." He leaned down to kiss her. "What are you thinking of?"

That I'll lose you.

Margaret forced a smile to her lips. "Mrs. Anderson is attempting to convince me to publish my sonata. I'm not sure she'll succeed. I don't feel it's ready yet."

Welles kissed her again. "You must, Maggie. It's a beautiful piece. And you've worked so hard on it."

It was a beautiful piece. She'd written it for *Welles,* after all, though she'd never told him. Would he send her away? Insist she get rid of the child before it could be born? She already knew he would go to great lengths to hurt the Duke of Averell.

Her fingers tightened over her stomach protectively.

"I'll see you at dinner," he strode through the connecting doors calling for his valet, "Maggie mine."

Margaret watched as Welles walked back and forth, various items of clothing coming off to reveal his beautiful form until his valet shut the door.

Maybe it wouldn't be as bad as she thought—telling Welles he would be a father.

No. It was far worse.

40

"I am with child."

Tony's head lifted from his desk to take in the tiny form of his wife, standing defiantly before him in the parlor which he'd been forced into using as his study. He'd only just returned from reviewing the Elysium account books with Leo and meeting with several wine merchants who were vying for a contract with the club. Winthrop had had the audacity to demand his membership be reinstated, which was highly amusing.

Tony had denied it.

"Excuse me?" At first, he thought he'd misheard her.

"I said, my lord," her chin tilted mulishly, and her eyes flashed dark fire at him, "I am with child."

The floor fell away beneath his feet while his vision narrowed on Maggie, the words ringing in his ears. A brief, tiny burst of joy tried to make its way out of the darkness rapidly enveloping him, but Tony viciously stomped the light out.

His eyes ran over every inch of her, searching for the

truth in her words. Tony was intimately acquainted with every inch of his wife's body, and—his gaze dropped to the abundant spill of her breasts over the neckline of her gown.

Bloody hell.

The news shouldn't be unexpected, given his inability to keep his cock in his pants when his wife was in close proximity. But Tony had ensured they took precautions, as he had for years, determined *not* to have a child before his prick of a father was in the ground and couldn't possibly delight in the knowledge he would have an heir.

He stood and went to the sideboard, not even bothering with a glass as he took a deep draught of the bottle of brandy he kept there. Pausing to wipe his mouth he uttered, "Well, that's bloody inconvenient." All the feelings about his marriage, his father, his mother's death, erupted once again after having been contained for so many weeks. At the moment, he detested his weakness for the woman standing before him. Resenting her and the child she carried.

"I know this isn't what you planned. But it isn't unexpected—"

"Because I fuck you so much?" He swallowed more brandy, feeling the burn go down his throat and into his belly. The bitterness, dark and ugly, gnawed at him. The promise he'd made to his mother as she lay dying in his arms echoed in his ears, that Tony would make the Duke of Averell pay for what he'd done.

Maggie flinched. "There isn't any need to be crude."

"Do you know I saw my mother's stomach move? My unborn sibling was trapped inside her, slowly dying along with my mother. I watched until the movement stilled and then, so did she."

His wife paled, her eyes fluttering shut against the picture he painted. "Tony—"

He was so enraged, so full of pain remembering the death of his mother. It had never really gone away. The coppery smell of her blood still lingered in his nostrils even after all these years. Maggie was stopping him from avenging her.

"Are you sure it's mine?" he said in a nasty tone, delighted to watch the oval of her face whiten until she resembled one of the statues his stepmother liked to collect. "After all, you were entertaining a mob of piano players while I stayed at Elysium. Are you sure you didn't give one of them lessons in something else?"

"You're being unreasonable. And horrible." She stepped back in shock, the woman who loved him with every fiber of her being. He was doing his best to destroy that love despite his soul screaming at him to stop.

"I understand," she clenched her small fists, struggling for composure, "you are less than pleased with this news, considering the steps we've both taken—"

"Did you, Maggie? Take steps?" He sounded irrational and didn't care.

"I can see we can't possibly discuss this calmly. This is a shock to both of us." Maggie went still. Like she used to with her aunt to avoid attention. That she was doing so now infuriated Tony.

"Can't you just get rid of it?"

Dear God. He wished the words back before they'd completely left his mouth.

Maggie sucked in her breath so sharply he thought she might fall over. Her hand went out to steady herself against a table. She was regarding him with horror, the kind usually reserved for monsters.

"Christ, Maggie. I—"

She shook her head and backed away from him. "Don't touch me."

Pain dug into his heart at the words. Tony held out his

hand to her as if Maggie were a small bird he didn't wish to frighten. "I didn't mean it."

Maggie clasped her hands over her stomach in a protective gesture and stayed out of his reach.

She's afraid of me. The knowledge stung.

"I think you did, Welles." Maggie shook her head as tears streamed down her cheeks and a tortured sound left her. He'd never seen her cry before, not really, and certainly not as if he'd broken her heart. "I think next you will be asking if you can get rid of *me*."

He swung up the bottle unable to look at her a moment longer. Tony had gone cold all over the chill of her confession hardening him to ice. Averell was going to win. There would be an heir to Cherry Hill. He had high hopes the child would be a girl, but he didn't think he'd be so lucky. If his wife didn't leave the room immediately there was no telling what other vile things he'd hurl at her.

"I love you, Tony," Maggie whispered. "Your mother would want you to be happy. She never meant—"

"Get out of my sight," he roared at the mention of his mother. "You have *no* idea what she would want." He turned back to the brandy, guzzling as much of the bottle as possible before needing to take a breath.

"Tony—"

"Leave." Wiping his mouth, he barely flinched when the door slammed shut behind him. When he finally turned around the room was empty.

Maggie was gone.

※

THE NEXT MORNING, AFTER A NIGHT SPENT CLOSETED IN the small parlor with only alcohol and a plate of scones to fortify him—the last done in a burst of anger since his wife liked them so much—he decided to seek out Maggie. He'd behaved abominably.

As he went upstairs to dress, ignoring the constant stream of chatter from his valet, Tony glanced at the door leading to Maggie's rooms. It was shut against him. The doors were *always* left open. He often joked Maggie's rooms had become nothing more than a large armoire to store her clothing and other fripperies because she no longer slept anywhere else but with him.

Because I get cold at night without her.

His heart thudded painfully in his chest as he stared, unsettled by the sight of the closed door. Tony waved off his valet and knocked softly. When there was no response, he flung the door open.

The room was empty. Strangely still and quiet. The sight unnerved Tony and filled him with a terrible foreboding. Where would she have gone so early in the morning?

He made his way to the breakfast room where there was still no sign of his wife. Fenwick greeted him with the morning papers but claimed to have no knowledge of the whereabouts of Lady Welles.

Tony suspected the butler was lying. Fenwick knew everything.

As he munched on a piece of bacon, he thought back to the mountain of scones and eggs Maggie had started consuming when they had breakfast together, which was nearly every morning. He should have guessed she was with child. He meant to beg her forgiveness for the way he'd spoken to her. And the utterly revolting thing he'd suggested in his horrible anger at her. At himself.

Filled with self-loathing, he pushed aside his bacon.

"You must be announced." Fenwick was agitated and speaking to someone in the hall.

"I don't need an announcement." Leo's amused voice

filtered toward Tony as his brother's dark head popped through the breakfast room door.

Leo rarely left his bed before noon. Maggie was nowhere to be found. Nor Daisy, her lady's maid, for that matter. He threw down his napkin, glaring at his brother as Leo came in and sat down next to him.

"Where is she?"

"As a greeting, I thought for sure you could do better. You look like hell, by the way." Leo's pleasant manner held an undercurrent of hostility.

"I fell asleep in my study, which is actually the parlor. Maggie needed a conservatory." Tony waved toward the sideboard, anxiety clawing at him. His wife had left him. Not that he blamed her after he'd—Tony winced again at the things he'd said. She couldn't have gotten far. "Breakfast?"

"Thank you. I'm starving." Leo sat down as a footman served him a portion of eggs and toast. "The jam as well." He pointed.

After a few minutes of watching his brother devour nearly everything on his plate, Tony finally spat out, "Where's my wife? I assume you know, or you wouldn't be here."

Leo sighed and took one more bite of his bacon before putting his knife and fork aside. Placing his fingers together in a point, he regarded Tony coldly.

His brother was furious with him. Leo and he rarely argued, though they did have their disagreements. This was different. "Leo—"

"I should beat you for the things you said to Maggie," he said, all pretense at pleasantry gone. "I don't care if you are going to be a bloody duke."

"I see you've spoken to her." Shame filled him.

"Yes, I have. I will only assume you were briefly out of your mind to have said what you did to Maggie. Who *loves* you despite every effort you've made to drive her away. You may have finally succeeded."

Tony rubbed at the sharp sting over his heart as he glared back at his brother. "You don't understand."

Leo slammed his fist on the table. "I understand your hatred of the duke. He's a selfish prick. A terrible human being. He's done questionable things."

Much like I have.

"You are punishing *Maggie*, not him. *She* is paying the price for your arrogance."

Just as my mother did.

Tony took a deep, painful breath at the realization, seeing far too many comparisons between himself and his father. Or at least the arrogant man the Duke of Averell had been.

"That you would be so *selfish* as to suggest such a despicable thing simply because your scheme against the duke might be infringed upon? Especially given you rut after her like a dog in heat?" Leo sneered at Tony in contempt. "You are becoming the very thing you hate."

Tony gripped his fork, resisting the urge to stab his brother with it. He didn't care to have Leo come to the same conclusion as Tony had a moment ago. "Enough, Leo," he snarled. "I take your point. I was angry and lost my temper. I didn't mean it. I *don't* mean it."

Leo calmed somewhat. "Maggie will *not* come home to you and I don't blame her. She is angry and hurt. If you decide to fetch her—"

"I have every intention of doing so."

"You should wait a week or two and then beg her forgiveness. She's very upset and doesn't want to see you at present. I hope you won't be foolish, Tony. I've no desire to see you become one of those jaded rakes who skirts around the edges of ballrooms ogling the young ladies before returning home to their empty houses." His brother stood and placed his napkin on the table. "I'm sure you can imagine where she is."

Tony sat back as Leo left the breakfast room, slamming the door behind him. He knew exactly where Maggie had gone, damn her. The one place he'd avoided for years. The last time he'd visited Tony had vowed never to return.

Cherry Hill.

41

Maggie walked slowly up the stairs, holding on to the railing as she did so. Every time she made her way to the second floor, she was reminded these were the steps Katherine, Welles's mother, had fallen down, and she took special care.

A large male cat, one ear partially missing and black as coal, shot down the stairs, startling her. A shriek followed the cat's departure, coming from the direction of the duchess's rooms.

Phaedra came around the corner, skidding to a stop as she narrowed her eyes. "Theseus!"

Margaret bit her lip to keep from laughing. The big tomcat's adoration of the duchess was well known among the household staff at Cherry Hill. No matter Phaedra's best efforts, Theseus continued to leave gifts of dead birds and mice for the mistress of the house.

Phaedra sped by her on the stairs. "Today," she informed Margaret as she passed, "it was a mole. Mama was horrified. She may have fainted."

"I shall check on her." Margaret turned sideways, placing

a hand on the small bump of her stomach, and continued up the stairs.

Margaret drank in the stunning beauty of Cherry Hill, the Duke of Averell's seat. She tried to imagine Welles as a child, growing up in this enormous house, perhaps running outside to play soldiers with Leo. Comprised of three separate wings and constructed of stone, Margaret had not yet walked from one end of the house to the other. Though the estate was grand, the furnishings were warm and welcoming, instead of the pretentious formality she'd expected from a duke. The downstairs was paneled in dark woods and jewel tones, with plush carpets thrown over the heavy wood floors. Margaret's rooms were bright and sunny and painted a lovely shade of cream with accents of rose and gold.

Cherry Hill was a study in understated elegance, just like the Averell mansion in London. She thought her new mother-in-law had something to do with the warmth to be found in both places.

Upon her arrival at Cherry Hill, Margaret had stepped out of the coach and immediately been embraced by the duchess and the rest of the family. The girls swirled around her, chattering and arguing. A splash of paint decorated Theo's cheek. Romy had been making something with feathers, for they were stuck in her hair as well as that of Miss Nelson, who had apparently been assisting her.

Phaedra had hugged her tight before taking off to run after Theseus, the cat.

Margaret had sobbed at that first sight of them. She hadn't been sure of her welcome but need not have worried. Romy had held her hand and admonished her not to cry.

"It's only that I've missed you all," Margaret had said before bursting into tears again.

The duchess had kissed her cheeks, cupping Margaret's

face between her palms. She wasn't easily fooled. "My dear daughter. Welcome home."

It had been an emotional reunion, to say the least.

Margaret continued to climb up the stairs toward the room at the far end of the hall, first stopping in to check on the duchess. Her mother-in-law was lying on a chaise lounge, one hand over her eyes, using the other to fan herself with a dramatic wave.

"Your Grace?"

"Good Lord, Margaret. Do you see the mole? The poor thing has more holes in it than one of Romy's pincushions. And no eyes that I can see. I rang for a footman to dispose of the creature. What is wrong with Theseus? Why can he not thank me by purring quietly in my lap?"

Margaret looked carefully around the room until she saw a dark pile of fur. Moving closer, she scrunched down to check for any signs of life.

"Is it dead?"

"Quite." Margaret stood. "Theseus is very devoted to you as evidenced by the gifts he brings."

"I would prefer an orchid. Or even a spray of violets." A trickle of laughter escaped her. "I assume you are on your way to see Marcus?" The duchess's pretty face grew anguished, and her lip trembled before she smiled bravely. "I'm sorry, my dear, I get melancholy. My husband would be very upset if he knew, so please let it be our secret. And remind His Grace," she said, her voice rough with tears, "we are dining together tonight so he should look his best." She winked.

"I will make sure not to tire him, Your Grace." Margaret stepped toward the door, eyes averted from the poor mole.

Margaret had been prepared to hate the Duke of Averell, despite the affection Amanda and the girls had for him. She felt quite the opposite now. Whatever type of man Marcus had been, the selfish father Welles remembered, the man dying inside the lavish suite of rooms, was that man no longer. The duke and Margaret had become friends during her stay at Cherry Hill. She found him to be loving and affectionate, a man who adored his wife and daughters. After being introduced and learning Margaret had only just begun to play faro, the duke had taken it upon himself to teach her every card game and trick he knew. Which was substantial.

The duke's nurse, Gladys, came out of the double doors carrying a basin of water. She bobbed politely at the sight of Margaret. "Lady Welles. His Grace is expecting you. He says he will take you for every bit of your pin money." She touched Margaret's forearm. "I've given him his medicine. Don't be alarmed if he nods off. I thought he should rest before dinner tonight with the duchess. He wishes to be at his best." The nurse's eyes grew watery, for she adored her charge as well.

Margaret nodded. "I won't, Gladys. Thank you."

She entered the darkened room, gratified to see the duke sitting up in bed, two fluffy pillows lodged firmly behind his back. He was already toying with a deck of cards, the elegant, tapered fingers trembling as he did so.

"Hello, Maggie." He looked up and winked at her, his wide mouth ticked upward in a smile she was more than familiar with. "I'll take your pin money today if you aren't careful."

The Duke of Averell was still a handsome, charming devil no matter the ravages of the disease which was slowly killing him. Just like his son. The eyes Welles had inherited from his father were still brilliant, the darkening rings of blue stark and glowing in his face, a sharp contrast to his withering, frail body. No matter the feelings of her husband for his father, it saddened Margaret greatly that the duke was not long for this world.

"You're very bold, Your Grace," she said in a saucy tone. "I may have a trick or two up my sleeve."

A rumbling laugh came from him, another thing he had in common with his son, except the duke's amusement ended in a bout of coughing. He waved toward a pitcher of water, and Margaret hastened to fetch him a glass. Holding the water to his lips, she watched him drink.

Once the coughing subsided, he gave a great sigh and sat back, taking her hand in his.

"Deal, my girl."

They played whist. The duke, she suspected, allowed her to win, for she only lost a bit of her pin money. After an hour or so, much sooner than Margaret wished, he laid down his cards and declared the game over for the day.

"I find I'm very tired, my child."

She nodded and turned her head, not wishing him to see her blinking away tears. The duke's face was etched with pain no matter how much medicine Gladys gave him.

Margaret stood to leave, and the duke reached out, his fingers encircling her wrist. "Wait, daughter."

"Your Grace, would you like me to read to you? Perhaps play you something soothing?" The conservatory was directly below the duke's rooms. Sometimes he asked her to play with the windows open so he could hear her.

"No, my dear. Did you know my first wife was a pianist?" He shot her a look. "We've never spoken of the past, but perhaps we should. Time is running out and I wish you to know some things." He winced in pain, lips tightening before he took her hand. "From my own lips. Amanda will white-wash my history because she loves me. Welles and Leo will paint me as the devil, which I fear is closer to the truth."

"Your Grace—" Margaret tried to dissuade him. His tone had all the makings of a deathbed confession, one she didn't feel ready to hear.

"I became a duke shortly before marrying Katherine," he said without preamble. "I was arrogant," he squeezed her fingers, "which I'm sure you find hard to believe. Handsome. Titled. I already had a reputation in London for the things I had done." His eyes took on a faraway look. "I was a careless father with Welles. I was absent for most of Leo's life, even though he was born on the other side of the estate. I was too busy being...a duke." He waved his hand. "Feeling important. Having women throw themselves at me and men court my favor. I was a poor husband to Katherine. More terrible to Leo's mother." He paused as another fit of coughing plagued him.

"We do not need to continue, Your Grace." Margaret patted a napkin against his lips.

"Oh, but we must. I will never have an opportunity to tell Welles or Leo." He took her hand again. "You must not blame Welles for his aversion to me. I accept his hatred, though it pains me. You see, Welles adored his mother. She taught him the piano. Coddled him. I took that from my son." A ghost of a smile crossed his lips. "Katherine saw him as not the duke he would be but the child he was, something my own selfishness and attention to duty did not allow. *That* Welles was a much gentler human being than the man you married. Another thing I took from him. But you see *Anthony*, I suspect. As Katherine did. It is a rare gift." A choked laugh escaped him. "Much as Amanda sees me."

Margaret blinked back a tear thinking of her husband.

I see you, Maggie.

She had never thought the same in reverse. Never assumed it was anything but her talent on the piano which had brought them together; instead, it was something much more profound. And beautiful.

"I wish to thank you for coming to Cherry Hill. Your presence brings joy to my family. And I especially thank you for the gift of my grandchild. I wish I was going to live—"

"Your Grace." She took his hands as tears ran unbidden down her cheeks.

"Don't you start behaving like Amanda," he snapped. "Watering pots, all of you."

"I'm sorry, Your Grace." He was telling her goodbye and Margaret was loath to hear it.

"Amanda despairs of my passing, but it was a foregone conclusion from the moment we met. I'm many years her elder. Promise me you will forgive Welles for whatever he did to bring you here. I do not wish to be the cause of another estrangement. You love him. And he must love you greatly to have put aside his hatred of me to wed you." His eyes were fluttering shut, his voice becoming thin. "I've left letters for both my sons."

"Your Grace, we can speak of this later."

"Amanda will not remember when the time comes," he continued in a whisper. "My beautiful summer strawberry will be devastated that I have left her—a duchess without a duke to fuss over. The girls will be distraught. I expect Theseus will be the only one who will not take notice of my death." A raspy chuckle sounded. "I must depend on you, my dear daughter, to take care of all the Barringtons in my absence."

Margaret pressed his hand to her cheek and nodded.

"Especially Welles."

42

I never expected to see this place again.

Tony looked out the window of the coach as the estate of the Duke of Averell came into view. A thousand memories filled his mind. Racing on horseback across the fields. His mother taking him fishing at the small pond they'd just passed. Sword fighting with his best friend, the maid's son, Leo.

His mother dead at the bottom of the stairs awash in her own blood.

Amanda would be furious he'd waited so long to come, he thought, as the coach began to ascend the long drive leading up to the house. Despite his brother's advice to leave his wife be for a bit and Tony's own reluctance at coming here, he should have left immediately for Cherry Hill. But he'd been a coward. Tony was deeply ashamed of the things he'd said, and he'd needed time to decide what he would say to the Duke of Averell.

As it turns out, the speech Tony had practiced in his head wouldn't be needed.

The news that *he* was now the Duke of Averell had reached Tony at a coaching inn halfway to Cherry Hill, the messenger recognizing his coach. He'd sent the man ahead to inform Leo and continued resolutely on, wishing now that he'd forced Leo to come with him.

As the coach rolled up the long drive, the main house came into view, as immense and majestic as it had been on the day he'd left, vowing never to return. One more thing to add to the list of things he'd promised never to do but had been forced to reconsider. Two nights ago, he'd played the Broadwood and drunk scotch while longing for his wife. He'd allowed the joy at having his own child blossom as his hands ran over the keys, the room filling with the sound of Chopin. He thought of his father and what he would say to him after all these years. Could he forgive the duke? Maggie would wish it, if only because it would bring Tony peace.

When he'd finally made his way to bed, Tony had fallen into a deep slumber. He'd dreamt of his mother. Not of her death but of playing the piano and smiling. Then her face had become Maggie's. He'd awoken feeling calm and ready to face the old duke.

Now his father was dead.

Servants in the duke's livery, all wearing black armbands, rushed out to greet the coach. As the door opened, Graven, Cherry Hill's butler, bowed.

"Your Grace, welcome home."

***

MARGARET SAT IN THE CONSERVATORY, HER FINGERS running over the keys, admiring the sound of the piano. The poor instrument had been woefully out of tune when she'd first arrived, which Romy had seized upon as an excuse for her poor playing. The duke had insisted the piano be tuned immediately for his new daughter-in-law.

Grief filled her.

Marcus Barrington, the Duke of Averell, was dead.

Amanda had been with him the night he died, cradling his head against her heart as the duke departed this world for the next. Gladys had found her the following morning, sobbing quietly and refusing to leave her dead husband's side until Romy had appeared to lead her away.

Margaret's hands banged against the keys as another wave of sorrow engulfed her. The late duke had told all of them, in a letter read aloud at his request by Margaret, that there was to be no wailing, banging, prostrations of grief or other nonsense. He loved them all and felt honored to be loved in return.

Welles had been sent for, of course. And Leo.

He's not Welles anymore. He's Averell.

Margaret's heart broke that the duke had died without reconciling with his heir.

She tried to play a few bars of her sonata, the one written for her husband, and stopped. Her entire body ached with pain for the Barringtons. And for herself. Her husband hadn't come for her immediately, nor had she had word of him. Amanda had already told Margaret to consider Cherry Hill her home. There was no need for her to ever return to London should she not wish it. She was a duchess now and could do as she pleased.

I need to remember that. I am now the Duchess of Averell. Her hand cupped her stomach for a moment. *You are likely Lord Welles.*

Her hands returned to the keys. Her father-in-law had requested no lavish wake. No grand funeral. He wished to be buried in the family churchyard, an old copy of the Iliad tucked beneath his arm.

When Amanda heard the request, she burst into tears and fled the room, Romy, Theo and Phaedra trailing her. It was Miss Nelson who told Margaret the significance of the book to the duke and duchess.

'She was reading the Iliad when he fell in love with her.'

Margaret's fingers hit a wrong key and she bit her lip at the desolation filling her heart.

"Have you not been practicing?"

The baritone trailed down her back and tingled at the base of her spine. Margaret's heart expanded and contracted with such happiness, she nearly wept. But wariness kept her from turning. "I have, Your Grace."

"Liar. You've been playing cards instead." The sound of his footsteps echoed as he came closer. "Did you play for him? Amanda always despaired she could not."

"Yes. And your father wished me to learn every card trick he knew."

He sat down and pressed a kiss to the base of her neck, nuzzling against her skin. The dark waves of his hair fell over his cheeks as he kissed her. "I was on my way to fetch you when I received word of the duke's death, lest you think I was in London taking mistresses and had forgotten all about you."

That was exactly what she'd been thinking. "Of course, Your Grace."

He looked away for a moment before returning to face her, regret etched in the lines of his handsome face. "I would *never* forget you, Maggie. Leo insisted I leave you be for a few weeks."

"It's possible I instructed him to do so." She had, as a matter of fact, said something to that effect when she'd sobbed out her heart on her brother-in-law's shoulder.

"I should not have listened, at any rate. If it eases your

heart, I went first to my father. It was the only time I recall in which I could speak my mind and have no worry he would rebuke me. I'm sure Amanda heard most of it. She refused to leave."

Margaret wondered what Tony had said to his father's body. Maybe someday she would ask, but not today.

"And now I must beg your forgiveness. Again." He took her hand and pressed a kiss to the pulse beating in her wrist before leaning down to press his lips to the small bump of her stomach. "And yours." He lifted her chin with his finger. "I never meant to say such a horrible thing, Maggie. It was only the shock of it. My own bitterness toward my father turned against me."

"I know." She knew his soul. His heart. It had only taken him longer to see himself as she did.

"I wish to start fresh and put the past behind us. I promise to stop being a complete ass if you will vow to continue playing the piano for me in your underthings."

She saw the hopefulness in his eyes, and something else Margaret had been afraid she'd never see. *Peace*. Whatever had transpired between Tony and his deceased father had calmed something within her husband.

"Even before I learned of my father's passing, I had decided I could no longer continue to be a man I would grow to hate. Worse, a man you would have no love for." He pressed a kiss to her forehead, then to her lips again. "Did you know this was my mother's piano?"

Margaret nodded, her happiness tempered with the loss of the duke. How she wished Tony and his father could have ended their estrangement. But maybe they had.

"She would tuck me in next to her like this," her husband said, grabbing her tightly to his side and positioning her under his arm. "And teach me my scales." He played down the keys, filling the conservatory with music. "Did you know," his voice lowered until it vibrated along the curves of her body, "I once compromised a young lady at the piano? She had designs on another man, but I didn't allow such a thing to stop me."

Margaret trembled as the hand at her waist slid up to gently cup her breast. "Did the lady in question object?"

"No." The low timbre softened into her bones. "She had an affinity for music, particularly Chopin. Horribly intelligent. Behaves in a wicked manner behind closed doors."

"She sounds marvelous."

"Oh, she is. That is why I ruined her intentionally." His tongue traced the curve of her ear. "I should have guessed, you know." He cupped her stomach before his fingers trailed up her waist. "Christ, you were eating all the scones, and these," he fondled her breasts, "have become much riper." His lips moved to inspect the skin of her neck.

"I'm not a piece of fruit, Your Grace. And I wasn't eating all the scones. Only most."

"All. Whatever our souls are made of," he kissed the line of her jaw, "hers and mine are the same. Do you know why I repeat such a ridiculous platitude to you?"

"It isn't ridiculous." It wasn't. Margaret found it terribly romantic. "Why?"

"Because I'm in love with you."

Margaret's heart beat harder.

"But *I love you* seems so trite. We are each other's music." His mouth fell over hers, lazily trailing over her lips. "I *will* be the husband you deserve. And I *will* be the sort of father my child will be proud of. You will have no cause to look to Henri for affection."

"You know there was never a wastrel Frenchman waiting for me," she whispered.

"Only this reformed rake." His eyes lowered, his voice thick with emotion.

Margaret wrapped her arms around his neck, inhaling the scent of her husband, and pressed herself to his heart, listening as it beat. For her.

EPILOGUE

Margaret bent over the piano, or at least as far as the large mound of her stomach would allow. The sonata, the beautiful swirling notes of blue and green, poured out of her. She closed her eyes, her fingers gliding over the ivory keys with ease, as the conservatory at Cherry Hill echoed with the music Margaret had written for Welles.

Averell.

She still couldn't get used to calling him Averell instead of Welles. She supposed it would take some time. In her heart, he was Tony.

Her husband had only briefly returned to London after the burial of the late duke, to close his house and handle some of the business of Elysium before returning. He would be a much more silent partner in the establishment moving forward. Tony had also wanted to check on Leo, who'd returned to London immediately after their father's funeral. After reading the letter the late duke had left for him, Leo had paled and walked stiffly to his waiting carriage, neglecting to say goodbye to any of them.

Leo was not handling the death of the late Duke of Averell at all well.

Margaret did not return to London. Town held no appeal for her especially since she grew rounder with each passing day. She was determined to fulfill her promise to the late duke and care for the Barringtons as best she could. At least once a week, Margaret walked with her mother-in-law to the small hill near the duke's grave and sat on a stone bench while Amanda spoke to her late husband. Several months after the duke died, a spill of wild strawberries had mysteriously sprouted into bloom atop his grave.

Margaret stopped and wiped a tear from her cheek. Amanda had insisted it was a sign from the late duke.

Strong arms wrapped around her, startling her from her thoughts, surrounding Margaret with warmth and love. She smiled, sinking into the familiar scent of leather, soap and the wind. A palm fell possessively over her stomach.

"How was your ride, Your Grace?" Her eyes fluttered open.

"Splendid. I had a heated conversation with my father."

Tony had gotten into the habit of visiting the late duke's grave. Always alone. Phaedra had ridden by one day and heard her older brother yelling at the headstone as if arguing with their dead father. Margaret supposed it was Tony's way of dealing with his father's death. After he visited the gravesite, he was often calmer. More at peace.

A ripple shot across her stomach, followed by a tiny kick.

His arms tightened around her. "He's hungry, my love. It's nearly time for tea."

"Will there be scones?"

A dark rumble of laughter erupted at her back. "Dozens." His fingers threaded through hers. "Pray don't eat them all. I'm hungry as well."

"Would you care to play a duet before tea?" Margaret gave him a saucy look.

Another chuckle escaped him. "Are you making an improper request? Madam, I'd no idea you were so wicked."

Margaret elbowed him.

Tony looked down at her and brushed her lips with his. "Whatever our souls are made of," he said softly.

Margaret cupped his cheek and whispered back, "his and mine are the same."

THE THEORY OF EARLS IS THE FIRST IN MY NEW SERIES, ***The Beautiful Barringtons***. Margaret and Welles are two of my very favorite characters from **The Wickeds**. I love the idea of an average girl capturing the heart (and the piano) of a rakish, handsome man like Welles. If you enjoyed **The Theory of Earls,** please leave me a review.

Join my readers group on Facebook!
https://www.facebook.com/groups/historicallyhotkathleenayers

Or subscribe to my newsletter at www.kathleenayers.com and be the first to learn about new releases, cover reveals and more.

https://www.facebook.com/kayersauthor/
https://www.bookbub.com/authors/kathleen-ayers
https://www.instagram.com/kayersauthor/

AUTHOR NOTES

The Royal Society of Female Musicians was a real organization and formed by Mrs. Lucy Anderson and Mrs. Anne Mounsey (among others) in 1839.

Chopin did attend a party thrown in his honor at the home of James Broadwood in London in 1837. While his music was being published in England at the time, I've taken some liberties with his popularity.

Broadwood was a piano maker of note (pun intended) during the time period and introduced a grand piano in 1827. Broadwoods were known for their quality of tone, something Margaret falls in love with besides Welles.

Lastly, fans of Wuthering Heights will recognize the quote Welles recites to Margaret instead of telling her he loves her. There are some who find the quote misused or overused, but I thought it the perfect way for Welles to express himself.

ALSO BY KATHLEEN AYERS

The Wickeds Series

Wicked's Scandal

Devil of a Duke

My Wicked Earl

Wickedly Yours

Tall Dark & Wicked

Still Wicked

Wicked Again